The Gingerbr

Kiley Dunbar is Scottish and lives in England with her husband, two kids and Amos the Bedlington Terrier. She writes around her work at a University in the North of England where she lectures in English Literature and creative writing. She is proud to be a member of the Romantic Novelists' Association and a graduate of their New Writers' Scheme.

Also by Kiley Dunbar

Christmas at Frozen Falls
The Gingerbread Christmas Village

Kelsey Anderson

One Summer's Night
One Winter's Night

Port Willow Bay

Summer at the Highland Coral Beach
Matchmaking at Port Willow

The Borrow a Bookshop

The Borrow a Bookshop Holiday
Christmas at the Borrow a Bookshop
Something New at the Borrow a Bookshop

KILEY DUNBAR

The Gingerbread Christmas Village

hera

First published in the United Kingdom in 2023 by

Hera Books
Unit 9 (Canelo), 5th Floor
Cargo Works, 1-2 Hatfields
London SE1 9PG
United Kingdom

A CIP catalogue record for this book is available from the British Library.

Print ISBN 978 1 80436 459 8
Ebook ISBN 978 1 80436 458 1

Look for more great books at www.herabooks.com

Printed and bound in Great Britain by Clays Ltd, Elcograf S.p.A.

1

For Kathleen Marr,

the reason I can do any of this.

Thank you so much.

Prologue

There's so much about my childhood that I can't help but see through a happy, rose-tinted haze, and it looks rosier the older I get. I happen to be sixty-five, by the way, the same age as Madonna, which I enjoy telling people. What I'm trying to say is that when I was little, I knew I was one of the luckiest girls on earth. Not only were my parents madly in love, and not only did we live in the prettiest village in the Cotswolds, but I was fortunate enough to be born the eldest daughter of absolutely the best gingerbread baker in the northern hemisphere, possibly the universe.

I can't attest to her Victoria sponges or her spotted dick or shortbread fingers; Mum had one recipe and one recipe only, her gingerbread. And I'm not talking about a batch of biscuity men rustled up every now and again to satisfy my sweet tooth either. That would be thinking far too small for Mum who every December could be found working away at our cottage's kitchen table, spicing and kneading, rolling and cutting, cooling and icing, industriously assembling her famous gingerbread cottages. Attached to her mixing arm, you could bet your baubles, there I'd be, her gingerbread village's Chief Spoon Licker.

I can still see the scene now, as clear as day, that Christmas after Granny died, when Mum suddenly

I

stopped in her stirring in our sugar-scented kitchen, glanced at my baby sister, Lydia, asleep in her Moses basket, and announced with eyes both absent and urgent, 'I should write it down for you. Quick, Margi!' She snapped doughy fingers and sent me to fetch a felt tip.

(That's Margi pronounced with a 'g', as in Margate, and not with a 'j' like margarine! I shortened it myself when I was five, rebelling against the association with Great Aunt Margaret who'd tell me if I kept eating gingerbread, I'd end up toothless like her and, laughing, she'd take out her dentures and scare me.)

So I, young Margi, had leaned over the floury tabletop watching Mum jotting down her recipe on a fresh page sacrificed from my colouring book. I watched the formula appear in her loopy handwriting, listening as she spoke the words, rendered exotic and homely at the same time, and so closely associated with my mother in my brain's pathways they'll never disentangle: demerara, cinnamon, fiery ginger, nutmeg, star anise, cloves, candied orange, angelica.

When she was done, I watched her re-cap my green felt tip, now greasy with butter, and slip the paper inside her *Mrs Beaton* – a wedding present she told me she'd never once read – and that's where her precious gingerbread spell would live for years, until it became mine. I hadn't understood it was a bequest at the time. A gift and a burden.

On days like that the village women would spill in through our (always unlocked) cottage door and Mum would greet them with a busy nod, her hands shoved in the mixing bowl.

'Plain flour, Mrs Frost. Two bags,' Mrs Cooper, the school dinner lady renowned amongst us kids for her generosity with the pink custard, would announce.

'And I've butter,' Mrs Jonson might add, struggling to shove the pram ferrying her chubby twins over the doorstep.

The woman us kids wrote off as 'Old Widow Davies' (it makes me gulp now to think she was probably only in her early seventies at the time) would step inside and lay down her offering of icing sugar or marzipan and she'd fill the kettle and light the gas ring like she felt thoroughly at home, which of course she did. Everyone did. There was always someone dropping round looking for a cuppa and a chat, no matter the time of year, and Mum always welcomed them like family.

Sometimes the younger village mothers would tell Mum apologetically that they'd brought nothing that day, but could they still help, and Mum would only smile and hand them an apron.

This was how it always went. Whole armies of Wheaton village women encamped in our kitchen all through Advent, bringing what provisions they could from their pantries, letting their kids toddle around and interfere with the Lego houses and gardens I loved making back then. Every one of the women offered up their time and their housekeeping money for the cause. All to help Mum turn her gingerbread village display dreams into a reality.

Standing by her side, I picked up all her special techniques. How to achieve different shades of gingerbread by using only caster sugar (when pale stuff was needed), or adding a patiently dropped dollop of black treacle for a glorious dark bronze bake, or folding in cocoa powder for a sweetly moreish golden-brown colour.

She demonstrated her rolling know-how too, always getting an even thickness by using the hardwood spacers Dad rustled up in his woodworking shed, and I learned how to prevent patches of dough clinging to pins by rolling it between two sheets of parchment or by using Mum's home-made dusting bags – little pouches of corn-flour made from a new cotton hankie tied with an elastic band (these always put me in mind of a powder puff and produced just as satisfactory a cloud of floaty white when you vigorously banged two together above your head).

I wasn't so much of a nuisance in the kitchen that I didn't pick up Mum's cutting-out techniques. The women worked off templates made to scale on tracing paper (again, that was Dad's handiwork) whilst I had the job of cutting the rectangular gingerbread supports which, once glued inside with royal icing, would stop our biscuit buildings collapsing in on themselves.

Over time I mastered her methods with the sugar-paste piping bag which Mum wielded with the speed of an old hand used to perfectly repeating lacy patterns of dots and dashes, drops and scallops, loops and fleur-de-lys, or lavishly thick beaded snail's trails like snowdrifts, all adding charming snowy details to her little houses in miniature.

While they worked, the women would share stories – whispering the ones I wasn't supposed to overhear but always strained my ears extra hard for – and some would break away to feed babies, and the radio played big band Christmas hits interspersed with blasts of Frank and Nancy Sinatra, The Monkees, and Sandy Shaw, and we'd bop along as the rolling pins *shush shushed* across the surface of glossy dough, and everyone's cheeks pinked from the heat and the Christmas sherry – concealed from no one in particular – sloshing in Mum's best china teacups, turning our little spot on the very edge of sleepy old Wheaton village into the laughter-filled, oven-warmed heart of the community.

Then, come the middle of December, a walking procession would leave our cottage, slow and careful on icy pavements sparkling under the street lights, a stream of locals transporting cottages, school buildings and shops, churchyard and gardens, the old forge and stables, every inch of our village recreated in iced gingerbread and decorated with boiled sweets, strawberry bootlaces, chocolate buttons, candied fruit and glacé cherries, and I'd skip alongside Dad, dragging Biscuits the dachshund beside me, all the way down the high street, enjoying the commotion at the windows where the other children pressed their faces or at front doors where the old ladies waved as we, the celebrated bakers, made our way to Wheaton Village Hall.

The hall was where our world in miniature took shape, laid out on trestle tables pushed together and covered in every white linen cloth the women could muster, and old Mr Paxton, the school caretaker, would be busy digging out his red suit and cotton wool beard, preparing the grotto corner for the little ones.

For the next two weeks, the whole of the Cotswolds would descend on Mum's gingerbread grotto, lit by fairy lights and candles for extra magic. They'd queue right down the high street to get in and pay a shilling for tea from the hall's big silver urn and another for a gift from Santa's pack, and everyone, literally everyone, would be exchanging festive greetings and chatting happily.

The spare money raised by Mum's adventures in baking would go to whoever needed it around the village. She was the sort of woman who always knew when so-and-so's eldest had gone through yet another pair of school shoes, or when there was an overdue grocery account at the village stores or a milkman's bill needing paying off urgently. She'd never see anyone struggling. That was my mum. *Is* my mum. These days, she's all about helping at the stray dog sanctuary in Mijas rather than making cookie model villages. Well, helping strays and lying by the pool with Dad and one of his jugs of sangria – so strong it's more a general anaesthetic than a cocktail.

Back then, though, she was the heart of Wheaton; at least that's how I remember it. Back when Christmas was still small and special and full of nothing but simple joy, when snow fell every winter and stayed until the snowdrops emerged, and the only thing us gingerbread grotto recruits had to worry about was where the next gumdrops and candy canes were coming from for next year's (bigger, better) display, and the next year's and the next, back when the prospect of all those future Christmases in my cosy unspoiled Wheaton village spread out ahead of me like a wonderful promise.

Chapter One

Friday 1 December: Tin-Rattling

The car horn makes me jump as the four-by-four slams to a stop immediately in front of my collecting spot at the Wheaton primary school gate, almost sending me spinning with its wing mirror.

I bite down the impulse to shout at the frowning father in the driving seat, telling myself that wouldn't be the best start to my morning of tin-shaking on the village high street. So I call him some very un-festive names under my breath and step back so he can throw open doors and bundle his tiny, uniform-clad kids out of their car seats. One of them's crying, and the other is on the verge. Nevertheless, he hustles them in through the school gates.

I hold out my tin to him as he huffs his way back to his idling car, but without even looking at it, he's gone, leaving me coughing in his exhaust fumes.

Izz, our committee treasurer and my best friend, was impressed when I first suggested a bit of school-run cash collecting to boost our gingerbread grotto ingredients fund. Flour, sugar, butter and spices have doubled in price this winter, even at the wholesalers, so we need to raise some serious funds or the gingerbread village will turn out tiny this year.

'Sounds genius to me, Margi!' Izz had said. 'Proper Elon Musk business-like thinking, that.'

She doesn't read the news so probably thought that was an encouraging thing to say.

Izz is waving at me right this second from her lollipop crossing fifty yards away. She's in head-to-toe neon which you'd think would make her impossible to ignore, but I've already seen her almost ploughed down by two school-run mums in sporty hatchbacks this morning.

Everyone's in such a rush, and I don't recognise half the grown-ups arriving for drop-off. Most of them are from the new builds that appeared on the green belt a decade back; most of them look very stressed and are glugging from big red takeaway coffee cups. Hardly any of them pay me any attention as I do my best to help the committee break even on baking powder. The ones who know me give me the thin-lipped, pitying smiles I've grown used to, and sure enough they rummage for notes. It's nice of them – lovely, in fact – but I reckon I know what they're thinking. It's written all over their faces. *That's her. The one whose husband left her last Christmas only days after their big white village wedding. Silly old woman.* I hear a group of mums laughing behind me and try to convince myself it can't be me they're whispering about, but still, I feel myself shrink a little.

I try to infuse as much positivity as I can into the thumbs up I'm giving Izz, and I watch as she enthusiastically returns one of her own. She's what you might call a true innocent: the kind of person who sees the good in everyone and everything. I have no idea how she's made it into her seventy-seventh year with that trusting attitude and wide-eyed gentleness. How does someone that jolly and at peace with life remain this sweet? Or avoid getting kidnapped with the promise of a van full of puppies?

I thank the universe every day that she's my friend.

Here come the on-foot families. Izz shakes an invisible tin at me by way of encouragement. I draw a deep lungful of chilly morning air and greet them.

'Merry Christmas!' I cry, rattling my collection tin in what I hope seems a cheerful way and not at all like a mugging. 'Support the grotto?'

'Christmas gingerbread… grotto?' one of the women, I don't recognise her, definitely one of the newcomers, reads off my home-made placard by my feet, giving it a puzzled look. She brightens before adding, 'Is that the stately home with the light displays and fireworks over Dunham way?'

I can tell from how her expression shifts that my reaction has already scared her.

I want to say, *No, it bloody isn't!* Instead, I tell her, 'We're a small *local* Christmas event, at the village hall. The model village display? All made from gingerbread? It's a Wheaton tradition.'

'So, no fireworks?' she says, innocently enough.

'Not so much as a sparkler.'

She slips a fifty pence into the slot – more to get away from me, I suspect, than out of any desire to support our lowly event, and she shuffles her kids in through the school gates.

I give my feet a good stamp to get the circulation going again. It really is freezing out here, and the temperature's falling by the second. Or that's how it feels to me.

'Do you have permission for this?' says a man's low voice, making me turn my back on the sudden influx of cars crawling by, all vying for a space.

It's another person I don't recognise, but his lanyard gives it away. He's the new head teacher, started last week. And from the looks of him, he's only just finished his A levels himself.

'Permission from who?' I say.

'Well…'

I reckon I've got him here; he's flustering.

'The council?' he tries.

'*Pfft!* I doubt any of that lot'll be interested.' I can't even remember the last time one of them popped by the grotto. They'll hardly mind me collecting a few quid outside the school.

The young guy's still not satisfied. He's all sharp dark tweed, pointy shoes, trendy round specs and nice sweepy-uppy hair – all of which would suggest a far warmer personality than the cold-eyed fellow currently pulling an unimpressed face at my home-made sign.

'You can't protest here,' he says.

'I'm collecting money for butter. It's hardly Greenham Common. I promise I won't be chaining myself to your railings.'

We both look around at the school perimeter. It's crumbly Cotswold stone, not a railing in sight, but I think my point stands.

'*Hmph.*' He's gearing up to say something else, and looking officious and weary all at once – again, it seems odd in such a young guy – but his attention is dragged away by a car pulling right up onto the pavement. 'Excuse me, you'll have to move,' he calls out, gliding away, and I turn back to my task with a laugh.

He doesn't seem village-headmaster material, somehow. Nothing like trusty old Mrs Fourmile who always supported the gingerbread grotto and was a dab hand with an icing bag herself.

'He won't last the term,' I tell myself.

It's as I'm shaking my tin once more that I spot it. Way along the high street, almost at the lane that leads off to Mum and Dad's cottage – well, my cottage – there's someone fixing a big green awning over a stall.

It's been years since Wheaton had any kind of market day, so this is a new one on me. Izz is closer to it than I am, and she's already checking it out. She turns to me and does an exaggerated shrug with a plumped lip.

'No idea,' she mouths.

The awning's in place now and I see the guy fiddling with a big white bundle and some kind of machinery on the ground. It's only when the sound from a puttering generator reaches me that I realise what it is. He's inflating a huge, bobbing snowman, and he's drawing a crowd.

Just as I'm craning my neck for a better view over all the heads, Lolla, the always-vaping landlady of Wheaton's only pub, The Salutation, approaches with her son, Ben, bundled in his red coat like Paddington Bear.

'What's all that about?' I ask her, nodding towards the stall.

'They're selling Dunham Gravey tickets,' she tells me through a haze of apple-scented vapour.

I peer even harder now and can just make out the pale green of the estate's crest. 'What? For their Christmas lights thing?'

'You'd know they applied for a pop-up licence if you ever came to any of the council meetings,' she says with a laugh and a touch at my arm, and she sails past with Ben.

I hear the new head teacher telling Lolla that vaping's not permitted in the vicinity of the school grounds, but I don't stay to hear her, doubtless, sarky reply.

I sneak my way along the pavement, passing the low Cotswold stone walls and prettily painted garden gates on my left – the blue one is Izz's cottage. The frigid winter's morning air carries the music coming from the interloper's stall all down the high street.

One of the school-run grandmothers with three kids in tow is opening her purse and buying a handful of tickets. The stallholder, looking very smart in a branded green gilet, has a proper sign that boasts of the *Dunham Gravey Christmas Illuminations Spectacular, Dec 1st–31st*. The whole set-up looks extremely professional.

I'm almost level with Izz at her crossing. She gives me a warning look.

'What?' I mouth. 'I'm not going to say anything.'

She shoos me back towards the school gates. I'd better obey. I'll never make any money at this rate. Not now Green Gilet Guy has arrived to steal all my donations.

'I should've had a branded gingerbread grotto gilet made,' I mutter to myself once I'm stationed back outside the school, dismayed that the traffic's clearing already (not great for business) but glad to see the grumpy head's stalked off into the school building.

Even if I did have the money, I wouldn't be wasting it on flashy fleeces. Every spare penny I've come by this year has gone into the grotto pot.

I can't help staring along the road again. There's a line forming for Dunham Gravey tickets. Gilet is delighted. Every time another person joins his queue the bloke's face lights up like Mariah Carey's Christmas tree.

I suppose I could've knitted myself an official 'event planner' jumper if it would mean more interest, maybe with little cookie houses all around the hem and the words *Wheaton Village Gingerbread Grotto* across my chest? Or would novelty knitwear be *too* weird?

There goes another bundle of his tickets! You know, I wouldn't mind the massive success of their magical-woodland-Christmas-lights-walk-with-live-orchestral-pyrotechnics-and-dancing-fountains-finale *quite so much* if it hadn't been dreamt up by the faceless Dunham bosses two years ago, immediately nabbing what was left of my festive regulars from the surrounding area.

Thirty quid their tickets start at. Each! Kids too. I don't know how the average family can afford it… Is that a card reader he's produced? OK, so he's taking Visa payments. Flash git. My trusty tinsel-wrapped tin looks sorrier than ever.

I shake it at another of the mums and receive twenty-five pence and a sheepish smile in return. 'All I've got on me, sorry.'

She's clasping Dunham tickets, I notice.

I suppose if you've shelled out a few hundred quid to treat your family to a great big Christmassy night out enjoying the Dunham Gravey lights, you're unlikely to be desperate to throw even more money at holiday outings. And certainly not our one. People aren't exactly dying to part with an additional twenty quid on the door (that's how much one of our family tickets cost) to come and stand in a draughty 1950s hall and look at our traditional gingerbread village display before receiving a Poundland pencil case and a net of chocolate coins from what is obviously Patrick, the primary school caretaker, in a synthetic beard and Santa suit.

Dunham Gravey's got outdoor pizza ovens and a festive fairground, all at extra cost, of course. We don't even have parking. Not now the school's dropped the bombshell they won't be letting us use their staff car park this year. Blasted *Drop a Dress Size for Christmas* boot camp in the PE hall every night this month.

Roadside parking in Wheaton's tricky at the best of times, what with our Cotswold village being a three-street, forty-cottages kind of affair. Even then, we somehow still warrant double yellows everywhere and our own weekend traffic warden. As if the council doesn't have anything better to do than preventing drivers popping into the village shop for a pint of milk and a Lotto ticket.

There are fields and fields of off-road, well-lit, accessible parking at Dunham flippin' Gravey. And a gift shop. And a cafeteria. The grotto's mulled wine stall can't compete with any of that.

Izz is giving me a puzzled look. It says, *Buck up, Margi!*

I *should* try to think more positively. If not for Izz, then for Patrick. He's going to do himself proud this year with his new hydraulics set-up and dry-ice machine, transforming my mother's once static display into a flying gingerbread sleigh scene, with real smoking chimneys and houses lit from the inside in an edible diorama to end all dioramas. *Oh!* It does promise to be so lovely this Christmas.

Ah, so I can still smile? Good to know.

I bring my hand to my cheek where there's a definite flush of heat going on. I can feel it through my glove. Nothing to do with Patrick, of course, just a little whoosh of Christmas joy.

Still, it's nice to think that I can depend on him, and his tool belt and hot glue gun. And he's not the only person the gingerbread grotto has fighting its corner. There's all the toddlers and schoolkids (who'll adore the display, as always). You can depend on the grotto bringing in the few locals who remember it from their childhoods. Only, with all the second homes and the house prices shooting up there are fewer of them every year, plus they're not the ones with the deep pockets and the sponsorship money.

Things being tight like they are, big donations dried up a while back, and now... well, now we're keeping going on our last reserves of Christmas spirits and, frankly, actual spirits. It's amazing the boost an own-brand Baileys can give you in the face of adversity.

I try not to wince at the sight of the bank cards being swiped down under that fancy awning and instead shake my tin at a gaggle of teenage girls sliding by on their way to the bus stop, each one carrying a big red coffee cup and all looking glacial in school skirts and blazers. Where on earth are their coats... is, uh, something my mother might say.

One girl gives my tin a side-eye glance, and there's a definite look of distaste on her face like I'm asking her to sniff a litter tray. There's a few shared smirks, and I hear a pitying, '*Eww, cringe!*' before they're gone.

Me? Cringe? *I'm the same age as Madonna!* I want to shout after them. But they might point out that's clearly where the similarity ends and I'd wind up swearing at schoolchildren in public.

As I'm left questioning whether they'd actually know who Madonna even is, I look down my body at my silver-grey cords (with added stretch – I'm not tackling the high street at Christmas in anything belted; I'm not a masochist), pull-on Doc Martens (Mum's called them my 'clodhoppers' since I got my first pair at nineteen), and my multiple layers of cotton and M&S merino wool. Greys and classic black, of course. Cosy and practical, and a little bit bobbly with age.

They're not seeing the real me, though. The old me, wherever she's buggered off to. I guess this is what's left of me now. They see a post-menopausal, twice-divorced, retired Home Ec teacher with an unhealthy obsession with spiced cookies, and yes, I've let my shoulder-length waves go their natural soft grey, unassaulted by the bleach bottle I was practically bonded to in my youth. These days, I'm not exactly someone those schoolgirls would want to emulate.

They should think themselves lucky they don't have an increasingly out-of-reach fundraising target, a painful bunion in spite of a lifetime of Doc-wearing, rollercoaster mood swings, or a bashed-about heart to contend with. They'll know soon enough how quickly time passes, and how broken hearts, like broken bones, are harder to heal the older you get. Not that I'd wish the way I've been feeling this year on anyone.

I suppose I do feel a bit 'cringe' after all.

I've just about had enough of this. Standing outside the school, at risk of losing digits to frostbite, not to mention limbs to parallel parkers, and has it been worth it? My tin's disappointingly light.

The school bell's ringing now. I reckon it's time to crack open the thermos of coffee Izz made for me.

I notice the bin by the school gate is stuffed to overflowing with Starbucks cups from that new branch out on the bypass where, according to Izz, they charge nearly five quid a pop for a soy maple latte with light whip and a dusting of cocoa powder.

If she's right, then literally everyone who's passed by me this morning clutching a green paper bag and a red cup like it's full of life-giving elixir has already blown an hour's pay in there. No wonder there's nothing left to spare for us and our little gingerbread venture.

Ugh! Grumbling about Starbucks! As if they give a monkey's. I'm turning into a sour old bat, and I hate that feeling. Only, it's hard not to indulge my grumpiness on days like this.

I don't like admitting it, but lately, I've lost that vital, burning, alive feeling I'd always had at my core, the part that made me get up in the morning and meet the day bravely. The best way to describe my emotions nowadays would be 'flat'. Steamrollered flat.

I'll pour myself a cup of Izz's coffee, turn up my collar and tell myself I'll give it another hour. The shops are opening now, and by shops, I mean Scrimengor's bakery, Jill's hair salon, Ted Olsen's bike repair place, the art gallery, and the newsagents. That's the entire retail and business offering of Wheaton village these days, not including the pub, and Bizzy Izz's Cafe, of course, which Izz will be opening up in a few minutes now she's on the move, waving as she goes to swap her lollipop stick for her oven gloves. I raise my steaming cup to her with a stoic smile.

I'll hang around long enough to catch the morning dog walkers and the newspaper-and-a-loaf shoppers, then I'm sacking it all off for a hot bath and a depressed scroll through Instagram reels of strangers' Christmas party charcuterie boards.

Gilet's crowds have died down too, I notice. He catches me staring and waves a gloved hand while his stall's sound system blasts out 'Frosty the Snowman'. A passing car pulls up beside him and he sells yet more tickets through the passenger window. Give me strength!

Half an hour more passes. I've begun to lose feeling in my calves, and I'm done. I pack up my home-made sign with my tin under my arm and trudge past the Dunham Gravey guy in shamefaced defeat. He's busy organising banknotes in a cash box chained to the stall like the ghost of Jacob Marley. The sight of all that money sends me spiralling, wondering why I ever thought this was a good idea in the first place. Nobody outside our committee cares about the future of our gingerbread grotto or the village's Christmas traditions, and why should they, really?

I'll have to tell Izz and Patrick that their fundraising faith in me was completely misplaced and there doesn't seem to be any way of breaking even on our baking ingredients this winter.

Maybe this is the year we accept the inevitable and let Wheaton dwindle away to become just another commuter-belt village with only its pretty scenery going for it. Maybe it's time to ring in some serious life changes all round.

If I was more like Mum was, back in the day, would things be easier? If I'd managed to hold on to my enthusiasm and tenacity? If I hadn't lost my community spirit? If I wasn't secretly planning on getting out of Wheaton?

How can you fundraise with a whole heart when you've already got one foot out the door – or one foot on the other side of Wheaton's thirty-limit signs, in my case. Still, that's my secret for now. No point telling the gang before there's something concrete to tell.

I plod on to the edge of the village where the double yellows end and the long road to Cirencester begins. That's where I take my familiar turning down the lane to my cottage. The mud is solid and ridged underfoot after last night's frost, the first of many to come this December.

A robin flits across the path in front of me, warbling in warning: a tiny, delicate thing shouting birdy obscenities at me, the giant, disturbing its morning's singing.

'Good on you,' I tell the plucky ball of rage eyeing me furiously from the holly hedge. 'Give it hell, little guy.'

I used to be like him. Bold, loud, fearless, loved. I mean, everyone loves a robin, don't they? These days, I'm more like one of those silly pigeons which has flown smack bang into sheet glass and sits, shocked, on the patio, feathers fluffed for protection, wondering why its head hurts.

I reach my gate in the stone wall that hugs my little garden. Here, all summer long, Dad's roses bloom in the sunshine. In December, the skeleton shrubs and looming evergreens do their best to look jolly, but I can't help thinking the cottage – with its threadbare thatch and its stone walls the colour of gingerbread – has the look of the house where Hansel and Gretel came a greedy cropper at the hands of the witch, who, incidentally, I am seriously coming to identify with: crotchety, sweet-obsessed, and increasingly isolated. The robin keeps his eyes on me as my phone receives a noisy barrage of notifications just as I'm slipping the key in the lock.

A quick glance at the screen tells me: *We have four Birmingham properties matching your search criteria.*

I shut the door on my little garden, frosted a sparkling white as though the sugarplum fairy has dusted every leaf with icing sugar. I'm too absorbed in my phone to revel in the beauty of it, scrolling through the properties. A mid-terrace and three little semis, all with nice, manageable-sized gardens, and all in my price range. All situated minutes away from Lucy, my darling niece's place, as well as being a snowball's throw from all the exciting stuff a big, bustling city has to offer.

It's all there on my screen; the promise of a new life. My burgeoning getaway plan. And why on earth not? I'm chilled to the bone by this year, and nothing will rekindle my enjoyment of Christmas or my faith that there's a future for me in Wheaton.

It's hard not to think that Don doing a runner was some kind of sign telling me to cut and run too. Starting over has never felt more appealing. There'd be no more pitying looks or gossipy whispers if I was in Birmingham. If I was miles away, I wouldn't have to watch everything I've ever known going under. I'd be blissfully unaware. I carry my phone to the bedroom and lie down with it.

Chapter Two

Friday night: The Gingerbread Committee

'How can you be glum when there's gingerbread needs mixing? Just smell that spicy loveliness!'

Izz is trying to cheer me up about my school-run collection, and, to be fair, it's working.

'I just hate letting you down,' I tell her, fixing her apron in a bow at her back. She's holding her just-washed hands like a surgeon prepped for theatre.

'Letting me down? You raised some money, didn't you? That's still cash in the pot; better than nothing.'

'*Hmm.*' Eight quid thirty-two pence isn't going to stretch very far, is it? 'How much have you made at the cafe?' I ask her. She's had a jar by her till point since September, though her regular crowd of local farmers and pensioners aren't renowned for being big tippers; I've seen Mr and Mrs Saddler make a pot of tea and a *Daily Mail* last three hours sat in one of the booths (all while charging up a mobile on Izz's energy bill, I should add), and they still won't drop their coppers in Izz's tips jar.

'Umm… seven… *ahum ahum.*' She fudges the rest in a fluttery cough directed into her crooked elbow.

'Seventy pounds?' I venture.

She shakes her head, making her way around my kitchen table to grab a bowl.

'Seventeen?'

She fixes me with a look that says she's tried her best. 'Seven pounds twenty, but add it to yours and that covers our golden syrup and sugar costs for this first batch, so...' Even *she's* struggling to sound positive. 'Come on,' she cajoles. 'Weigh out the butter and let's get started. Have you got your mum's recipe out?'

It's not as though we need the recipe; I know it by heart, but yes, I do. I prop it against the scales, her love song to gingerbread in green felt tip.

Mum started the whole gingerbread village thing the year she got married: just a shelf with a few prettily iced houses inside the porch of the church, when 'It was just something nice for the kiddies', before it all got a bit out of hand. Over the years her gingerbread display grew until it included nearby landmarks – Broadway Tower, Tewkesbury Abbey, a very ambitious attempt at Sudeley Castle and grounds, that sort of thing – until, by necessity, it had to be moved into the village hall where she could really let her imagination run wild.

'Shall we listen to *The Archers* while we bake?' Izz interrupts my thoughts of missing Mum, thank goodness. I don't want to get misty over the bread mix.

'Must we?' I say.

'I've got an emergency Christmas hits CD?' she offers instead. 'Should I break it out?'

'I'm not sure that's any better, Izz,' I tell her, but she's already pulling it from her tote bag and, I'm delighted to say, that's followed by a big bottle of red. 'Now you're talking!'

Within twenty minutes we've got a cosy red-wine glow on, we're up to our elbows kneading sweet, spiced, bready cookie mixture in Mum's huge old earthenware bowls in my lovely little cottage kitchen and Alexander O'Neal's knocking out 'My Gift to You' from the stereo. It's nice in here. Cheerful, even. Izz is doing a sort of soulful two-step as she works and I've gone for the traditional white-lady hip sway.

Wet ingredients combine with dry, and the familiar heady, spicy scent fills the room right up to the wonky beams above our heads. Everything about the process is easy and warm, and I'm eight years old again every time I watch the golden syrup stream off Mum's old tablespoon, reserved especially for gingerbread nights. I can almost hear Old Widow Davies saying this looks a good batch, and I can see Mrs Cooper sifting the flour while toddlers chew at sneaked gingerbread stars and snowflakes. And I'm by Mum's mixing arm once more; my hands are her hands. 'A pinch more ginger,' Mum says. 'It wants to be fiery.' This is my favourite place to be, and I let the lovely delusion linger as long as I can.

I meet Izz's eyes, and she sends me a smiling wink. She knows I'm only half in the here and now, half back there in the rosy haze.

We've known each other long enough to be able to work in silent concentration and not feel awkward; this is, after all, our twelfth year running the grotto together. My twelfth Christmas without Mum here, and the eleventh after Lydia, my younger sister, took a nursing job in New Zealand and never looked back. I was suddenly the only Frost family member left in Wheaton to carry all of this on, and that was the year the council gave up subsidising the village hall, so the building's been getting increasingly run-down since then, not that it hasn't been well used, what with Bobbie's 'chairobics' sessions for seniors, and there's all manner of baby-group things, breastfeeding drop-ins double-booked with jumble sales and beetle drives, and that's before all the local produce competitions and summer fetes. You can't get moving in the hall come the end of July for officials with clipboards judging jams or pinning rosettes on offensively girthy courgettes.

Come Christmas, the hall's less in demand: too chilly. I doubt the 'A land fit for heroes' blokes who built the place after the war could ever have foreseen it shut up for four months of the year except for the one fortnight when some lunatics fill it with confectionery.

The council let us have the keys early in December, and we open the grotto exhibit on the middle Friday of the month and run all the way up to Christmas Eve. Getting the place cobweb-free and set up before then is no mean feat. So, we're women on a deadline. We've a whole village to rustle up.

'Mine's ready for the fridge,' says Izz, bundling her gingerbread into a cloth to rest. Never cling film, as per Mum's instructions. 'You're quiet tonight?'

'I'm fine.' I do a really convincing shrug, but at the back of my mind, I'm still distracted by those alerts on my phone.

Those properties in Birmingham have left me feeling seriously unsettled. One of them had a conservatory on the back and a little veg garden. The estate agent called it a 'potagerie', which is, for the West Midlands, I reckon, pushing it a bit. Still, it did look nice.

If I'd started thinking this way sooner and put some 'For Sale' signs up in the autumn, I could've been taking Lucy to Wagamama's right now. It's her favourite place, and I've always wanted to try it out. Maybe we'd be watching *The Nutcracker* at the Birmingham Royal Ballet. Or we could be pottering round the Bullring doing our

Christmas shopping together, happily sipping overpriced coffee in red cups like the rest of the world.

'It's not Don, is it?' Izz says.

'*Hmm?* No. Well, not really.'

'It can't be easy, this time of year and everything.' She shuttles her dough into the fridge and makes for mine. 'Shove over. Let me finish that for you. You sit.'

'Fine by me,' I tell her, moving over to top up our glasses. I perch on a tall stool at the table.

'You haven't bothered with a Christmas tree this year, then?' she persists.

I know what she's getting at, of course. This time two years ago I was being swept off my feet by Don, and within a fortnight we were engaged. I remember the whole thing feeling distinctly festive, and I went all in celebrating. Then, cut to last Christmas, and I was up to my eyeballs in organising it all: white roses and baby's breath bouquet; floor-length ice-white satin gown overlaid with Cotswold lace; all ready to flounce down the aisle – or rather straight down through the gingerbread grotto tables – with Don on December twenty-fourth, head over heels with festive feels.

'Just a bit Christmassed out,' I say into my glass.

Izz is now slapping and knuckling my gingerbread mixture better than any Magimix could. 'If I could get my hands on him!' she says, but then, with a wary glance at me, she adds, 'Still, it's nearly twelve months since he…' She leaves a pause which my brain fills with suitable words. *Bolted. Did a runner. Absconded.* 'May happen you're thinking about…'

Again with the pausing. Her eyes are sparkling wickedly.

'What?' I say, not really wanting to know.

'May happen you're thinking about meeting someone new?'

'May happen *you* are?' I say, like a child, and then I feel stupid because Izz has shown precisely zero interest in anyone other than her ill-fated 1960s sweetheart. 'Here, pass that to me,' I say, relieving her of her dough and wrapping it for the fridge.

There's a knock at the front door, and it only fuels Izz more. She's raising a knowing eyebrow at the sound of it. Precisely *what* she knows, I couldn't say.

'Don't do that,' I warn her, turning for the door behind me. Typical Cotswold cottage, it opens into the kitchen.

'Do what?' She fails to feign innocence, taking off her apron and gathering the glasses and wine bottle. 'I'll grab a clean one for Patrick,' she chirrups and makes her way through to the den where the log burner is making the room glow a cosy orange in the absence of other lights.

I unlatch the door for Patrick. Right on time as always. My friend. My fellow fundraiser. Reliable, easy-to-get-along-with Patrick.

'Where d'you need these putting?' he asks as he steps inside, bringing the nicest smell of wood sap and winter chill with him.

Of course he's brought logs, and of course he's hefting them over his shoulders like a lumberjack posing for the type of calendar I'd definitely be pleased to find in my stocking on Christmas morning.

'Oh, uh, just through in the basket by the wood burner, thanks.'

He nods his understanding (he's not the grinning type, not like Don was), and he follows Izz's voice to the den where she's switched on the lights and is asking him if he's ready for a wine.

I shut the door behind him, noticing there are a few strands of Christmas bulbs twinkling in some of the back windows down the lane. Give it a few days and everyone will have their houses decorated except me.

I wash my hands and head for the den.

'Felled a tree on your way over?' Izz asks Patrick as she moves from the sofa to the lone armchair, leaving the seats side by side for me and Patrick.

'It's from one of the schoolyard oaks,' he tells her, laying down the wood by my log burner. 'Whole limb was damaged in the October storms. Been drying in my workshop ever since.'

We all look stupidly at the logs. Izz isn't even trying to hide the fact she's enjoying the curious awkwardness in the air. Patrick's oblivious, though. I lift his glass from Izz's hands and pass it to him, telling him to sit and get comfy.

I thank him for the firewood as he settles himself, and, as always when he's here, the den suddenly looks like a hobbit house with his tall, broad frame inside it.

'I nominate Izz to take the meeting minutes,' I say, giving her a smirk that immediately stops her delightedly observing the pair of us. What is she up to?

Patrick's mouth hitches into a smile at the corner, which he hides in his wine glass.

'You know as well as I do we never get further than the first five minutes before we forget to take notes,' Izz complains. 'Anyways, we've got to start the rolling soon. Gingerbread's in the fridge.'

Patrick's been around for enough Decembers to know what this means. The first of the gingerbreads are being cut and baked tonight.

27

'There is actually something I need to add to the agenda,' Patrick says in a voice that doesn't sound quite like him somehow.

Izz, too settled in my armchair to search for our minutes book, pretends to pull a pencil from her glorious orb of black hair shot with patches of white and mimes turning an invisible page, ready to write.

The light leaves his eyes as he sits forward. 'I don't foresee it being a problem for the grotto, not really,' he begins.

'Oh no, what?' I say. Just what we need, more problems.

'It's my caretaker job at the school. That new head, Mr Bold, called me into his office today, and well… he says the board have decided they can't afford to keep me on during school holidays. They're changing my contract to term time only. Effective immediately. And if I don't like it, I can lump it.'

'What?' I have to put my glass down I'm so cross.

'He can't do that. Can he?' Izz demands.

'I checked with my cousin, the one that works in employment law,' Patrick goes on. 'They're within their rights to do it. I don't have to accept the new contract, but if I don't, they can let me go entirely, if they want to.'

'So, you're not going to get paid over the Christmas break?' I say, blinking in outrage.

He shrugs like he's already accepted his fate. 'The head's going to get a surprise when he realises the school boiler needs bleeding weekly through winter, but I'll let him find that out for himself when there's icicles on the gymnasium windowsills.'

'Who is this person?' Izz wants to know.

'The new head teacher?' Patrick replies. 'Some bloke from down south somewhere. Barely out of uni, I'd say. He's the only one wanted the job when Mrs Fourmile retired. The board loved him and his cost-cutting ideas. He was the one came up with the December boot camp thing, renting out the gymnasium and bringing in some much-needed money.'

'Yeah, and it's lost us our grotto parking!' I say, feeling my face heat. I need to calm down.

'He won't stay long,' Patrick says with the air of a man who's overheard something confidential in some meeting or other. 'He's only here biding his time before fast-tracking himself into a superhead job in some city primary. A country school's not for the likes of him.'

'A superhead?' Izz squints.

'You know,' I tell her. 'An educational troubleshooter? Like the SAS but for underperforming schools. They parachute these superheads in and within weeks there's no such thing as bullying, turkey twizzler lunches, under-performing teachers...'

'Unnecessary caretakers,' Patrick adds wryly.

I fight the urge to reach out and touch his arm, though really, why shouldn't I comfort a friend in a friendly, not weirdly-touchy-feely, way? I reach for my glass once more and grip the stem tight.

'If he thinks I'm telling him where the grit's kept, he's wrong.' Patrick forces a smile to show us he's OK. 'Hope he likes ice skating.' He takes a drink, and this douses his agitation a little. 'It's only three weeks without pay. Seventeen days, in fact. I counted.'

'You don't need to worry about money,' I say. 'I can help.' I really mean it, but saying the words makes me feel like a mum offering a grown-up son some of their

29

savings. I'd say I've never felt more aware of the gap in years between us (fifteen years, eight weeks and a day, not that I've done the sums), but that would be a lie.

'God no,' he blurts. 'Thank you, but no. I'm fine. I can always pick up something seasonal if I need to.'

Izz joins in. 'That's the spirit, and you can do literally anything. Electric stuff, woodwork stuff, building stuff...' She tails off, thinking hard before enthusiastically adding, 'Baking stuff too.'

Patrick takes another big gulp of wine before saying, 'Speaking of baking, did anyone respond to your flyers, Izz?'

It was her idea to have them printed and shove them through every door in Wheaton, a call to arms, or rather, spoons, for the grotto. *Santa's seeking some little helpers*, it said, which Izz thought was cute, but even with the promise of *All ingredients provided*, I wasn't hopeful.

'Turns out Margi was right,' Izz tells us.

Patrick is more of an optimist than me. 'What, nobody?' he says.

Izz shakes her head.

'Just us three, then,' I say, and I wonder if it's time to mention this is going to be my last year on the committee. Soon they'll be down to two, and, realistically, that will make the whole thing unfeasible. It's already exhausting and expensive without losing one of the ringleaders.

'Then we should crack on, shouldn't we?' Patrick says, offering a reprieve before I've taken the huge breath I need to blurt out the truth: that I'm not only giving up on the grotto but getting out of Wheaton too.

'You're right. Come on,' I say, feeling a little wobbly as I try to stand. I drop back down again. Another chance missed. How am I ever supposed to broach the subject?

Actually leaving Wheaton? I can hardly believe it myself, but the whole idea's gathered pace now I've had this place valued and the estate agent assured me they'd be able to sell it without even advertising it. 'Be snapped up in seconds by any number of our contacts,' he told me. 'Historic old property like this, original fireplaces, old world Cotswolds setting. It's a dream home.'

It was mine too, all my life, but once Mum and Dad left for Spain it lost so much of its magic, and then Don shipped in and shipped straight back out again, playing the man of the house for all of twelve months. The place just doesn't feel like home any more. Izz, for one, will be devastated. It's harder to know what Patrick will feel. Maybe he won't mind. It can't be fun for him, hanging out with us all Advent, then being forced to play Santa Claus when he could be having a normal Christmas with his own family, whoever they are, or going out on some festive dates, maybe. He's not even fifty yet. Why bother with us and all our gingerbread nonsense? I just don't know what we did to deserve his help. I really don't.

He's towering over me. I find I can't risk looking up at him from this angle in case he notices me goggling. I have, however, already clocked how nicely dressed he is. Dark khaki pants rolled a little at the ankle – a reminder if it was needed that he's still in his forties and dresses like it – and brown boots with a dark jumper I've never seen him in before.

'Been shopping?' I ask as I rise to my feet too.

'Hmm?' He tips his head.

'This is new.' I gesture at his sleeve, which he immediately pushes up, I'm guessing in an unconscious response, to reveal a leather watch strap and some forearm that makes me want to bite my lip and scold myself for being like this.

'Oh, uh, yeah,' he remarks, and leaves it at that.

Oh no, is he scowling or... blushing?

Suddenly, I'm not sure what's going on, but I'm aware he's just standing there looking at me like he's trying to figure out what I'm thinking, or maybe he's unsure what else to say.

Izz's smirking face rises from around his shoulder. 'If you two are finished with the scintillating chat, how about we get our pins out? Hmm?' And she leads the way to the kitchen again. 'Meeting adjourned on account of there being tons to be getting on with.' As she glides by, she replaces the imaginary pencil in her hair.

'After you,' Patrick tells me, sweeping a hand in front.

'Right!' I yelp as I follow Izz, bringing my hands together in a decisive clap. 'Ovens on, let's get rolling.' I try not to think about Patrick following behind me, eyes on my back. *Hopefully*, they're only on my back.

The three of us huddle around the table ready to bake into the night, the last people in England who give two fruit cakes about the Gingerbread Christmas Village and, since I'm the only one amongst us who knows this year will be the very last of its kind, I'm secretly determined that we'll go out with a big festive bang.

Chapter Three

Four a.m. is the worst time to be single and sixty-five. However, my brain chemistry decided months ago that this was absolutely the best time to wake me up. Its favourite ways for startling me awake include: phantom wee (an urgent bladder that turns out to be a false alarm, but by the time I know this, I'm face to face with myself in the bathroom mirror), a good old-fashioned creak at the windows or rafters (in a 400-year-old cottage there's nothing but creaks all day long but at night my brain interprets every one as an intruder set on murdering me in my bed), or – and this is its favourite method by a long way – a horribly twisted dream. And that's what my grey matter served up for me tonight, a sort of nightmare mixed in with real memories in all their glorious technicolour realism. So here I am again, wide awake in the dark, counting the minutes until morning, and an article Izz read to me in *Prima* promised this will only get worse the older I get. Sleeplessness, just one of ageing's many bountiful gifts!

This time, though, my clever old brain got so many of the details right, replaying the scene for me like an old cine film, and I got to watch the whole thing over again, exactly as it had unfolded that night in The Salutation.

It had all started out so promising too. Two Christmas Eves ago, after the grotto closed for the season. Everyone had a drink inside them, and people do things they regret when they're well into a bottle of Tia Maria, not that that's any excuse for my behaviour. The whole village was in, it seemed, standing room only, and we'd burst through the doors, flushed with (moderate) success and the relief of shutting up the exhibit for the year.

We'd raised about three thousand pounds, not bad at all, a slight increase on previous years, but that increase had been absorbed by Patrick's new Father Christmas costume. The old one had been moth-eaten, and one of the grotto's predecessor Santas had left a humbug in the trousers sometime in 1990, and it had melted and glued the pocket shut ever since, so it was beyond time to replace it. Patrick was still wearing it, the suit, and I remember thinking he looked handsome in his scarlet velvet breeches and with the matching jacket all undone and those black boots and the big leather belt.

What my dream-mare helpfully filled in for me tonight was how rosy his cheeks had been and how his eyes were shining while he twirled me on the pub's dance floor. I'm still not sure if those are things I actually saw and must have packed away in my unconscious only for them to come back out in my vulnerable alone-in-bed state, or whether my brain enjoys embellishing these things out of a sick preoccupation with paining me.

Either way, I got to experience it all over again, dancing under the pub's party lights while Lolla the landlady (exhaling enough apple-scented vapour to give any smoke machine a run for its atmosphere-making money) kept the drinks coming.

There was a definite moment where we stopped under the big ball of mistletoe one of the farmers had hung from the rafters over the dance floor. Cerys Matthews and Tom Jones were crooning about it being cold outside, and I was laughing and feeling my absolute happiest in that moment.

Dream Patrick told me he liked me in a dress. I had worn a dress that night (berry-red and short); the first time I'd bared my legs in public in years, actually. I can't remember if he really did say it in real life or not. The music had been too loud for chatting, so I doubt it somehow. Maybe he said it right in my ear. Was that what set off the electrified feeling inside me? Thanks, brain, for capturing all of that so accurately in the rerun.

That night, Patrick had ditched the beard and the glasses, and everyone was buying him drinks and toasting the village's own Father Christmas, the man of the hour, and he was playing along, saying how he'd better be setting off in his sleigh soon, what with it being Christmas Eve.

He definitely asked me what I wanted for Christmas as we danced – my brain's got that spot on – and I know I laughed, and his palm, I distinctly recall, spread across the small of my back in a way that made my nervous system malfunction completely.

Then, and this is where my dream took liberties because this categorically did not happen, I rested my cheek against his, and we slowed in our dancing while he said things in a voice sunk to a hazy, gruff kind of rasp that I hadn't imagined coming from Patrick before tonight – again, thank you, brain. He was saying things about liking me, how he couldn't hold back any longer. I won't go into detail. It never happened, of course. It's just four a.m. me getting lost in a silly fantasy. But what happened next,

I will never forget. This bit was one hundred per cent accurate in all its awful detail in the replay.

Patrick had suddenly stopped dancing, and I was sort of blinking in his face, wondering why the pub lights had come up, and he pulled away looking kind of cross, frustrated maybe, and it's possible Real Patrick *had* been saying something along the lines of 'I know things are getting serious with Don, but—' when everything else got lost in the sudden commotion in the pub, and people were cheering and whooping and Lolla cut the music for some reason.

I hadn't remembered until tonight, but I think Patrick's face kind of froze, and he stepped away backwards, disappearing into the crowd of laughing, tipsy locals in Christmas jumpers who were all looking at me for some reason, and Patrick was just... gone.

I turned around, wondering what the hell everyone was shouting at, and there, kneeling on the floor at my feet, was Don holding up a ring box, and he was smiling his most winning smile, and that's when I jolted awake tonight, at the part that is supposed to be every woman's dream: a big, romantic proposal.

That's it. I'm getting up and putting the kettle on.

The bedroom floorboards are cold under my feet, but the kitchen flagstones are downright freezing, enough to banish the very last hazy clouds of my dream state.

I watch the kettle on the gas ring, waiting for it to boil, and it's still there: the heavy sinking sensation in my chest that I had that night in the seconds that followed Don popping the question. It seemed at the time to last an excruciating hour while I was assaulted by a rush of feelings, most of them happy, excited, dizzy ones, and only some of them anxious, cautious and embarrassed ones telling me not to mind all the people gathered around watching, waiting for my response.

I knew I could walk right out if I wanted to. I don't know why I didn't. Don's smile? His confidence that we were perfect together? The feeling of being really alive and actually desired for once?

The racket that went up when I heard myself saying 'yes' kind of blasted everything else that happened that evening into insignificance.

I'm opening the Christmas biscuits, sod it. If I'm going to be sleepless, I'm at least having some lebkuchen to console me. I make my tea extra milky, hoping that will settle me.

A whirlwind. That's what the *Wheaton Parish Newsletter* announcement called our engagement. That's one way to describe it, even though now, with the divorce papers on my computer and everything dissolved between me and Don, I know it was more of a category-five hurricane. Catastrophic damage. Risk to human life. Loss of power. Homes levelled. I should get him a storm warning printed on a T-shirt to scare off the next dizzy woman he plans to sweep off her feet.

Turns out, Don was a serial monogamist, addicted to the thrill of falling in love. When the buzz wore off, he'd ride away. At least, that's how me and Izz figured it, during the marriage post-mortem. It certainly explains why he had Interflora set as a 'favourite' phone contact.

Funny how only after it was all over did I recall him enthusing fondly about old girlfriends and impromptu trips to Paris or Rome that he'd surprised them with. He must have left a trail of romantic destruction in his wake wherever he drifted. I wonder now how many of them he actually married. I can add that to the long list of things

37

I simply don't know about the man I was fool enough to marry. Stupid woman!

I carry my tea into the den. There's a special bleakness in an English winter night when you're alone with your memories and there's nothing but sixty-watt bulbs buzzing in their shades, too harsh and hurting my tired eyes.

'I should have got a tree,' I tell the night, pulling the blanket over me on the sofa where Patrick was sitting only this afternoon.

Izz was right. Being miserable by fairy light has to be better than this glare. Even Scrooge had candles to soften his long night's reacquaintance with his past mistakes.

But no. I won't be indulging in decorations this year. There's too much faffery goes into Christmas as it is, and I'm still remorseful about how I overdosed last December when I thought it'd be a good idea to combine my wedding with the opening night of the gingerbread grotto.

Last year there wasn't a wall, a gatepost or a hedgerow left un-fairy-lit from my garden path all the way down the lane and on to the high street and past the schoolhouse to the village hall. It took me days to string them up, marking my bridal passage. It's safe to say my nuptials tipped my love of Christmas décor over into 'dangerously twee' territory.

Looking back, I think I was aware of the looks on some of the villagers' faces as I paraded through town that crisp winter morning in my satin, lace and faux fur, past all my pretty lights and down to the hall where Don was waiting. At the time, I was blissfully unaware, but I should have *heard* those looks. 'She's no spring chicken,' they said. 'Barely knows the fella.' 'Who even is he?' 'I give it a year,' they said. Even behind the locals' plastered-on smiles. I should have known.

Maybe, deep down, I was intent on proving the world wrong. You *can* get the whole fairy tale in your sixties, course you can. Don and I were going to last, and we'd show them what love in later life looked like. We'd put on a show for all those young ones thinking they invented attraction and held the monopoly on romance. I couldn't have been more deluded.

Only I didn't know it until two weeks later when Don slipped from our honeymoon bed right here in my cottage and hopped on his Harley, riding off into the Christmas Eve dawn with as little warning as he'd swept into my life just thirteen months earlier.

I sip my tea and ruminate. Patrick was away for the whole wedding, thankfully, so at least one villager missed my humiliation. He was using up two weeks of his remaining holiday time to visit his parents in Cheltenham. But Mum and Dad were here to help with everything, little knowing they were flying over to give their daughter away (again) *and* to help pick up the pieces when it all went wrong (again). Dad even filled Patrick's Santa boots that year and didn't do a half-bad job of it, though the grotto wasn't quite the same without him. Yet everyone else in the village was here to witness my hopefulness turn to humiliation. Most people, and especially Patrick, have been kind enough not to mention Don since. We all just pretend he never existed.

I've drained my tea, disappeared three biscuits, and am feeling distinctly dozy again when I find myself speculating about Dream Patrick.

Why now? After knowing him for getting on for five years of companionate friendship, why does my brain want to play tricks on me now? Making me dream like that. When there's almost fifteen years between us, and when he's become one of the firmest friends of my entire life. Why not back then, when he first moved to the village, taking the job at the school? When I was still in my fifties. Maybe then we could have... no.

No, this isn't helpful. There's no use in asking 'what if?'

If we were going to be 'something', it would have happened then, back when I was a different person without a reputation in the village for reckless love matches, when I could be classed as officially still young(ish) and, even if I say it myself, really quite fanciable. Back before he became indispensable to me, a true friend I couldn't bear to lose.

The dream sensations linger, the feeling of his hand firm at the base of my spine, the insistent thoughts about how nice it would be to be held like that again while his eyes are shining and we're both laughing and breathless from dancing.

The jolt I receive from the phone ringing in the kitchen makes me almost throw my empty mug across the floor. Its piercing sound cracks open the night.

Four forty-five? Not a good time for a phone call. Not good at all. I sprint for it, dragging the blanket with me.

'Auntie Margi?' a small voice trembles and sniffs.

'Luce? What's the matter?' She's trying not to cry.

'It's Craig. He's gone.'

Ugh, no surprise there. I only met him once, right at the beginning, and I didn't like him even then. Another flop of a man, and years of my clever, talented, beautiful niece's precious time wasted.

'Oh, darling. Where are you?' I ask, and that's when I hear the tapping at the cottage door.

Chapter Four

There's only one thing for it during an ongoing heartache situation: a trip to Bizzy Izz's, another Wheaton institution holding on for dear life. It's the sweetest tea room in the Cotswolds, and I'm not talking intentionally shabby chic, either. This is old-school, hangover-from-the-1970s stuff; all copper kettles on the walls and cabbage roses on the curtains, as though *The Country Diary of an Edwardian Lady* and Laura Ashley had a chintzy tea-room baby.

I wasn't sure how Lucy would react to the suggestion of popping out to eat, but she followed me dutifully down the lane and into the village. I saw her tired red eyes light up when we let ourselves inside a moment ago and were immediately assaulted by retro (read: 'so old they've become cool again') decorations and a blast of Christmas FM on the cafe radio.

Now the hugs are out of the way – Izz has known Lucy since she was a baby – she asks if we want some tea.

'Maybe a hot chocolate for me? Large, please,' Lucy replies, and I get a flash of the little girl she used to be.

'Righty-o,' Izz calls, disappearing again, but I make sure she hears my order for two big breakfasts as well.

'I'd have thought Izz would have retired by now,' says Lucy, pulling up a chair by the cherrywood grandfather clock that hasn't ticked in decades but is nonetheless shiny and gorgeous.

'She should have done,' I say, 'years ago, but, between us, I'm not sure she can bring herself to sell the place.'

Lucy's looking around like she's seeing it for the first time. I'm not surprised, really. It's been a while since she visited Wheaton, and she usually spends her trips out in the fresh air with her easel and paints.

'It's cute,' she says, but her eyes fall back to her hands in her lap. She's more exhausted than me, poor thing.

When she stumbled through my cottage door long before dawn, she cried, and I managed to get a few details out of her, but not many. Craig had upped and left at some point in the last twenty-four hours and their on-again, off-again relationship seems to be well and truly off for good this time. He even went to the trouble of taking the telly they had bought together, so I reckon he really isn't coming back. I try not to feel too pleased she chose to come to me in her hour of need, but it's nice to be wanted. I hope it doesn't mean she didn't have anyone else and I was her last resort.

Wheaton was never really her home. When my sister Lydia (a nurse) and Terry, her husband (he's a pharmacist) left Wheaton for Birmingham to take jobs at the hospital, they of course took Lucy with them. She was only a toddler then. Later, when the prospect of a living wage and comfortable working conditions in shiny New Zealand hospitals and dispensaries proved too irresistible for either of them to turn down (and who can blame them?), Lucy was leaving for uni and didn't want to go with her parents. It caused a lot of tears and guilt on both sides, but everybody's fine about it now.

Lucy's boyfriend at the time probably had a lot to do with the decision to stay. I can't even remember his name. He was what Mum would call a 'flash in the pan' kind of fellow.

And, right on cue, there it is again. I have to push thoughts of Don, my own flash in the pan, to the back of my brain. He emerges at every opportunity to remind me I have no more relationship nous than a teenager.

Anyway, Lucy's uni days are far behind her, and she's been settled in Birmingham in her own place for a few years now, doing bits and bobs of substitute art teaching and tutoring, and every now and again we get days like this, me and her, catching up. They are a beacon of light for me. I adore this girl, and I am – even though I am her only auntie – still regarded by her as her 'cool aunt'. Got the birthday mug to prove it and everything.

'One hot chocolate.' Izz puts the mug down between us. It's peaked with cream and marshmallows. 'And tea in a mug, strong and black. Breakfasts won't be a minute,' she says, but at the rate she shuffles off, I wonder if perhaps it's going to take longer than usual.

'Is your hip still bad, Izz?' I ask, and she turns in a slow half-circle to face us again.

'Bit creaky now it's turned colder.' She adjusts her stance in a pained way. 'But I've got one of the farmers' daughters coming in today to help out. Trial run.'

'That's good,' I say, trying not to sound too enthusiastic, because I've been begging Izz to look for a helper for ages and she wouldn't hear anything of it, she's so protective of her little world, and I suppose, up until recently, she's managed fine on her own.

Izz grimaces. 'If she comes. She's late.'

'The roads were icy on the way here,' puts in Lucy. 'Maybe she's having trouble getting into the village if she's coming from one of the farms?'

'Well, let's hope she's a dynamo when she does get here,' Izz says as she hirples into the kitchen. We watch her go, Lucy's expression mirroring my own.

'Not good,' Lucy says, as Izz disappears into the kitchen.

'Izz likes her independence and to be kept busy, but' – I lower my voice to a whisper – 'it's getting too much now.'

Izz's voice rising in song with the kitchen radio makes us both smile. I'll bet she knows we're talking about her.

'So, did you bring your art supplies?' I venture, but Lucy only looks at me, a little surprised, and shakes her head, like the idea hadn't occurred to her.

'That's a shame. You could have done some painting today.'

My den wall has, over the years, become a bit of a Lucy gallery. They're all hanging there: from her first messy attempts with crayons and poster paints; through her teens when she was experimenting with portraiture in acrylics; to her more recent work, wonderful water-colours, mostly landscapes with a dreamy, unreal touch to them. Combined, they'd give the rather snooty Wheaton Gallery a run for its money. Only Lucy's paintings are actually priceless in my opinion.

She just shrugs, and it strikes me I haven't heard her mention anything to do with art in a very long time. She was forever entering her work into competitions or local exhibitions, but that's all gone quiet now. Not for the first time, I hear alarm bells ringing about how she's been living. I try to hide my concern with a smile.

'How are you now? That was quite the overnight dash you made.'

She takes a drink of hot chocolate, considering this.

'I'm all right,' she says eventually. 'I'm good, actually. Glad it's over and done with.' She doesn't look nearly as decided as she's trying to sound.

'Good for you,' I say anyway. 'And you're staying? The spare room's all yours.'

'Can I?'

I saw her suitcase in the back of her car as we walked past it a moment ago. I didn't mention it. 'Always,' I tell her. It's on the tip of my tongue to say I wish she could stay forever, but then I remember my Birmingham escape plan and keep my lip zipped. I haven't mentioned the idea to Lucy yet either, and this doesn't seem like the right time. She's always loved coming here for visits. It might add to her upset if I tell her that won't be an option any more someday soon.

'I might stay the night, then. If that's OK?' she tells me.

We clink our mugs to seal the deal just as the door opens, not with its usual screech at the hinges but with a slow, drawn-out mouse squeak that makes me turn in my chair.

Ever so gradually, a pair of wide eyes peer around the door, scanning as if for predators. Then, even more cautiously, a slight little body emerges too, squeezing through the narrow opening they've allowed themselves as though they don't want to let in any more chill December winds than strictly necessary.

'There you are!' Izz calls from the kitchen hatch, and the delicate person, now on the doormat and seemingly trying to close the door without being the slightest incon-venience to anyone, flinches. 'You're Fern,' Izz informs her, and the girl nods, her eyes darting around the cafe from customer to customer.

It's an averagely busy day; half of the ten or so tables and booths are occupied, enough to make the place steamy. There's condensation clouding the windows behind the nets.

'Well, come in, then,' Izz coaxes, and the girl clasps her own elbow with her hand, her head low.

The petrified thing steps further into the room where everyone examines her. Out of pity, I turn back to my mug of tea, but I keep my ears trained on the pair.

Izz is asking the girl, 'So, what have we here?'

To be fair to Izz, I haven't seen anyone quite like Fern before either. For a painfully shy scrap of a thing, she's dressed like she has the confidence of a town crier.

I glance at Lucy, worried I'm being judgy too, and find she's simply smiling at the girl in the ankle-length brown plaid smock dress and umpteen layers of flouncy, woolly things that seem so out of time that even my granny might have found them old-fashioned. She's wearing modern jewellery, though, and big specs that make her light eyes moley and rather endearing. And, impossible to miss, there are what look like little mushrooms and acorns dangling from her petite ears. I take the quickest glance back just to check she really is wearing some kind of lacy drape over her red hair too. Yep, she is. I don't understand it at all.

As Izz bustles the girl to a vacant table, I take my chance to ask Lucy in a whisper exactly what is going on there. 'Is she a cartoon character?'

'I thought you had Instagram?' is all Lucy has time to hiss at me. None the wiser, I decide I've been nosy-parkerish enough and I'd better leave the poor girl to her induction, but Izz is just as bewildered as me, evidently.

'So what's this get-up you're wearing?' I hear her ask.

The girl whispers something inaudible that prompts a 'Come again?' from her inquisitor.

'It's cottage core,' the girl breathes out. 'Little bit of forest core. It's my aesthetic.'

'Oh, 'tis, is it?' Izz says in a jolly, well-I've-seen-it-all-now kind of way.

Both Lucy and I are conspicuously not conversing. In fact, everyone in the cafe seems to be silently earwigging as Izz asks the girl what sort of things she makes at home.

'Uh, petticoats, obi belts, tried a few bits of corsetry,' the girl says.

'What *food*?'

'Oh! Um…' There's a long wait before Fern ventures timidly, 'Avo' smash on toast?'

There's another moment's silence for the death of Izz's hopes of finding a waitress to take the strain off her this winter.

'Can you manage a full fry-up?' Izz asks. 'Or kippers? Omelettes? Home-made soup? Toasties and the like? Could you do a Victoria sponge?'

'I don't know,' the girl says in such a defeated, delicate way that I just know it's accompanied by a shrinking shrug.

'Well,' Izz says, standing. '*Ooft!* My knees. You'll be needing an apron to cover your pretty dress. Come on. I'll show you your way around my stoves.'

Lucy and I have to pretend we've been chatting. Lucy goes so far as to fake a laugh in response to something I didn't say as Izz and the girl slope across the cafe and into the kitchen.

'Cottage core?' I say immediately after they've gone.

'Yeah, you know? It's for people who like vintage, countryfied lifestyle stuff.'

'Granny stuff?'

'Well, yeah,' Lucy says. 'It's nice. Lots of young people are into it.'

'But...' I'm baffled. 'She looked about eighteen and was dressed like the ghost of a nineteenth-century milk-maid. When I was her age I wanted a pin through my nose, and I ripped all my mohair jumpers so I could look like Vivienne Westwood. Last thing I wanted was to live like some fantasy grandma.'

'Auntie Margi!' Lucy playfully scolds. 'What annoys you more than anything?'

It's such a change of topic I give my head a shake.

'Um, when all your laundry jumps inside the duvet on the spin cycle? Why does it do that?' I venture, then change my mind. 'No, when your apples come in little individual moulded cup things. All that packaging drives me mad. No, scrub that. Jacob Rees-Mogg, the rotten little...'

'Nope.' My niece cuts me off. 'You hate when people expect you to be all old-fogeyish, right? *Right?*'

Lucy pulls a face, waiting for me to connect the dots myself. I pretend I can't see what she's getting at just so she'll roll her eyes and smile.

It's true, of course. Just because I have my bus pass doesn't mean I wouldn't use it to get to a Buzzcocks reunion, not that that can happen, but you get my meaning. Not that I do go to gigs these days. Anyway, you shouldn't assume I don't go to gigs just because of the greys in my hair.

Lucy interrupts my thoughts. 'So, let's not judge young people just because of the way they look? Or because of their interests.'

'You are young people!' I tell her, and she shakes her head.

'The kids I teach are Fern's age. I could almost be their mum.'

I suddenly feel extremely old, and Lucy looks sad again, so I drop the subject and reach for her hand instead, giving her a reassuring pat before our food arrives.

Fern sets my plate down in front of me. I whisper my thanks in case I startle her.

'Plated it up herself,' Izz tells us. 'Mostly.'

'It looks delicious,' Lucy tells Fern, who can't meet her eyes. Instead, she blushes and screws her mouth to the side like Lady Di. It's unpractised and a bit disarming.

'Which of the farms are you from?' I risk, straining my ears to hear her answer over the thrum of chat in the room.

'Brambledown.'

'Brambledown Farm? Does that make your dad *Tommy Brash*?' It's out before I can stop myself and I wonder if it sounded rude. I can't imagine this will-o'-the-wisp coming from bristly, brusque Tommy's farm. Mind you, he's a man of very few words as well. Grunts and grimaces, yes, but very few words. Maybe it does make sense after all.

'Dad said I had to get a job now I've left school.'

'And you don't fancy being a farmer?' I ask, and it's clearly a question too far. The girl withdraws like a snail into a shell.

'What do you reckon then, Fern?' Izz asks. 'Reckon you could manage nine till three thirty every day 'cept Sundays? I'll teach you all my recipes.'

'Cakes too?' Fern says – the loudest thing to come from her mouth yet.

'Cakes too.'

'And bread? I'd love to bake my own bread.' Fern's getting animated now. 'I live with Dad and Grandad. They're not into baking much.'

'Ah, um...' Izz looks to me for help.

'What's this?' my niece wants to know, looking between us.

'It's tricky, the bread thing,' I say, and Izz guides Fern through to the kitchen with her arm across her shoulder, explaining. Izz daren't be overheard speaking about it in public, not after all the fuss.

Me however, I have no qualms. I lift my cutlery and make a start on the fried egg. 'Didn't you know?' I say to Lucy, all arch and enjoying myself. 'The only person baking any kind of bread in this village is Scrimengor.'

'The bakery at the far end of the village?' says Lucy.

'That's the one.'

'Bakery' makes it sound cute. It's not. It's a breeze-block lock-up with industrial cooling racks lined up along its glass front, totally out of keeping with Wheaton's chocolate-box rows of ramshackle Cotswold stone cottages. When locals want a loaf they have to knock at the bolted door and pay in cash. It's been that way for easily fifty years, maybe longer.

I pop a bit of eggy toast in my mouth. 'This is his granary bread,' I say, and I have to admit, it is delicious. 'But Mr Scrimengor got all bent out of shape during lockdown when Izz, trying to keep her head above water like everyone else, attempted selling her own bread rolls and pizza dough kits. He said Izz was trying to put him out of business.'

'There's a Bentley parked outside his shop, though?' Lucy observes. She's shrewd, my niece, notices everything.

'That's him. The licence plate spells *DoUGH*.'

'Classy.'

Lucy's eating happily now. It warms me to see she still has an appetite despite her broken heart.

'Man's a pillock,' I go on since she's enjoying this particular bit of village lore. 'You know he and Mum had a huge falling out?'

'Really? I can't imagine Great-Aunt Nancy ever falling out with anybody.'

'When she moved the gingerbread grotto from the church porch into the village hall, absolutely yonks ago, when it was becoming obvious it wasn't some small-scale baking affair, he took exception to the fact she hadn't asked him to make all her gingerbreads.'

'Why didn't she? It would have been easier than doing it around the kitchen table.'

'Because he saw helping out as a money-spinning scheme for himself. He wanted to charge her umpteen times the cost of doing it all herself, and when she said she couldn't afford it – it was just a local charity event sort of thing, you know, for good causes in the village? – he took the huff. Hasn't so much as offered to help ice a gingerbread cottage since. He won't even let me put a grotto poster in his bakery window, and it's been decades since they fell out about it.'

Lucy's moved on to her bacon now. 'Dough boy can hold a grudge?'

'Certainly can.' I move one of my sausages onto her plate and get away with it because feeding her up is one of my auntie privileges. 'Anyway,' I tell her. 'He has the monopoly on all things baked, and to keep the peace, Izz only ever does her own scones, Victoria sponges, a bit of fruity flapjack and jam roly-poly – stuff he doesn't bother with at the bakery.'

'And he supplies all of Izz's bread?'

'Of course. Not worth the hassle of crossing him.'

'That sounds ominous,' says Lucy, giving me her black pudding, which I know she doesn't like, but I love. 'Are we talking Cotswold mafia here?'

'Good as. I mean, he's on the council. Holds a lot of sway. I never managed to get him on side, but once an enemy, I guess your family's always an enemy. It's a shame because his gingerbread men are seriously tasty. At least, I remember them that way. The Asda delivery driver brings my bread. Haven't bought anything from Scrimengor's on principle since the Grottogate nonsense.'

'You sound like a pretty good match,' Lucy remarks with a laugh, covering her mouth with her hand holding her fork.

'What does that mean? Me and Scrimengor?'

'I mean you're both stubborn.'

'*Pfft!*' Rubbish.

She's not finished with me yet. 'And taking the whole *support local businesses* thing to new heights? You're obsessed with your grotto; he's obsessed with his bakery.'

'You can't compare our gingerbread grotto to his miserable bready existence. Honestly, no one around here's even seen him smile. A match? What a thing to say.'

Lucy's really laughing now. She's always enjoyed winding me up, even when she was tiny, and I've always loved pretending she's got me. Still, she's not the first person to point out I can be a tiny bit stubborn, and it didn't go unnoticed by Don. Ugh, there he is again.

'Eat up,' I hurry her, circling my knife at Lucy's plate. 'We've got to go to the cash and carry over Stow way. We're out of flour, and we're baking tonight.'

'Tonight? What about *Strictly*?' she protests.

'Well… I suppose we could make a little gingerbread Anton Du Beke? And Claudia Winkleman's fringe will come up lovely in glossy black icing…'

Another eye-roll and a laugh.

This girl has no idea how much light she brings into my life. My Lucy. The best person I know. My December's looking up now she's in Wheaton, and hopefully, I can keep her here for a bit too, do us both good.

–

The Cotswolds really are at their gentle best at this time of year. Seeing it through Lucy's eyes as we make our run in her car to the wholesaler is a good reminder of that.

Sure, in the summer everything is lush and blousey, and the miles and miles of fields as far as your eye can see are soft and rolling, and the cattle are dotted around picturesquely like the whole thing is staged. In July, it's easy to feel like you're living in some Arcadian idyll. Unfortunately, we have to share the summer months with ten million tourists and their noisy, stinky coaches.

But, on days like today, when everything is stripped back by the cold weather and short, dark days of winter, the locals are left with the real, raw Cotswolds, and it is breath-taking. We live amidst unspoiled countryside, so landlocked it's hard to remember the sea even exists, right in the middle of what the lifestyle magazines call 'the heart of England'.

Fluffy clouds and summer skies are all very well, but December's glaring whiteout, hinting at snow waiting for its moment to fall, has an atmosphere all its own.

It's especially nice to go out for a drive on days like this, more so with Lucy's music playing and the heaters on. I take the wheel, letting Lucy rest, and we make our way extra slowly past the big duck pond on the green at Snowshill and take a long detour around Broadway where we keep our eyes trained on the tree line, looking for the resident herd of red deer, glimpsing only one peering back at us from a distance.

It's possible to drive for miles and see nothing constructed more recently than the sixteen hundreds. Repairs are carried out with our own thatch and locally-quarried slate and butter-coloured soft stone, and because of that, there's nowhere on the planet that looks quite like the Cotswolds. At Bourton-on-the-Water, I pull off the road and we nip into a cafe for a cream tea served with sweet cranberry jam as a nod to the season, and we gaze out at the wide, shallow river that runs right through the village, commenting to one another that we really ought to have brought some bread for the greedy mallards. Then it's back in the car and on our way.

Leafless, the oaks and ashes dominate the landscape, stark against the bare fields, like one of Lucy's pencil sketches before she adds the sweeping green watercolour foliage. It's wonderful; I'd forgotten quite how wonderful.

It's what Mum calls a 'pocket day', a few precious hours of warmth and comfort to be kept safely stored away in the memory for when you need it. I resist the urge to tell Lucy every ten minutes how glad I am that she's here. She's contemplative and quieter than usual, and I hope that means there's some recuperation happening.

We manage to enjoy ourselves even when we hit the main roads and the industrial units with the big ugly cash and carry where we don't forget to stock up on Christmas chocolates and wine for ourselves. This makes me hopeful Lucy's not leaving any time soon, but I don't pry.

Lucy takes over the driving on the way home as the sun sets, the boot loaded with plain flour and demerara.

We enter Wheaton, passing the church all in darkness and sidle alongside Scrimengor's bakery which happens to be lit up. We have to slow to a crawl to squeeze past the ridiculous *DoUGH* Bentley, but when Lucy spies the tractor coming towards us, we have to pull right into the side to let it pass, and we both say the obligatory 'Rush hour?' at the same time.

There's someone in the bakery. They're sweeping along the big glass frontage. Lucy stares in. 'He doesn't look like the misery guts you described,' she says.

The sweeper isn't stone-faced Scrimengor but a really rather handsome lad, probably in his mid-twenties, with the kind of cool, sculpted hair you'd see in a salon magazine.

'No, that's his grandson,' I tell her. 'Haven't seen him in years. Thought he'd left Wheaton.'

Lucy's still watching him, even now that the tractor's gone and the road's clear.

'Feeling peckish?' I joke. 'Shall we pop in? Maybe an iced bun would be nice?'

'Hmm?' Lucy isn't listening.

We watch as Scrimengor Junior — no idea what his name is, like I said, it's been years — is joined by the lowering figure of his grandfather who hands him what looks like a blue hairnet. There's a bit of an unheard altercation and the elder baker wins as the poor guy pulls the cover over his hair, looking less than impressed.

'So, Scrimengor's grumpy treatment extends even to his own grandson?' I say. 'No wonder that lad's stayed away.'

'Hm?' Lucy turns her face to mine with a slightly glazed look.

I only smile knowingly and point to the clear road ahead.

'Oh, right.' She hurriedly slips into gear and we pull away. Not before, I notice, Lucy takes one last glance at the unfortunate guy miserably working his broom across the bakery floor.

Chapter Five

Sunday 3 December: Keys

'What did you get this morning?' Izz asks me. She's bundled in so much wool the sight of her should really make me warmer than this. It's tipping rain, and we're sheltering beneath the stone lintel at the top of the village hall steps.

'Hmm?'

'Behind your advent door?' she beams. 'Mine was a gingerbread house. I took it as a good sign.'

We're waiting for Mr Scrimengor to send over the keys so we can get into the hall and start cleaning. I'm dreading seeing the place after a few damp months locked up, but Izz is clutching a bottle of Dettol like it's the answer to all our problems.

'I didn't bother with an advent calendar this year,' I tell her, and of course, she's horrified.

'Not even a chocolate one?'

I'm halfway through telling her I still don't feel all that festive, that there's some kind of block spoiling it for me, making me numb, and she interrupts, offering me one of her calendars. She's got four on the go, apparently.

'You can't be numb when there's a tiny work of art behind a paper door every morning and a chocolate reindeer for breakfast,' she insists. 'Ah, here's Lucy!'

Sure enough, plodding through the slanting rain beneath that golf umbrella I picked up in a charity shop is my niece, and sharing the brolly is the diminutive figure of Fern in a pair of moss-green corduroy dungarees, looking like a far sweeter, shrunken version of her dad. Now that I've noticed the family resemblance, it's hard to unsee. Though I can't picture Tommy Brash with frilly, lacy stuff clustered at his neck like Fern is wearing this morning. She's in green wellies, also trimmed with lacy stuff, and a long, ivory-coloured padded coat with delicate embroidered flowers which I'm a hundred per cent sure began life as an Edwardian tablecloth.

'How was her first shift in the cafe?' I ask before they reach us.

'She's timid as a mouse with the customers,' Izz replies. 'I'm afraid of making any sudden movements in case she scurries away.'

'Coffee's up!' Lucy shouts as they draw closer.

Lucy's been doing a great job of pretending she's fine, but when it came time for her to leave this morning she was pretty reluctant and she practically dived back under the blanket on my sofa when I asked if she fancied staying a few days more. She even offered to help out today, and her first job was accompanying Fern on the caffeine run.

'She needs the practice on the espresso machine when nobody's watching,' Izz whispers with a fixed smile of welcome.

'Not even you?'

'Better off finding her feet without an audience, I reckon.'

'Mine's a tea, yeah?' As I reach for my takeaway cup, I give Lucy a look that asks whether Fern got the cafe locked up properly. She nods discreetly.

'Yep, and one for Patrick. Milk, no sugar, didn't you say?' she says.

'He's not coming this morning,' Izz butts in, and I'm surprised how disappointed I am. 'He texted to say he had something to do today out Dunham way.'

The prospect of opening up the hall is even more daunting now I know he's not coming. Things are just easier with him around.

'Izz said I can look around the hall,' Fern all but whispers. 'Is it all vintage inside?'

'It's all old and knackered,' I tell her and immediately feel bad when her face falls. Like the other youngsters in Wheaton, she didn't see it in its heyday, and I don't recall Tommy Brash ever bringing her down to see Santa either. 'All the original features are still there,' I relent. 'If we ever get the keys, we'll show you.'

She can't be expecting olde worlde Cotswold splendour. Even just a cursory glance at the outside tells a different story. The builders did make a nod to our village setting by using our lovely local stone all around the double doors and in the steps leading up to them, but the rest of the building is brick, and round the back where appearances didn't matter so much in a post-war, money-saving world there's quite a bit of prefab sheeting and pebble-dashed breeze block – the reason the place doesn't have listed building status, poor thing. I still feel it deserves it for all the hundreds of whist drives and strawberry tea dances it's hosted over the last eight decades.

Fern is gazing up through the rain at the tall windows either side of the oak doors. Both panes are topped with leaded sunbursts of yellow glass, two halves of the same shining sun, and an absolute pain to clean, they're so delicate with age – it's a lot easier when Patrick's here with his ladders. Fern's smiling at the sunburst windows like it's her first time seeing them. Has she never left that farm until now, I wonder. How small has her world been?

Just as I'm cursing Councillor Scrimengor for forgetting about us, I spot one of the bakery vans trundling closer, backfiring and wheezing.

'He's never driving a delivery van?' Izz gasps.

'Not when he can lord it around the village in his shiny car,' I agree. 'Maybe he's sent a minion? One of the delivery men?'

The van ploughs through the puddles along the kerb-side, making us flatten ourselves against the hall doors to avoid the splash, and that's when I turn to Lucy and flash her a grin that I'm sure will annoy her no end.

'It's the grandson,' I announce meaningfully, and Lucy pretends not to understand what's going on.

We make a pretty strange welcoming committee as he noisily applies the handbrake. He's scowling and shaking his head at his vehicle, and when he steps out, dodging the puddled water, he looks like he'd rather be anywhere but Wheaton.

'Are you waiting for keys?' he asks, nipping under the porch.

'Sullivan Scrimengor?' Izz asks in reply.

He admits to it with a nod.

'I remember you at my crossing, years ago,' she tells him.

'I know,' he tells her reluctantly. 'I remember.'

'But you've been gone from Wheaton a long time?' Izz is mining him for details but isn't going to get anywhere with this one.

'I'm back to help Grandad,' he says.

60

Makes sense. Scrimengor must be way past retirement age too. He'll need someone to pass his baking empire to, and his rotten attitude has already chased off his own daughter so she's unlikely to be interested. As far as I'm aware she's in Scotland with her new bloke.

I take the keys and remark how Scrimengor must be glad of the help, but all I get is an uncertain look, so I try a different approach. 'Anyway, thanks for these. I'm Margi, and this is my niece, Lucy. That's Fern.'

He greets everyone properly. At least he's got some manners. 'Sully,' he tells the girls.

'Goodness, what an influx of youngsters for Wheaton,' Izz presses on, chuckling and looking from Sully to Fern and Lucy. 'Where have you all been hiding yourselves?'

I catch Lucy fidgeting and dropping her eyes to the ground, and I don't know how to read that.

'Can we go in?' Fern pips, surprising us all. Her voice may tremor like a leaf on the breeze, but there's real determination in there.

'Fancy a peek inside too, Sully?' I ask, turning for the lock. 'You must have come to the gingerbread grotto when you were little?'

'I've to get back to the bakery.' He hikes his thumb behind him, looking like a man who'd far rather potter round a mildewed village hall than spend the day sweeping up after his grandfather.

'Thank your grandad for us,' Izz throws in. She's less inclined to hold grudges and is kinder to Scrimengor than she needs to be.

'Ah.' Sully stops himself leaving, grasping an awkward hand to the back of his neck. 'Grandad told me to tell you you're not to light the fire in the hall, not unless you want a bonfire instead of a grotto.'

'Oh, he says that every year,' I say, swiping my hand through the air. 'As if I would.' I mean, I've been tempted, the hall's always freezing but I'm pretty sure that chimney hasn't been swept since the Sixties.

'Right, then,' Sully says, and he's gone, making a dash through the rain before throttling the engine, making it splutter and bang.

Lucy waves as he manoeuvres through a painfully slow four-point turn on the empty road, and he raises his hand in reply.

The church bells ring for Sunday service.

'OK, say a little prayer,' I tell Izz as I slip the key into the lock.

I'm suddenly aware of Fern by my shoulder, champing at the bit to get inside.

'Are you… are you filming this?' I ask. She's holding up her phone.

'Can I? It's a live stream for TikTok.'

'You can do what you like; just watch your step,' I reply, and I see her eyes widen. She's positively bursting with intrigue as I push the doors open, perhaps a little more dramatically than I might have done if she wasn't here. 'You first,' I tell her, and we all pile inside behind her, creeping along in a bunch like this is an episode of *Scooby-Doo*.

Fern's whispering a commentary with lots of wows and gasps as her lens probes all the nooks and crannies of the entrance hall. I wish I could see the place through her romanticising lens. All I see are the effects of yet another winter's neglect.

The hexagonal black and white floor tiles in the entrance foyer are dulled with dust, the kind that accrues in thick layers and turns sticky with moisture. The wood panelling is damp with a worryingly milky sheen that screams out for a good month of dehumidifying and polishing. The high white ceilings chevroned with neat beams (painted some time ago in a yellow ochre) are excellent for gathering spiders' webs, and I roll my eyes at the sight of them hanging in dewy loops high above us.

'Got your extending duster, Margi?' Izz chuckles, seeing my horror.

There's nothing in this first room, other than a collection of framed photographs and newspaper clippings from days gone by displayed in an arch around the door of the cloakroom, and there's a desk where tickets are sold and guest lists checked off, and that's it, other than the clusters of brown leaves in the corners that must have blown inside back in October during the pumpkin weighing – the last event of the gardening year in Wheaton. You'd be surprised how the promise of a few oversized gourds can attract a small crowd in an out-of-the-way village hall come the darker months.

A further set of doors awaits and above them hangs a painting of an aged King George the Sixth in what I think you could call 'the naive style', i.e., not very good and definitely done by a local. But, still, I've always loved the way the artist gave him the look of a goggle-eyed, stoical bear.

'Just look at this lobby! It's amazing,' Fern is telling her phone audience, to my surprise.

She's a bit young to appreciate mid-century rural shabby chic, isn't she? Nevertheless, there are red love hearts lighting up her screen to show that viewers also like what they see.

In spite of the December rain, this room is flooded with golden light, even if the sunburst glass *is* a little green with algae on the inside and the place itself is frigidly cold. There is still a warm glow. An undeniable (if rather faded) glamour.

Fern's trying to open the doors, all honey-coloured polished wood and frosted glass, that will lead into the main hall.

'They're stuck,' she says.

'It just needs a yank,' I whisper, not sure I want my voice on camera. 'It's swelled with the damp.' I tug the door for her and the handle comes off in my hand. 'Oh!'

No amount of jiggling fixes it back in place, so I lay it on the ticket table – another job to add to the growing list of repairs that the council should really be addressing – and I decide it's time to face the music.

Putting my shoulder firmly to the door, it swings open, and I take everyone through into the main hall, and that's when Fern nearly bursts into flames with excitement.

'Oh my days!' she cries, gliding past me, her phone aloft, capturing it all.

'She didn't know about the mural, then?' says Lucy.

We wait while she shows her viewers the wall covered in painted scenery. I wonder if they're getting bored yet and are turning back to scrolling pet stories.

'I had no idea this stuff was in here,' she's saying. 'Look at this. It's a huge painting. The whole wall's painted. The colours! What *is* this?' she says, looking to me. I hang back, letting Izz answer.

'They were painted in fifty-one,' says Izz, 'the year after the hall was opened by the King.'

'The King came here?' echoes Fern, still pointing her camera at the mural.

'And the Queen – well, the Queen Mum, you'd know her as.' Izz falls suddenly unsure, considering Fern's young age. 'Would you?'

I can see from her screen Fern's followers are being treated to close-ups of the summer scene of Wheaton village sitting in its green and yellow landscape of undulating fields against a blue sky with wispy white clouds. An orchard of apples (long since dug up and built over with Scrimengor's bakery) stands by the familiar churchyard and takes up much of the left side of the jaunty scene. A red-ribboned kite flies over this two-dimensional depiction of Wheaton, and there's a total of one car, a sporty thing in blue, on the broad high street (captured just before we were tarmacked and double yellow lined). A picnic is taking place in the schoolyard, and there are passers-by on the street. None of their faces can be seen, and there's no attempt at exact realism, but still, every time I see this mural I can't help smiling, thinking of my younger self gazing up at the Wheaton mural and taking in all the little details.

'It was painted by a bunch of local artists, not trained or anything, just enthusiasts, and it's been here ever since,' Izz concludes, before Lucy steps forward, clutching her coffee cup in one hand, her arms folded.

'Looks like it was painted straight onto the plaster,' she says.

'That's right,' says Izz. 'The other walls, they painted the murals onto stretched linen. That's why they're long gone, sadly. They faded terrible, and then the damp got to them.'

Fern pans her phone to show her viewers the three white emulsioned walls. 'I know, it is a shame,' she says,

I expect in response to the sudden burst of comments appearing over her live stream.

My niece isn't done yet. Inspecting the brushwork more closely, she says, 'It looks like oil paint, maybe diluted with paraffin wax or turps. You know, so the paint works more like watercolours or pastels.'

We all observe her. There's that shine in her eyes that's been missing lately. That's my Lucy. The art college graduate. The expert. Not the pale, tear-stained girl who turned up at my door in the middle of the night.

Fern ends her broadcast promising more from the 'little village hall that's about to get a big transformation', and we all roll up our sleeves and muck in.

The hot water isn't working, it turns out, and neither is the electricity, so we fill our buckets with cold water and disinfectant.

I mop while Fern and Izz wipe down the panelling. The folding tables all need doing too, but we're a man down, so I'll have to come back for those.

Izz takes the lobby where, out of sight, she wipes down the tiles and the woodwork. By three, we're losing light and feeling decidedly grubby.

My back's getting twingey by the time I announce we're calling it a day.

When we pile through the doors into the lobby, Izz is standing by the cloakroom looking at one of the pictures in a frame. I know exactly which one it is too.

'Ready?' I prompt her, but she doesn't break off her gaze.

Fern's already on the move to stand beside her – she has a serious case of what Lucy calls 'FOMO': fear of missing out – and she's already asking Izz what she's looking at.

'Oh, I was miles away,' Izz tells her, her eyes still glazed.

'Where were you?' Fern asks breathily, looking between Izz and the little gallery.

'There.' Izz lifts a finger to one of the pictures, singling out a girl behind the glass, dainty and alive with motion even in the still monochrome that captured her all those years ago.

'Is that you?' Fern asks, though we all know the answer already.

I give Lucy a warning look to say we really ought not to stand around here much longer, but even she's getting drawn in by the black-and-white image of our village hall, back when the whole room was wrapped in its murals. There's bunting strung along the walls too, and a big crowd of people.

'Is it a party?' Fern asks.

'Saturday night dancing. Nineteen sixty-five.'

'Who's he?' Fern asks, and my shoulders drop. Poor Izz.

Fern has her pearl-varnished, clipped-short fingernail against the glass, pinning the boy in the picture right beside the young Izz.

It's an image I've examined myself many times. The pair of them, Izz and the man, are squashed arm against arm for the photo, and they're both beaming, only if you really look closely – if you've an eye for detail and romance; if you're someone like, say, Fern Brash of Brambledown Farm – you'll spot it: the thing they thought they were getting away with. Their hands are clasped together between them, almost hidden in the folds of Izz's dress. The telltale sign that these two had a secret to hide, but there it is for the eagle-eyed to see, nailed to the wall.

Izz clears her throat, her eyes fixed upon the faces smiling back at her. 'That's Alexi Thorne.' Her voice is dry and cracking like the name is escaping a locked vault after years hidden away, and I suppose that's exactly what is happening.

It would be impossible to forget the night she told me about Alexi, the only man she ever loved. It was years ago now and after a lot of Chardonnay, back when Chardonnay was the 'in' thing, so you know how long ago that must have been. It came out of a boozy conversation at Izz's when she asked me if I ever thought I'd marry again. My first husband, John, had been long gone by that point. I told her I couldn't see it happening, marriage isn't for everyone, and she fell quiet, and the curiosity inside me finally took over, and I had to ask her if she'd ever had anyone special that she'd have liked to marry.

Instead of laughing and shrugging it off like my happy-go-lucky, breezy old Izz I thought I knew so well, I watched her considering the question for a moment, then her face crumpled, and a soft sob burst out. She threw a hand to her mouth to stop any more escaping, but it was three glasses of wine too late. Within five minutes she'd told me the whole thing. And after that, she never mentioned it again, except for the next day when she made me promise not to dwell on it, it was all forgotten and in the past, silly really.

Yet, here she is now, telling her story to a stranger. Maybe it's something about the soft, innocent Fern, a girl not entirely unlike wide-eyed, light-hearted Izz, now I come to think about it.

'We were neighbours. Honestly, we were,' Izz says, and there's amusement in her voice. 'He was the boy next door, Alexander. A few years older than me, enough for me to have thought nothing much about him. Well, not until he was suddenly very handsome indeed and marrying a factory girl from out Oxfordshire way. We'd been friendly, he and I, but not in the way he'd been with her. I was just a child.

'I watched them walk down the aisle and everything, not really thinking much of it, other than it was a shame the village's best-looking lads were all wedding their sweethearts, and I watched him go off with some of the other boys for national service a week later, and that was it. He liked the army life and was soon stationed in Malta. Only, his wife – she was young herself – got bored living here with Alexi's mum and went home to her parents and her pals.

'I didn't pay him any mind, not until he passed out after two years' service. His wife wasn't waiting for him when he got here so he gave the perfume he'd brought home for her to me.

'He was alone a lot, at a loose end most days, looking for work, doing bits and bobs here and there, and I'd finished my schooling and was helping Mum around the house. And it just happened. The falling in love. We kept it to ourselves, of course. Imagine the scandal around here if folks knew. You can't imagine what a whispering place Wheaton used to be.'

I can't help reacting to that. 'Used to be?' But Izz ignores me. She doesn't agree that people round here are still gossiping about me and Don, but why would she? It's me that gets the funny looks.

'Anyway,' she goes on, 'after a while, his wife just admitted it was a rum do and wrote to tell him so. She was never coming back. Of course, I thought my luck was in. But his mum twigged what we was up to and said he must either go after his wife or make himself useful somewhere out of harm's way, me being the harm.'

'What did he do?' Fern's eyes are as round as saucers. 'What happened?' The spell breaks. Izz blinks like she's waking from a dream.

'He enlisted again. Took another posting to Malta. That's what his postcard told me, anyway. And that was that. Stayed in the services out there, as far as my mother could glean from his mum, Mrs Thorne, next door. He never did come home, not even after his mum passed. Something good must have been keeping him away from Wheaton. Or someone.'

'But…' Fern begins, and I wish I could cut her off. 'You loved him?'

Izz's eyes mist. 'Loved each other. Beyond doubt. You'll know all about it one day. When it happens, there's no denying it's there.'

'Oh, I know,' Fern says, her cheeks turning pink. 'I have a girlfriend. Shell.'

'You do?' I say it out loud before I can check myself. 'What does Tommy Brash think of her?' I'm struck by the sudden realisation Fern might have her own family problems to deal with, but I needn't have concerned myself. She's smiling.

'They're in the big sheds together right this minute, tending the early ewes.'

Izz presses her hands together delightedly, and I find I'm the one getting misty now. If Tommy Brash, the last of the miserable Brashes, has moved into the twenty-first century, then Wheaton really has changed vastly for the better.

My heart warms for Fern and her open-heartedness. Nothing's private with these young ones, and it's quite refreshing really. I expect she lives half her life on a live stream to strangers, sharing her world with them. She's grown up in a time where young people are encouraged to talk about their inner world and their worries, and goodness knows they've had a lot of things to worry about in recent years.

I wish Lucy had this kind of frankness so maybe I could help her out more, make her happier. She's barely mentioned Craig since she got here, but the breakup must be getting to her.

'That's enough storytelling for one day,' Izz says, giving Alexi's picture one last glance.

We all make our way out into the December twilight and down the hall steps. The rain's stopping and there are a few more cars about. Everything is dripping and the rain has chased away the frost, warming the air a fraction.

Fern says she's getting picked up, so we leave her, but not before I catch sight of the phone screen in her palm where there's a close-up of Izz and her fella holding hands and facing the probing lens with their secret burning behind their eyes. It seems a strange thing for her to want to keep a memento of. As much as it's a heart-rending moment between Izz and her Alexi, it's still a reminder of a thwarted love, one that would have been allowed to blossom had it happened nowadays.

At Izz's gate, I ask her if she'll be all right.

'Goodness, yes. Nothing a nap and a cuppa won't sort.'

'See you tonight for baking?'

'*Hmm.*' She hesitates. 'I might give it a miss, if you don't mind, just this once? Bit tired.'

She leaves me and Lucy on the pavement, making her way slowly to her gate, looking further from the smiling, silver-lining-seeking Izz than I've ever seen her. Hopefully, she'll forget all about Fern's prying by the morning.

I tell Lucy to take the umbrella and walk ahead to get the heating on and the cottage pie in the oven. I have an errand to run.

I watch her walk away before crossing the street to the gallery, another beautiful old Wheaton building in a high street handsome enough to rival any Jane Austen BBC adaptation. The gallery is all honey-coloured stone with two big, curving windows jutting out over the pavement. I have to ring the bell before I'm allowed in.

The woman in front of the shiny oak console looks at me expectantly while I drip onto the doormat. There's only me and her in the silence of the white showroom. She's probably not that much younger than me and is in head-to-toe loose black drapery with huge black specs. They don't get many locals calling in, I suppose. It's more 'by appointment only' connoisseurs and collectors, I imagine, but today I want something in particular.

'You're interested in the Wenham-Ford catalogue?' the woman asks, doubtfully, before gesturing to a wall of gilt-framed images of hunched grey abstract figures.

I shake my head, feeling sorry for anyone who gets one of those for Christmas. She scans my body, stopping at my Doc Martens.

'Or the Ivo Brisks?' she tries, and we both turn to look at the ceramic sculptures on white plinths. These are definitely more interesting in their glossy colourfulness, but no.

'I'm only after a little present,' I say, making for the shelves by the furthest window.

It's slim pickings but what they do have is luxurious-looking. There are no prices on anything which means

72

they're going to be eye-wateringly expensive. Lucy deserves something special, though, so it won't matter.

I scan the coloured inks in squat bottles, slim brushes, rainbow tubes of oils, mysterious sticks of wax, and various other bits and pieces I'm not quite sure the use of. I pick out a long, narrow spiral-bound pad of handmade paper and a tin with a palette of heavily pigmented shimmery metallic paint blocks inside.

'Pretty sure I had eyeshadows that looked like this in the Eighties,' I tell the woman who's been conspicuously trying not to watch over me like I might be a rural art supplies shoplifter.

She only smiles tightly.

I notice there's no brush included with the tin, so lift a thin, pointy one from a jar. Years ago, I'd have bristled at the obvious stand-offishness of places like this and the feeling of being an outsider. I might have noisily rummaged in the brushes and bought two more I didn't need to spite someone like her, to show that you should never make assumptions about people. I could be arty, and loaded. There's no saying how many Ivo Brisks, or whatever his name is, I've got stashed in my attic. But I behave myself. One pretty brush is all I need.

There's no till, only a flat pad sort of thing on the console table where I'm invited to tap my card. I refuse the gift wrap but let her tie everything with a grey bow, and I carry Lucy's gifts back to the cottage.

Seeing her absorbed in a creative project would be the best Christmas present I could get. It would mean the old Lucy was still in there somewhere, waiting to come back out to play.

Chapter Six

'You want the strings suspended from that rafter there?' Patrick asks me as he sets up his camping floodlight. He is absolutely the kind of man who'd keep a floodlight in his workshop just in case a crazed lady friend wanted help hanging a gingerbread reindeer-led sleigh from the ceiling in a village hall without all its amenities connected.

'Thereabouts,' I tell him, and he sets up his stepladders right in the middle of the village hall. 'And you invited the superhead over to see the place?' I ask.

'Mr Bold? I did. He said he'd try to call in after the school governors' meeting but, I have to tell you, if you're hoping to appeal to his community spirit, you're barking up the wrong tree.'

Patrick climbs his ladders until he's in touching distance of the main beam that runs across the hall ceiling. I watch as he pulls the ball of catgut and the penknife from his pockets and sets to work measuring four floor-length strands to tie up there.

'It's just icing a few biscuits,' I protest. 'The little ones help us do it every year. He won't object.'

'He's not even having a nativity for the Early Years kids this year,' says Patrick dryly, his eyes fixed on the task above his head.

'No!' I've heard it all now.

'Says it interferes with their learning.'

'What about learning what it feels like to stand on a stage, or to speak in public? Or learn all the Christmas songs and make fairy wings from coat hangers and a halo from tinsel? That's learning.'

Patrick's deftly tied the four strings and is making his way back down the ladders. I admit, I've stood around watching him and achieved precisely nothing so far. I hurriedly pour the bleach into the water bucket and pull on my Marigolds.

'Sounds like someone enjoyed their own nativity as a kid?' he says, and he's smiling with his eyes. 'I'm guessing you were Mary?'

'How did you know?'

'Always at the centre of things, making stuff happen? Then hugely overshadowed by others?'

'Hah!' I laugh. 'I didn't realise I gave off "Mary complex". Does that make you Joseph?' I quip, and I *swear* I was thinking of the whole carpenter thing, not the husband thing, but Patrick still pauses in folding his ladders to raise a questioning eyebrow at me. 'Because of the tools and stuff,' I blurt, too late to stop the awkwardness. I start to witter to take the heat off. 'Seems a shame, though. For the little ones. Maybe if I have a word with him, he'll see sense.'

Patrick gives me a level look that says he wouldn't be willing to bet on it but against the floodlights, what I'm really seeing is the way he's all fine angles, cheekbones and thick, wavy brown hair. I make myself concentrate on the bucket, plunging the cloth in.

He's unfolding tables and setting them out in an elongated horseshoe shape ready for the exhibition, just as they've been set out for years.

'Your gingerbread sleigh will be above head height right in the middle here,' he says.

'Don't know how I'd manage without you,' I tell him.

A silence falls as we work our way down the rows of tables, cleaning off the winter's dampness and dust. By the time we reach each other in the middle of the horseshoe I'm wishing the electric was connected and we could play some music or something.

It's so quiet and cold, and we're the only ones in here, so there's the air of a secret twilight mission shared between us. I feel the warm easiness of our friendship so deeply I'm overtaken by a compulsion to confess about my Birmingham property search. It doesn't seem right, him not knowing. If I do go, he can come and visit, stay over, maybe? Him and Izz. It wouldn't mean it'd be the end of everything. Just the grotto.

I'm aware of breathy white vapour curling from our lips as we stop working and straighten our backs to look at one another.

'Patrick?' I say, just as he's saying *my* name, and we both laugh and say, 'You first,' and I laugh again, only Patrick's fallen serious and is looking at me hard.

'Listen, um, Margi…' he begins, and I'm suddenly half-afraid, half-bursting with intrigue. What's he about to tell me? He looks so stern and determined. Just as he's taking a breath ready to talk, my mobile rings.

'Oh! It's Mum!' I say, having wrenched my phone from the pocket on the front of my dark denim dungarees. I don't have time to assess whether I'm relieved or annoyed at the interruption.

Patrick's already stepped away and is busying himself making final adjustments to the layout of the tables.

'Margi?' Mum says, very loudly. I turn the volume down a bit. 'Floodlights? Where on earth are you? A football match?'

'Huh? Oh, no.' I turn my phone to show her the lamp. 'I'm tidying up at the hall.'

'What's wrong with the electrics?'

'They're not on yet. We're waiting for someone at the council to get us connected up for Christmas.'

'Do you need me to phone them?' she threatens.

'Not yet,' I tell her. 'We'll give them a chance to sort things before we unleash the big guns.'

'Hmm, well, don't take any nonsense from Scrimengor and his lot. Rodney Carruthers has wanted that hall demolished for as long as he's been on the council. Suits him if it's mildewed and rotten. He's got friends in the construction industry, if you know what I mean.' She mimes someone accepting a backhander, then taps the side of her nose.

I've heard all this before, many times, but it's never come to anything, so I try to divert her. 'How's Dad?'

'He's still having his siesta. Getting longer and longer these days, and then he's up rattling around the villa half the night, keeping me awake.'

'You should come here for Christmas,' I say. 'Get into an English winter routine.'

'Hibernating in the dark?'

'That's the one. So why don't you?'

It's not the first time I've asked, but with Christmas so close, I know it'll have to be my last attempt to lure them home.

77

I don't understand why they'd want to spend midwinter in a new-build retirement community of white breeze block and cold floor tiles where all the summer season businesses are closed up when they could be right here in the middle of England doing the traditional stuff they used to love: midnight Mass, cooking stews on the Aga, bundling under blankets on the sofa with a book and a brew. I suppose what I'm thinking is that I miss them, but I've learned not to say so. It makes us all sad.

'Can't leave the dogs,' Mum's explaining yet again. 'We've had a Dogue de Bordeaux come in this weekend in a right state, found wandering the Playa de Torreblanca. We're trying to get him an adoption in England already. Lots of paperwork to sort out. Besides, you've got Lucy with you, haven't you? And you've the grotto coming along. That's plenty to be getting on with.'

I stifle a sigh. Patrick makes a clattering noise in the background, hitting the bucket against his folded ladders.

'Oops, sorry!' he shouts, coming into shot, and Mum's set off, bringing her face right up to the screen.

'Who's that?' she wants to know.

'It's Patrick, our grotto's Santa?' I say, knowing full well this'll have her on the edge of her seat.

'Oh yes, Patrick. Let me see him, then.'

I bite back the protest and instead hold the phone out, mouthing my apology to him behind the screen.

'Hello, Mrs Frost,' he says with all the politeness of a teenager meeting his girlfriend's parents for the first time. He waves into the camera, coming closer.

'Ah! There you are, Patrick. I remember you. Like a young Patrick Swayze. Don't I always say that, Margi? Margi?'

'Yep, you do,' I tell her off camera, and whenever she says it, all I ever hear is the 'young'.

'You're a dog person, aren't you, Patrick?' she says.

'He doesn't want to adopt that beach dog, thanks, Mum,' I cut her off. You can see why she's indispensable at the dog rescue. Everyone she knows succumbs to the pressure eventually and ends up collecting their own Spanish mutt fresh from Heathrow quarantine.

'Oh, I'd love to, only I work out of the house. Maybe one day,' Patrick tells Mum.

'Margi won't take him, so there's no point asking her. We always had dogs in our family, you know?'

'We know,' I say.

'Margi's in the foyer, you know, Patrick, with Gingersnaps, her sausage dog.' She's still shouting, loud enough to awaken every stray from Mijas to Malaga.

'In the foyer?' he repeats.

'In the big frame.'

That's when he catches on. 'Oh, in the pictures?'

'Yep, big gold frame, the royal wedding. That'd be nineteen eighty-one. Go and have a look.'

Oh no. I know exactly what she's up to. It's the Face-Time equivalent of showing him my embarrassing baby albums. Patrick's way too polite to say no, so we both traipse through the doors and across the foyer to the cloakroom.

Beyond the sunburst windows, the street lights are just coming on and the sky isn't completely dark yet so there's enough light in here to find the picture Mum's talking about.

Patrick examines the image in the frame. It's an enlargement of a picture that appeared in the newspaper of Wheaton's street party, a wash of faded red, white and blue. The whole village was there that day.

'Can you see Margi and I at the front?' Mum asks. 'With her dad and little Gingersnaps?'

I oblige by pointing us out. I'm a gangly thing in a short kilt, Doc Martens and – oh Lord! – massively backcombed hair. I can smell the Elnett hairspray just looking at myself.

Patrick looks at me, and his eyes light up. 'Nice hair,' he tells me, not unkindly but definitely laughing. 'Was Izz there too? I can't see her.'

I look again. 'There.' Izz is right at the side in her sundress and strappy sandals. She's smiling broadly and waving a Union flag.

'Were you two mates at this point?' he asks me.

'Not yet. We didn't really fall in together until Mum left for Spain.'

'You'd be twenty-two or thereabouts when that was taken and studying at college,' Mum's saying.

'What was twenty-two-year-old Margi like?' Patrick's asking through a grin, enjoying my discomfort, I reckon.

'Never there,' Mum jokes, but she's not wrong. I was always out with friends at that point or hopping on National Express coaches to see Blondie in Birmingham or Kate Bush in Hammersmith.

He's really listening, like always, and looking closer at the picture. 'What's that you're holding?' he asks.

'That?' I draw my face close to the glass. 'That is a red Sony Walkman. Tell me you know what a Walkman is, for God's sake.'

He bursts into laughter. 'Of course I do. I'm forty-nine, not fourteen. Be worth a fortune now if you'd kept it. What do you think you were listening to that day?'

I know exactly what I was listening to, as clear as day. 'Bit of Madness, some Gary Numan, and The Specials.' I search his expression for recognition, and thankfully he's pulling an impressed face. 'I suppose you were rocking out to "The Birdie Song" around about this time.'

'No, actually.' He acts offended. 'I was a cool kid.'

'Oh yeah?'

'I was at the very least into Adam and the Ants.'

'When you were... seven?'

'Yeah!' he insists. 'Asked my mum to paint on a white stripe and everything.' He draws a fingertip over the bridge of his nose to his cheek.

'Ahem!' Mum interrupts us from the phone screen. I'd almost forgotten she was there.

To stop her sharing any salacious conclusions she might be drawing, I tell her I'll have to call her back later when I'm doing the evening's baking. 'I'll need some pointers about this flying gingerbread sleigh I'm trying out,' and she squints her eyes at us but thankfully only says she'll be waiting by her phone when I'm ready. I tell her I love her and hang up.

'You OK?' Patrick asks in the silence afterwards.

'Uh-huh, just thinking.'

'About?'

'Doesn't matter.'

We're still side by side in front of the visual reminder that Wheaton's street party days of neighbourliness and celebrations are long gone, but he's not looking at the picture. I let my eyes lift to Patrick's and realise he's reaching a hand to my hair.

'Cobweb,' he says, brushing his fingers close to my temple.

I feel myself frozen for a moment.

81

I don't know how to act. It's not fair, this younger guy acting all friendly, not knowing the effect he has on me. I lift my own hand to my hair, then look to 1980s Margi in the picture. 'Bit different-looking these days.'

'Are you? You look about the same to me.'

'Hah! What is it Lucy says? I'm a "boomer" now – only without the baby – and she's a "millennial", apparently. What does that make you?'

'Dunno.' He shrugs, his eyes alive like he couldn't care less about all that stuff.

'You don't have an older brother, do you?' It's out before I know what my mouth's doing.

I think he's going to laugh but he's firm when he replies. 'No. I don't.' He seems to think for a moment, then adds, 'Have you eaten? I'm starving.'

The awkwardness is suddenly over and we're back to what we had been before whatever that little moment of uncertainty was. 'Me too. And I'm freezing. Pub?'

'Pub,' he agrees.

Once we're outside in the dark locking up, someone approaches. They come all the way up the steps to meet us.

Patrick makes the introductions. 'Ah, Mr Bold, our new head teacher; this is Margi Frost, chair of the ginger-bread grotto committee.'

'We've met,' I say, trying to keep the grimness out of my voice.

The young man gives me the blankest look through his smart, round specs. 'Gingerbread grotto?' he says.

There's something weary around his mouth like he spent last week being introduced to new people and I'm the last straw testing his stoicism. He's searching his mind for mention of me, probably churning through all the other local nonsense us yokels concern ourselves with: gingerbread villages, nativities, harvest festivals, summer fetes, pinning rosettes on giant inedible veg. He'll have heard it all since he arrived in Wheaton in what's been, I'm guessing, a bewildering introduction to village life.

'What I wanted to talk with you about, Mr Bold...' Patrick begins. It's odd hearing him call this younger man 'Mr'. Shouldn't it be the other way around?

'Hm?' the man replies absently, and his eyes flit to what is surely his sporty Golf straddling the pavement. He's probably dreaming of getting out of here for the night.

'We'd hoped the school might be able to support us, support me, what with me being the handyman and all, with a bit of sponsorship, but...'

Mr Bold looks unmoved.

'But I understand that's probably not an option at the moment,' adds Patrick.

Now that my friend has begun the negotiations, I take over. 'We could do with some icers,' I say.

'Icers,' the head says, looking more tired by the second.

'You know, the tinies? Reception class, or kinder-garteners, to ice some gingerbread men of their own, get them involved in the exhibit. We've been doing it every year for... well, ages.'

Mr Bold looks relieved it's such a simple request. Easy to refuse it, I'm guessing.

'Listen, as much as I'd love to help, I can't,' he says. 'There's SATs prep and Ofsted looming. I can't very well have inspectors turning up and finding Key Stage One making a mess with food. You understand? It's a crucial year for me. For the school,' he corrects himself. 'Maybe next year?' He runs a hand through his hair, suddenly absent, stressed even. Now this guy makes more sense.

He has the weight of the world on his shoulders, so much is riding on his making a big splash at the school.

He's already making his way down the steps and wishing us a good evening.

'He'll be promoted out of here by next year,' I say under my breath as we watch him retreat into his car, making it burst into light and music before he races away, heading out of Wheaton. 'Where does he live again?'

Patrick's by my side on the top step. 'Out Cirencester way. Crashing with friends, apparently. At least, that's what they're saying in the school kitchens.'

If anybody's going to know, it'll be the dinner ladies. 'Not exactly committing to village life, then?'

'Doesn't need to, I suppose. It's temporary for him. He'll be on some inner-city academy's reality TV show before next Christmas. Destined for big things, the board thinks.'

'Too big to help us anyway.' I grit my teeth and stare through the exhaust cloud he's left behind. 'And he's the one that cut your contract to term time only?'

'The very same.'

'I should have said something.'

'I'm glad you didn't. Don't need you going all Scrappy-Doo on us. I still need to work for the guy come January.'

I'm smiling, glad he thinks I'm scrappy, when I notice he's fixing me with an odd look. 'What's the matter?'

'I, uh, I've got something to tell you, actually. About work.'

'Go on, then. It can't be that bad, can it?' I laugh, hoping he'll join in, but he's so serious.

'Yesterday, when I couldn't come to help open up the hall… it's because I had a job interview.'

'That's great,' I say. 'Izz didn't mention it was an interview. Top secret, is it? MI5? Or one of those secret shoppers ratting about rubbish service? Oh, I'd love that job; much more fun than spying for MI5!'

'Margi.' He cuts me off, impatient. 'I was at Dunham Gravey, interviewing for their Christmas spectacular. They desperately need more technicians to maintain the light displays and keep the whole thing running over the holidays.'

'Right.' I'm nodding, processing what this means, and possibly looking a bit weird.

'Are you OK?' he says.

'You've taken a job at Dunham Gravey?'

'Yep.' He bares his teeth with an inhale, cautious and apologetic, waiting for me to react.

I'm trying to be happy for him. I really am. Only I'm not finding it right this second. 'How are you going to help with the gingerbread set-up or our Santa grotto if you're at Dunham Gravey?'

'Uh…' He's startled, definitely looking a bit scared. 'I'm still not sure of the exact details…' he begins.

'When does it start? Your contract?'

He swallows before he answers. 'Tomorrow, after I'm done at the school. Five until midnight.'

'Every night?'

'Not *every* night, but… most of them, until Christmas. I can still pop into the grotto and help out, when I can.' He's clasping his hands together. 'Look, Margi, it's not that the grotto isn't important to me, that *you're* not important to me… uh, I'm trying to say… I wish I could be in both places…'

'Got it,' I utter, stopping him with my hand held up. 'You've taken a proper paying job at Dunham Gravey, quite rightly. It's not like our grotto pays you or anything. And I'm sure the Dunham bosses will appreciate you just as much as I...' I stop myself. 'As *we* do. It's just, I mean, Dunham Gravey? *Really?*'

Not only has the light spectacular nabbed my grotto visitors these last couple of years, now they've stolen Patrick too.

This year, which I'd determined was going to be the brightest and best Gingerbread Christmas Village to date, isn't even going to have Patrick now.

'You know, I'm not all that hungry,' I tell him.

'Margi, come on, let's head to the pub. You'll feel better when you've had something to eat.'

I want to, but I can't seem to relent. I can't think of anything I'd rather do than eat Lolla's lasagne in front of The Salutation's open fire with Patrick. Only, everything seems to be unravelling. I'm losing Patrick to that over-the-top, high-tech, fancy-pants lights spectacular, of all places, and Izz is so tired and distracted these last few days and should really be allowed to enjoy Christmas in peace and not work herself to death at the grotto all month long, and Lucy's just not herself *at all* and it hurts to see her so lost and lonely, and there's still most of the village to recreate in sodding gingerbread *and* it's supposed to be extra special this year so I can say goodbye to it all without letting Mum down any more than I already am, and that's before I even consider the school kids and how much they'll be looking forward to the grotto next year and the year after that.

I'm suddenly short of breath, and my head's swimming at the thought of doing all of this by myself, and there's still my own big confession to tackle – a much bigger thing to admit than Patrick's holiday job. I'm running away for

good, and before I go, there's everything to sort through…
I press my hands to my head to stop the thoughts.

'My whole life has been Wheaton and gingerbread and preparing for Christmas, Patrick.' I gasp out the words.

He tips his head, totally bamboozled. 'Margi, just calm down, take a breath…'

'Forget it. I'm fine. I'd better get home and crack on with the grotto arrangements, now we've lost our…' I was going to say our 'best person', but I swerve for 'Santa'.

'I might have been able to make it work, somehow,' he calls behind me as I leave, and we both know that splitting his time between the grotto and two jobs wouldn't have gone in the grotto's favour.

He doesn't follow me as I rush home through the first heavy splashes of sleet, ignoring every Christmas tree twinkling from the cottage windows along the main road. I'm not in the right headspace to think any deeper about why I'm so wounded and annoyed and out of breath; what I do know is that Christmas this year, and that bloody superhead, and Dunham effing Gravey, can absolutely get knotted.

Chapter Seven

Tuesday 5 December: Love technically

'And you don't think you overreacted a tiny bit?' Lucy asks, bang on as usual.

I don't reply straight away, only stirring the bolognese on the hob and glancing at my phone. I texted Patrick first thing after I'd had a chance to sleep on it all and decided I've no right guilting him for filling an employment gap at the most expensive time of year during the most expensive year in history. Of course he should take the job, grotto or not. He's done enough for us over the years.

'Maybe it was a bit of an overreaction,' I concede.

It's still there on my phone screen. My message.

> Hi Patrick. Sorry for snapping. I was shocked and disappointed. But not with you. You're a good friend and I'm a dozy pillock. Sorry, again. Good luck with your new job! M

There's still no reply from him. Not that I'm going to read anything into that. He'll be busy juggling school and his induction with the Dunham lights spectacular people.

Lucy's at the kitchen table tossing salad in one of Mum's big mixing bowls now we're done baking for the day.

There are a few cottages fully constructed in trays on the kitchen floor. They'll need transporting to the hall soon or they'll warp in the cottage's central heating.

Lucy's been a great help, even though I tried encouraging her outside for a bit to do some sketching. She said she'd far rather stay in the warm with me.

I'm still secretly hoping the pretty art supplies are going to give her the push she needs, but I daren't risk giving them to her yet. I'll have to pick my moment, when she's opening up a bit more. I don't want her to think I'm interfering and have her driving off home before we've had a proper talk about the break-up, and about my Birmingham plans. Only, every time I think I can do it, I chicken out, and I'm not sure why. If anyone needs to know sooner rather than later, it's Lucy. I'd have done it by now if there wasn't this new feeling of distance between us. She's still barely speaking, at least not about the big stuff.

'What are you up to?' I ask. She's done with the salad, picked up her phone and is swiping busily. 'Playing Space Invaders?' I joke because she loves it when I pretend I'm a hundred and clueless.

'Bumble,' she says.

'Come again?'

'It's a networking app. You don't know it?'

'Networking? As in… as in *dating*?' I'm not sure that's a good idea. She needs to recover and to give herself some space after Craig. 'Can you be bothered with dating right now?'

'I'm just looking. Reminding myself there's still nice people out there. See?' She pauses on a picture of an outdoorsy-looking man up a mountain in a beanie hat.

'He seems nice. Dad of two. Rock climbing, strength-training and running, travel.'

'Are you going to… click on him?'

'Nope. I want a drama-free Christmas.'

I breathe a sigh of relief. I know it's selfish but part of me is hoping we can simply keep each other company this winter. Having her here has filled a big lonely gap in my days since Don scarpered.

I'm about to ask the question I've been meaning to for days – will she stay for Christmas – when Lucy looks sharply at me, her eyes narrowed.

'You know?' she begins, and I can already tell this spells trouble. '*You* could meet somebody nice on an app, I reckon.'

I snort. 'Good one, Luce.' The spaghetti's ready, so I drain it and send up a big puff of steam that clouds the kitchen window. 'Can you grab cutlery?'

'I'm not kidding. Have you ever tried the dating apps?'

'Darling, apps didn't even *exist* when I was first swimming in the dating pool.' It's true. When I started meeting men it all happened down The Salutation or at parties or gigs.

'Analogue dating is like looking for a needle in a haystack,' says Lucy, grabbing plates and helping me serve up. 'You should give online a try. I don't like to think of you all alone here,' she says.

'I don't like the feeling of being pitied.' Ugh! Not by Lucy, at any rate.

She's supposed to think I'm fabulous. She's supposed to tell stories about me at parties, about her cool, fun aunt. At least, I *used* to feel cool and fun. This sense of sudden ageing that's been plaguing me lately has a lot to do with my decision to dive in with Don if I'm honest.

He rode in on his bike, same age as me, and wearing it really well, all leathers and bristly beard, and for a while we were living it up, hosting parties of our own, or always on our way out somewhere, zipping across the Cotswolds on his Harley, meeting his biker friends in country pubs. I loved it. I felt alive again. He took a lot of that spark away with him when he disappeared.

Lucy's watching me, so I compose myself in case the wobbly feelings show on my face. Her eyes are still on me as I pull up a stool at the kitchen table and tear a hunk of garlic bread. She serves me some salad.

'Think about it,' she persists. 'You can flick through profiles, bin the ones you don't like the look of, and take your pick of the nicest guys... maybe go on a few romantic Christmas dates?'

'With strangers?' I say, weary, wishing we could just eat instead of this.

'They won't be a stranger by the time you go to meet them. You can chat and get to know each other first, see if you're a match.'

I'll have to nip this in the bud quickly. 'Lucy, I'm not cut out for online anything. I like real life. Real people.'

'You mean a real *person*?' Lucy cuts in, one eyebrow almost popping off her forehead she's being so arch.

'*Hm?*' I fork a big bundle of spaghetti into my mouth.

'You like Patrick, don't you?'

I'm chewing, so I only have to pull a *don't be daft* face, but I realise Lucy's going to take advantage of the fact I'm incapacitated by pasta.

'You were disappointed he wasn't at the hall the other day. Plus, you wouldn't be this bummed out that he's taken a job outside of the village for Christmas if you didn't want to spend more time with him.' She spreads her hands out and does a sweet smile. 'I'm just stating facts.'

I swallow and chase the pasta with wine. I think of the royal wedding picture. 'He's in his forties,' I say.

'Late forties. Almost fifty,' she says. 'Have you really ruled him out?'

'He was never even considered in.'

'You want to date men your own age, is that what you're saying?'

I shrug. That's not really what I'm saying.

'Don was the same age as you, wasn't he?'

I don't want the humiliated feelings spoiling this really nice food. 'Eat your dinner,' I tell her, and she rolls her eyes. I reckon it's time to draw a line under this dating speculation, so I launch in.

'Humans have evolved for thousands of years to get really good at social stuff, Lucy. We use our instincts to suss people out, judge character, detect if there's any chemistry there. And now the internet's arrived to sweep all that away in a few clicks and swipes? Algorithms can't replace instinct.' I nod to show that's my last word, feeling pleased I've made my point. I take another mouthful.

Lucy lifts her head, hesitating. She's weighing up her words. *Don't say it*, whatever it is. I feel like a moth under a microscope already.

'Have your instincts served you well up till now?' she says, and it's so blunt I splutter a bit.

I grab for my wine, and Lucy shoves a napkin towards me.

'Sorry, Auntie Margi. Are you all right?'

'Fine, I'm fine.' But as we finish our meal and I steer our conversation to what's on the Christmas telly, it's still there at the back of my mind. How well *have* my instincts served me?

They certainly didn't help out with Don. And back when I met John and we got married fresh out of college – I studied food technology, then teaching; he was an agricultural engineer – it had nothing to do with instinct and more to do with just going along with what everyone else was doing: a simple wedding, a honeymoon, a house. Except the whole babies thing didn't appeal to me one bit, and that's where it turned rocky.

John and I styled it out, of course, all the questions and pressure. People seriously like to pry when you're a newly-wed. I still feel queasy when I hear the phrase 'the pitter-patter of tiny feet'. Yuck.

In the end, John wanted to be a father, and I wasn't able to give him that. Wasn't willing. It didn't even hurt all that much in the end. He just left one day after years of living together like housemates. And that was it for me. I was suddenly approaching my forties, divorced, busy teaching in the comps, not much time for men, really, other than a few no-strings things here and there.

Maybe it's true to say my instincts have served me well when it comes to protecting myself, to knowing when to say no – to babies and those expectations upon me – but in regards to love and attraction? They've been kind of rubbish.

After dinner, Lucy tells me she'll clear up and I should go pick something for us to watch. As I get settled by the glow of the wood burner, my brain nags at me to pick up my phone.

Lucy catches me when she comes through with our wine glasses.

'Tinder?' she says, spotting me sussing out the dating apps, and I know she's trying to hold back her surprise in case she startles me. 'Can I?' She gestures for my phone, and I surrender it. 'Tinder's waaay too aggressive for you, trust me. And you don't want to be bombarded with messages, right?' Lucy has the phone in her hands and a fevered look on her face. 'Happn's too young too, sorry, but it is. You want to meet nice men your age.'

'O-kay? I guess.' I'll have to defer to her expertise. Watching her type and scroll, a pang blooms in my chest for her. She knows all about this stuff.

It makes me wonder about the phone chats we've had lately when she's been bubbly and bright, telling me she was fine, busy at work, looking forward to the future. Was any of it true? She's always had a solitary, quiet place inside her where she'd retreat. It used to worry my sister, and I'd always say that Lucy's introspection would be the secret to her success eventually. All soul searchers and arty types have that shadowy side to them. But here she is, just turned thirty, alone and cooped up at her auntie's house, refusing to talk about her life and meddling in mine as a distraction from whatever's going on in her head.

'Lucy?' I begin. 'Did you have any teaching lined up for this month?' She's absorbed with my phone, so I keep probing. 'Only, I wondered if any schools had been in touch since you arrived? Looking for substitutes? *Hmm?* Lucy?'

'How about Countryside Cupids?' she replies with a quick lift of her eyes to mine, as though she really hasn't heard me. I'm not fooled. She looks about fifteen years old sitting there, her hair falling over her face, hiding.

'Oh, Luce, I'm not sure.'

'There, you're in!' she says, turning the phone towards me. 'All you have to do is fill in this questionnaire thingy.' There's desperation in the air. Her brows droop. I can feel her begging me to drop my interrogations.

I give in and take my phone, reading the first question on this fancy-looking app. It's all in pastels with a beachy, palm-tree background, designed to make you think of all the romantic, exotic, sandy walks you'll take with your new geezer, I suppose.

'Where would I rather live?' I read out loud, and Lucy settles back onto the sofa. 'A cosy country cottage? A townhouse in reach of an allotment plot? A low-rise apartment community with a buzzing social scene? You do realise that means a retirement community, Lucy?' She ignores this, so I read on. 'Or a coastal retreat?' I look around the room. 'I mean, I already chose a cosy country cottage, so that, I suppose?'

'Click it, then,' Lucy urges.

The screen eats up my answer and throws another question at me. 'What is your love language?' I have to read that one twice. 'My love *language*?'

'You know? How you show love to people. I already know what yours is.' Lucy looks proud of herself.

'You do?' I look down at the choices. 'Acts of Service, doing little things to show you care; Gift Giving, spoiling someone with material things; Feeding, bringing comfort with your cooking; Touch, reassuring hands-on kindness; Words, you wear your heart on your sleeve; or Quality Time, showing you care by setting aside time for someone special.' I look at Lucy, uncertain. 'And you think one of these is me?'

'Obviously, it's the Acts of Service one.'

'It is?'

'All you ever do is do things for your community.'

At first that sounds kind of nice but after a second's thought, I say, 'Why am I Acts of Service, and not any of the other ones? Are you saying I'm closed off and can't simply tell people I love them?'

'Of course not…'

'Because I really love you. See? I said it. Easy.'

'Can you say it to a guy?'

She's got me there. *Dammit*.

'I would,' I protest. 'I might. If there was someone nice enough to say it to.'

She's right, though. That was the one thing I struggled with when it came to Don. Letting him move in? No problem. Sharing a bed? That was fine too. Letting him park his bike and all its paraphernalia in the lock-up round the back, even if it meant moving out some of the old furniture I've had in storage for years? I told him to knock himself out. But somehow, even on our wedding day, I felt horribly bashful and squirming when it came to the big declaration. I don't think I ever actually said it out loud, instead saying 'you too' every time he said it gushingly to me, which was often, actually. I was right to be wary. Looking back, Don's love language must have been Bullshit.

'OK,' I concede. 'I'll pick Acts of Service.'

The questions keep coming, on and on, increasingly quirky ones designed to draw out my personality so it can be filtered and profiled and broken down into matches.

'What are the top two traits you look for in a partner?'

Lucy doesn't laugh when I joke about their own teeth and a pulse, so I plump for patience and understanding, things you definitely need to deal with me, if my dating history is anything to go by.

By the final question I've had enough.

'If you were a season, which would you be? Oh, for God's sake.'

Lucy pulls an insistent face, and I sigh dramatically.

'Oh, Ok,' I sigh. The old me would have put 'winter', but having grown desensitised to Christmas cheer for obvious and increasingly piled-up reasons, I select 'spring' instead. That's what this is supposed to be, isn't it? This time of life? A second spring. That's how the leaflet in the menopause clinic described it anyway and I'd fought hard not to gag.

'Next, profile image?' I say, following the app prompt. 'I haven't taken a selfie in my life. Maybe we should give this up as a lost cause?'

'No, no, no,' Lucy chides, and tells me she has some great photos of me in her phone – which is news to me – but it's touching that she's kept them. 'Here, let me.' She does something clever with her phone (called 'AirDropping', apparently), and now she's uploaded to the app a shot of me three Christmases ago when I was in a phase of dying my hair red.

She crops herself out of the image, and suddenly there I am, fixed inside a little circular window. My profile picture. Just a handful of pixels to be judged. Because, let's face it, any bloke's going to be more interested in what I look like than which element I consider myself, right? (I chose fire over earth, air and water, if you're interested, only because I hate being cold.) That was around about the time Lucy scolded me to put more effort into my answers, in case I 'threw the results', and I felt like a kid and wanted to stick out my tongue in revolt.

What is this role reversal thing that's happening? I feel like Lucy's the watchful adult and I'm the youngster.

Izz warned me about it; the moment people start to 'hover', she called it. One minute you're an independent, kick-ass woman ploughing her own furrow, the next, people are suddenly 'concerned' and meddling in your business.

The whole thing, this shift, and all the recent changes in my life, have left me as dizzy as the wheel circling on my phone screen in front of me, where the words *Searching for your perfect match* are fading in and out in lilac font.

'Give it a second,' Lucy's saying, and I suddenly have no idea how we went from bolognese and night-in-front-of-the-telly-in-our-jammies to matchmaking for rural seniors.

In spite of myself, there's that old curiosity of mine, making itself felt with an adrenalised rush of excitement. Suddenly, I have an intense interest in the app's ability to accurately locate the absolutely ideal man for me (should they be solvent, child-free – I have zero desire to become a stepmother – and living within a forty-mile radius of Wheaton, that is).

'It's exciting, isn't it?' Lucy says as the database does its magic.

It's taking too long for my liking. 'It is,' I reply, wishing the rising sicky feeling in my stomach would go away. What if nobody matches to me? What if they're all on the hunt for younger women? And, now that I think of it, surely if there were crowds of handsome, eligible men living near Wheaton I'd have bumped into at least one of them by now? (I find I'm pushing thoughts of Patrick out of my brain at this.)

'Hah! There you go,' Lucy yelps. 'Thirty potential matches in your area.'

'Thirty?'

I watch her enthusiastically scrolling their profiles; the happiest I've seen her in a long time.

'You're glad?' I ask.

'Of course I am. All I really want is for you to find somebody good so I don't have to worry about you any more.'

This pulls me up. 'Hold on. You worry about me?'

She shrugs. 'Little bit. We all do.'

I was right. This is how the hovering begins.

'At least pick your favourite and arrange one date, won't you?' she cajoles, and of course, I'm powerless.

If being cast out into the dating wilderness at sixty-five makes Lucy happy or proud of me or even a little less worried, I'll just have to do it for her. And a tiny bit for me, I suppose.

Maybe mathematical principles and personality tests and psychosocial metric doodads *can* succeed in a few short hours where I, Margi Frost, have clearly failed over the course of my entire lifetime.

We're about to dive into the profiles when the doorbell rings. Instinctively, I shut the app and shove my phone between the sofa cushions.

'You think it's Patrick,' Lucy says, watching me.

'Patrick? It could be anybody,' I say, cool as a cucumber because, as usual, she's read me like a children's picture book.

I pointedly don't check my face in the mirror as I make for the door in case Lucy's still watching.

It's only just after eight but it feels much later with the wintry darkness and sparkles on the windows where the sleet has frosted in pretty, jagged patterns.

I pull at the door, and there, so slight on my doorstep, is Fern, in her tablecloth coat, and beside her holding a large cardboard box is a smiling, freckled, healthful girl I don't know.

'I'd have texted first, but I didn't know your number?' Fern says like it's a question, still a bundle of jangling nerves.

'Come inside. You must be freezing. Did you walk all the way from the farm?'

'Shell drove,' Fern says, and the girl with the box frees one hand to give me a spread-fingered wave.

'Is this your girlfriend?' I ask, but I already know. These two have that obvious youthful magic between them. I can tell they're a match. See? Instinct and chemistry; it's A Thing. It can shift the air around people, crackling like static, drawing you in.

I can't help smiling at them both. 'Do you want an… orange juice?' Then I remember Lucy drank the last of it. 'Or tea?'

Both of them enthusiastically respond to the idea of tea, and I see Fern's gaze drifting around the cottage.

'This is so nice,' she tells me in a tiny voice.

It makes sense that she'd like the place. You couldn't get closer to the faded charm of real old-fashioned Cotswold living if you tried; or, in other words, everything in here is ancient.

'My mum decorated it before I was born,' I tell her. 'I never changed it.' I quickly fill the kettle. 'What's in the box?'

Lucy's joined us now, and I'm surprised to see her hugging Fern. They're unlikely pals, I think, from totally different generations. Mind you, Wheaton sort of throws people together. We're a big mishmash of oddities trying, and so often failing, to make a community, and I guess you take connection where you can find it round here.

'It's the farm,' Shell tells us, patting the top of the box. I'm surprised at her loud, easy way. She's planted herself by the kitchen table, comfortable and confident. She makes me think of the advice Mum always gave me whenever I felt I was getting in the way somewhere. She'd say, 'This is the space you occupy, so fill it up and don't make yourself smaller for anybody.' Shell occupies her own space, totally unselfconsciously, and it's lovely to see. I'm glad terrified little Fern has this straightforward person by her side.

'The farm?' Lucy echoes, peering inside the open top of the box.

I make the tea in Mum's oldest china pot, just to tickle Fern. She'll love that. I get my Christmas cake from the cupboard too and slice into it.

'Yep, for the grotto,' Fern says, signalling to Shell, who puts the box on the floor and carefully lifts out a ginger-bread model of the Brambledown Farm cottage, setting it on the table.

'Took us all day,' Shell says. 'That's why we're here so late.'

'Oh, that's amazing,' Lucy coos, her eyes lighting up, taking in the intricate icing – all different shades of browns and greens. 'You've even captured the moss on the barn roof. It's beautiful.'

I listen in, setting Mum's best teacups down in their saucers – again, they're for Fern's benefit.

'You've worked so hard, you two.' I tell them and give Fern a little hug that makes her cheeks bloom pink. 'You would make smashing committee members.'

'We would?' says Fern.

I sit and look levelly at the three young women. This feels like a moment for letting them in a little. I breathe and exhale sharply before telling them the truth.

'You see, the thing is, this might be the last gingerbread grotto, unless someone new takes over running the whole thing. Izz is too busy with the cafe to do it and should have retired years ago from all this nonsense, truth be told, and Patrick's moving on, I think, and…' I don't know how to finish this sentence, and the worried look Lucy's giving me makes it impossible to tell her I'm ready to jack it all in and up sticks for Birmingham where we could be near neighbours, popping to the museums and art galleries, or strolling by the canals, whenever the mood took us.

Fern's looking between me and her handiwork a few times, struck wordless, it seems.

'The last grotto?' Shell says. 'But everyone loves the grotto. I've been every year of my life. The whole fam drive over, and we get a chippy tea on the way home. It's, like, a tradition. Christmas without the gingerbread grotto?' she says again in disbelief.

'I know,' I say, 'but times change. Just because it's been a tradition forever doesn't mean it can carry on, not without massive support anyway.'

I pour the tea and plop a slice of cake on each plate. The scent of sweet marzipan and booze mixes with the fresh gingerbread in the air.

'I feel bad,' states Fern bluntly. 'Me and Dad haven't visited it. We're always with the ewes in the barn in late December. Maybe if we'd made the effort…'

'We'd still be skint and struggling,' I say.

Shell reaches for Fern's hand under the table. It must be nice having someone to comfort you like that.

I reach for the one idea that's been in my mind for a while now. Only it doesn't appeal as a solution for this year. Maybe when I'm out of here it would work? 'The project *could* be saved by going back to its roots, only decorating the shelf inside the church porch. That's how it all began, when Mum started it.'

This catches Fern's imagination. She wants to hear more, and before we know it, I've got the albums out and we're poring over pictures of Mum when she was younger. There are newspaper clippings too, from the days before the grotto established itself as a Wheaton institution, when it was just one woman's way of making the world sweeter.

Turning the sheets, Fern stops at pictures of Izz and me during our first Christmases working together on the grotto.

'Do you think Izz is OK?' Fern asks. 'She was really quiet this morning in the cafe. Is it Alexi, do you think? Does she still miss him?'

'She'll be all right,' I offer. 'She just needs a bit more time to herself, and to stop running around like a mad woman, doing far too much.'

We're taking our last bites of cake and draining our cups. It's getting late and Lucy's stifling a yawn. I can see Fern wants to pursue the story of Izz's broken heart but I stand up to clear the tea things in hopes of putting her off.

Suddenly, there's a pinging sound. And another.

'What is that?' Then I realise it's coming from the sofa. 'Oh, it's me! 'Scuse me a sec.'

In the quiet of the den, I check my messages. Nothing from Patrick, but there are two app notifications. I open them and have to fight the urge to chuck the phone into the log burner.

Kenneth, 69, wants to meet up. Then another. *Rusty, 62, wants to meet up.*

'How do I get rid of these?' I say to myself.

'What is it?' Lucy shouts from the kitchen.

'Oh, nothing.'

'Is it the app?' she says, delight sneaking into her voice.

I carry the phone back to the kitchen table like I've found an undetonated bomb.

'What do I do?' I say.

The girls immediately cotton on to what's been happening here tonight, and I'm amazed to see they're not smirking. They're genuinely interested.

'Let's have a look,' says Shell, who is extremely good at making herself at home. 'Ooh, it's definitely Rusty for me,' she says.

Fern agrees that he's 'adorable'.

'Is he? Let me have a look.' I take the phone back, feeling less silly now I know they're not going to take the mick.

Rusty is pictured in a dark jumper, almost-white hair slicked back. He's so good-looking I think there's been some kind of mistake. He looks just like the model Countryside Cupids uses in its advertising, all white teeth and cheekbones. There's another picture of him in shorts and a sporty hoodie like he's on his way to the gym. He's smiling in this one too.

'Seems legit,' Shell says to Fern.

'What does that mean? Why wouldn't he be legit?' I ask.

Fern looks to Lucy like she's uncertain what to say.

'What does she mean?' I turn to Lucy this time.

'Well.' My niece hesitates. 'I read somewhere that around ten per cent of dating profiles are catfishing.'

I repeat the unfamiliar word, blinking.

Fern helps out. 'Scammers, out to rip you off.'

'They ask you for money, after you've been chatting for a bit,' Shell adds. 'Usually, they say it's so they can come and visit you.'

I turn back to Lucy, outraged.

'It's true,' she confirms. 'You have to watch out for sob stories that end in someone asking you to transfer cash. Some of them just pretend to be someone else for fun, then they disappear.'

'What? Don't they vet these people?'

'Did they vet you?' Lucy shrugs.

I swallow hard and look again at Rusty, 62, and Kenneth, 69, and now I'm seeing them in a whole new light. A suspicious one. 'How do I know for sure they're real people?'

'You get a feel for it,' Lucy says like an old hand.

'And, like, you should avoid the ones obviously using filters,' says Fern.

'Yep, and make sure you ask for recents,' Shell adds.

Again, I look accusingly at Lucy. 'Recents?'

'Pictures taken recently, and not a decade ago when they were actually hot.'

'Oh God.' It's not too late to get my money back. *Fourteen-day cooling off period*, it said. I'd made sure to read the small print.

'Yeah, you need to suss them out a bit in the chat,' Shell's saying. 'Or you just don't know what you're dealing with IRL.'

'In real life,' clarifies Lucy before I have to ask.

Shell seems to be enjoying herself, at least. She's shovelling in a second slice of cake that she cut for herself and telling me, 'Some of them will turn up at the date then leave without even approaching you.'

Fern gives her a wide-eyed warning.

'What'd I say?' she says, still munching.

'Don't worry,' Lucy pitches in, trying to curb my panic. 'You'll meet them somewhere public, and we'll make sure we know where you are the whole time. And I'll be sure to ring you thirty minutes in with your get-out call, so if it's awful you can just leave without looking rude. Say there's a family emergency or something.'

I'm nodding, absorbing this madness. None of it sounds like the excitement of dating that I've been used to. I vividly remember doing my make-up and picking my outfit the first time Don called for me. It was all fresh and exciting, and I'd been chatting to him in The Salutation the night before, so I knew what I was getting. This Kenneth, whose surname remains a mystery, the air sign with an interest in travel and cooking, could literally be anybody. And now I have to worry about him turning up at a date, taking one look at me and hightailing it.

'Why didn't you mention this stuff before I made my profile?' I ask Lucy, as I get on with clearing the cups. I have to do something with all this agitation.

I can tell Fern's flown into a panic. She's standing and signalling to Shell they should leave.

'And you're already on these apps, Luce?' I say, clattering about and pouring the dregs from the pot into the compost bin. 'It sounds like a nightmare.'

'Not any more,' Lucy says. 'I told you I was using Bumble to network.' She's adamant when she adds, 'I'm happily single.'

'Romanticise your own life,' Shell says, pulling on her uni women's basketball team jacket. 'That's what you always say, isn't it, Fern?'

I look to the girls, wondering what this might be young-person code for. I've already had a whole education tonight.

Fern takes pity, casting her big, soft eyes over me. 'For some people,' she says, 'it's good to be single and romanticise your own life, rather than being left on read for days by some random who isn't interested.'

'Left on read?' I sigh wearily, the teatowel scrunched in my hand, knuckles on my hip.

'You know, when they've read your message but they don't reply. They've left you on read.'

My eyes flit of their own accord to my phone abandoned on the table where Rusty's handsome face grins out at us.

There was a little tick beside the apology I sent Patrick this morning. That means he read my message hours ago and he hasn't replied.

'And that's a bad thing?' I say, and my voice comes out pitchy. 'Who said we have to reply to messages instantly? We don't have to be available twenty-four hours a day. We're not the Samaritans.'

'But if someone really cares, they reply, don't they?' Fern says, perfectly innocently, with the air of a girl who always gets a reply from her lovely, dependable, simple Shell. They smile at each other with crumpled lips and make for the door. 'Thank you for the tea and cake,' Fern says. 'Can I have the recipe?'

'Oh, uh,' I mumble, wrestling with my thoughts. 'It's Izz's late mum's. I'll copy it out for you through the week.'

Lucy lets the girls out into the dark of the night, waving after them until Shell starts her car engine.

Once they're gone, and I'm wrapping up what's left of the cake, I'm faintly conscious of my niece stopping by the table and lifting my phone to her face, turning her back on me, presumably having one last look at the men's profiles. Then she exaggeratedly says she's tired with a yawn and a stretch and slopes off to bed.

'Night night, darling,' I say.

When I've wiped round the kitchen and put the clean cups away, thinking all the time about Patrick making the choice to ignore me – his annoying, mad old colleague on the gingerbread committee – because I chose to offend him instead of congratulating him on finding work, I click the lights off.

As I'm putting my phone on charge for the night by the bread bin – I don't understand the urge to keep a phone by your bed like Lucy does – I notice the status updates.

You have accepted two dates, it tells me.

'Have I?' I scroll in alarm.

There, underneath, are pictures of Kenneth and Rusty, the con man and the catfisher, joined to my profile picture with overlapping pulsing hearts and the words *Click here to chat with your date* in gaudy pink.

I shut my phone off as quickly as I can and head to bed.

Chapter Eight

Thursday 7 December: Kenneth, 69

A date at Christmas. It should be romantic, right? Only Fern, Shell and Lucy's advice the other night has freaked me out, and I've come to think of the app as little more than a who's who of murderers, weirdos and pathological liars.

But, as Kenneth approaches me in the restaurant at the back of The Cotswold Lass pub (chosen because it's a twenty-minute taxi ride from Wheaton where The Salutation is doing a roaring trade on Lolla's pie, peas and pub quiz night, so there's little chance of anyone I know spotting me), I'm relieved to say he looks sort of normal and not at all murdery.

Glasses, closely cut and tidy salt and pepper beard and a moustache, a dark navy suit like he's just come from work, open collar. He's stocky and about the same height as me when I stand to greet him, all very unintimidating. So far, so good.

Only, I sort of fumble an air kiss beside his cheek because I'm not sure if he's expecting a kiss or not. He's thrust out a hand to shake but because I was lunging forward for the kiss, his knuckles end up squashed against my ribs in a weird way, and I have to laugh it off.

He doesn't laugh. Is he disappointed already?

'Sorry. I'm not used to this. Do you… um… go on many dates?' I ask, sitting myself down and lifting the menu card for something to do.

He hoicks up his trousers before he sits opposite me. 'You're the first in a while.'

I wonder if I should be flattered. 'What made you pick me?' I venture. Am I supposed to ask that? He'll think I'm fishing for compliments.

'I've met all the rest,' he says. It takes me a beat to figure out what he means. He's a serial dater, already exhausted the app's stock of local women. 'You popped up and I thought, I don't know this one.'

He looks around for a waiter. Nobody's come to meet us yet. The bar room's getting busy but we're the only ones through here in the dining room. Even with the tinsel strung around the walls there's not much Christmas atmosphere.

'Shall we go sit by the bar instead?' I offer, but he speaks over me.

'Drink?'

What was it Lucy told me? I should get the drinks in; that way I know they're not spiked. God! To be a young woman on the dating scene today. It must be a nightmare.

'I'll get them,' I say, but he's waving this suggestion away like it's ridiculous.

'No, I will,' he tells me. In this guy's world the man buys the lady's drinks and that's that.

I have to relent or I'll look paranoid. 'Aperol Spritz?' I say, not sure he'll have heard of it.

He only nods and is gone. That's when my phone rings.

'Not now,' I tell Lucy down the line. 'He's just gone to the bar. Try again in about half an hour.'

'What's he like?' she asks.

'Uh.' I inhale, thinking hard. 'Just a bloke, really.'

'Not impressed?'

'Haven't had a chance to be impressed yet,' I say, trying not to appear judgy, but I can admit to myself, I already know there's nothing there, no magic spark. Because, as Izz said about her Alexi, when you know, you know.

'Ring you back,' she says and hangs up.

Noddy Holder's singing from a jukebox through in the bar room. He's wishing it could be Christmas every day and I'm wondering what on earth I'm doing here.

A couple, already a few drinks into a Christmas date, stumble past me and find their 'reserved' table in the corner by the sparkling artificial tree. They're talking animatedly and knocking back a bottle of bubbly. She's touching his arm and they keep their heads close together. Definitely newly in love. I'd say a few months in and still in the first giddy flush of it all.

I fix my eyes on the bar where Kenneth's lifted our drinks and is turning back towards me with an impassive expression.

The contrast between us and the loved-up couple feels too much to bear. I think I'm going to accept Lucy's call and make my excuses and dash home. It's not Kenneth, though; it's me. I want magic and connection when, realistically, I already know they're in drastically short supply and aren't things you can force. Still, I'll give him thirty minutes and see if I can tease out some attraction.

'Tell me, what sort of thing do you like doing?' I ask as he drapes his jacket over the chair back and sits down.

'I like a pub quiz, actually,' he says, and I regret not arranging to meet him at The Salutation. It would be livelier than this, but that would mean people seeing us.

'There's one at my local tonight,' I tell him. 'I usually go with my friend Izz. We never win.'

He takes a sip from his pint and I realise he's not saying anything. Hasn't asked any questions either. I abandon sucking at my straw, forced to keep talking. 'The Stubborn Greys,' I say. 'That's our team name.'

He doesn't laugh, doesn't even seem to get it. I take a long drink.

The couple in the corner are kissing behind their menus. I'd think it was sweet if I wasn't stuck here in stilted conversation with Kenneth.

I notice he's looking at me, or specifically my hair. Has been ever since I made the Stubborn Greys quip.

'What is it?' I ask him, already feeling myself shrinking.

'If you don't mind me saying,' he begins, and I know I am definitely going to mind. 'In your profile picture you had red hair.'

'And now it's not,' I agree. 'I stopped dyeing it a while back, when I realised I was covering up something I wasn't actually ashamed of.' I make sure to direct my eyes to his greying stubble so he knows not to push it.

'Right,' he says, not at all impressed with my stance on ageing without shame. I look at my phone on my lap. Ages till Lucy's get-out call.

Slade fade out on the jukebox and something much more my style comes on: 'Wuthering Heights'.

'Do you like music?' I try, pointing a finger into the air in case he somehow doesn't know what music is. What is wrong with me?

'Hmm.' He nods, lowering his pint like I've actually managed to interest him. 'Tamla Motown, mainly. Northern Soul, bit of blues,' he says.

'Nice!' I over-enthuse. 'I love a bit of Stevie Wonder.' Then, out of nowhere, I sing a bit of 'Superstition' before I force myself to stop. 'Sorry, bit nervous,' I tell him, but he's clamped his lips closed and I realise I'm more annoyed than nervous now. 'I love a bit of Kate Bush,' I attempt in desperation, and he seems confused, so, unbelievably, I point into the air yet again. 'This is one of my favourites.'

He grunts as if to say, *It takes all sorts, I suppose.*

'We're the same age, actually. Me and Kate.' This elicits no response either, so I add, 'You know, my niece Lucy has only just discovered her?'

He plumps a lip like he's not following.

'You know? Because of *Stranger Things*? They're all into it.'

'Nope, you've lost me,' says Kenneth, and we both take a long drink in the awful silence that cannot be filled even by the magnificence of Kate Bush and the clamour of the busy bar room beyond and the audible smooching of the couple in the corner.

'Should we order some food?' I say because nothing else comes to mind. I could get mine to go.

'Big lunch,' he says, patting his belly.

That's when my phone chirps into life, only it's not Lucy with my escape call; it's a text from Patrick.

'Sorry,' I say, lifting my phone, but Kenneth's looking round at the way he came in like he's readying himself to stride back through it.

Sorry I didn't reply to your messages. Crazy busy with school then heading straight to Dunham at night. Not getting home till way past twelve. Hope the gingerbreads are coming together OK, Patrick

I smile for the first time tonight.

'You know, Kenneth,' I say, suddenly inspired to just be myself. 'I reckon romance isn't on the cards for us... and, you know, maybe we could just be friends?'

That's when Kenneth's phone rings and he stands up to answer it, putting on his coat from the back of his chair before he's even spoken.

'Really? Oh no,' he's saying.

No! This can't be! *He's* faking the emergency call? *He's* flaking out on our date? Kenneth, 69, who doesn't like my hair?

'Sorry.' He shrugs. 'Something's come up... at work?' He doesn't even try to sound convincing.

'Yeah, yeah,' I grumble, waving him away. 'Off you trot.' And I watch him leave.

'Oh,' a waitress with tinsel round her head says as their paths cross. 'Is the gent coming back?' she asks me. 'Didn't you want to order?'

I think of the pie and peas and the Stubborn Greys back at The Salutation. It's enough to get me on my feet too.

I apologise to the woman, but at that moment our eyes are drawn to the couple in the corner who've got extremely caught up in 'Wuthering Heights' and are fervently clawing fingers through one another's hair as they kiss.

The waitress looks back at me with a sorry nod – she gets it – and, wordlessly, we leave them to it.

I'm already ringing for a cab as I let the pub doors shut behind me, leaving the disaster that was my first attempt at online dating behind.

–

There's a space for feedback on the app. As if we all ought to be rating our dates out of five like they're a takeaway pizza, as if that's a reasonable thing to do.

I shudder at the thought of Kenneth looking down the options and selecting 'one star' for me. That would hurt more than the date-and-dash thing he pulled, honestly. He doesn't even know me. Even though – Lucy takes care to remind me over our post-pub-quiz hot chocolates – I was also, technically, prepared to make a run for it as well. So I suppose I'm just as bad.

'Except I was honest about things,' I say, wanting to believe I'm a better person.

'How'd you mean?' she says, curling her legs under her on the sofa while the fire crackles.

We're warm in the light from the burning logs and a tree which Lucy's decorated with the help of Fern and Shell as a surprise while I was on my way to meet Kenneth. It's got Fern's signature foresty touch all over it with its pine cones and threaded cranberries and popped corn. It's beautiful, actually.

'You didn't *let's be friends* him? Did you?' Lucy says, grinning.

'Of course I did. That's what you do, to be polite.'

'They're not on the apps to make friends, though.'

'Did I make a fool of myself?'

'You don't have to be so nice.'

'It's nice to be nice.'

But then I'm reminded of all the stupid scrapes I got myself in when I was younger, trying not to hurt men's feelings. Laughing at jokes I didn't find funny, agreeing to a drink with a persistent guy because I couldn't think of a way to put them off asking a second or third time, as if the words 'No thanks, I'm not interested' weren't allowed somehow.

For a while, in my forties, I'd lie and say I had a boyfriend if someone I didn't fancy asked me out, but that didn't serve me all that well. Sometimes blokes would come over all hurt or offended, as though I'd led them on just by chatting with them, or like I owed them something because I'd listened to them boring on about themselves at some party or other.

'Lucy,' I say. 'Promise me you won't ever pretend to be interested in some fella just to be polite, OK?'

'I wouldn't.'

'Good. Life's too short.' Look at me, passing on relationship wisdom. 'I wish I hadn't said to Kenneth we could be friends.'

'I wouldn't worry,' Lucy says over her mug. 'He won't have thought too much about it. And he won't message or anything. He's long gone.'

'All right, all right, I get your point. It's just that friends is such a precious thing, isn't it? I don't go offering it to just anyone, or at least, I don't and mean it.'

Lucy's just listening now, clutching her mug to her chest, looking through the door of the log burner. I join her, watching the flames dancing.

'When you're young, you have loads of friends,' I say. 'At school and college, at work, that kind of thing, but as you get older you get more… selective and you trim off the ones you realise maybe aren't all that great. Fair-weather friends, the ones that bring you down or aren't pleased for you when things are going well, the ones that pick at you or make you feel like you're walking on eggshells? Ever had that?'

Lucy shrugs, non-committal and quiet. I wonder if she's thinking of Craig.

'Some you lose and you never know why. Some don't have the good fortune to grow old with you and you have to go on with your life, just missing them. And by the time you're my age, if you're very, *very* lucky, you'll maybe only have one or two real friends left who you can rely on. Lots of people don't have anyone like that.'

'Like Izz, for you?' Lucy says sleepily.

'Yeah, and Patrick too. I'm lucky enough to have two good friends and I don't know what I'd do without them. I'd be all alone.'

'You've got me,' she says.

'I do, thank goodness.'

'And a whole village of familiar faces. That counts for something?'

I think about that for a moment. She's right. Here in Wheaton, I do have the comforting familiarity of our generations' long history. What people might call roots. Only it's not as comfy-cosy as Lucy imagines. People can know too much about a person.

Not for the first time, I brood over where all my neighbours got to when Don left me in the lurch. They were hardly lining up to offer me a conciliatory cuppa. Errol Burford from number nine practically jumped into a hedge to avoid talking to me the first time he spotted me after Don had done a runner. My sticky situation made people feel awkward instead of provoking the community spirit everyone thinks you find in a small place like this.

You can be in each other's pockets in a small village, what with all the curtain-twitching and passing on news that isn't yours to pass on, but are we really looking after one another? I'm not so sure any more.

If I go ahead with the big move and ship out of here for Birmingham, I'll be leaving all of it behind, a whole lifetime of familiarity, knowing every little detail about people, all spread in whispers behind their backs. Will I miss it when I'm gone? Will they miss me?

I don't like to think about how Izz will be devastated. But I will visit her, very often, and Patrick too. I'll be their friend in the city and it'll be like being on holiday, coming to see me. And the hassle of selling this place, uprooting and shipping my stuff sixty miles away, will be worth it to be closer to Lucy.

'Luce,' I begin. 'You're happy in Birmingham, aren't you?'

She tips her head like I've asked a funny question, and before she can say anything there's a buzz at her phone.

'It's a text from Mum,' she says. 'I think I'll go call her before bed.' She hikes a thumb to her bedroom and I smile, letting her go.

I hope she shares more with Lydia than she does with me. Things seem to have changed recently. We'd talk about everything before, to the extent my sister would get hurt feelings about it, but now Lucy's clammed up. Maybe it's the distance doing it? The fact we only see each other a few times a year now. When I'm in Birmingham it'll be different. I can help her out, be a friend to her. I never hear her mentioning her own friends any more. Did Craig chase them all off? Can I ask her?

I hear Lucy's voice through the bedroom door and pull a blanket over my legs. I quickly fire a message back to Patrick.

> Hope work's going well. About half the exhibit is in place, almost ready for your technical additions. Don't worry if you don't have time, though. I can probably figure out how to work your dry ice machine.

I stop for a second and consider how to sign off. I don't want my friend thinking I'm still upset with him, or that I'm blaming him in any way for us having to start the search for a replacement Santa Claus. I definitely won't have a clue how to do the dry ice thing or any of the lighting setup, but Patrick doesn't need any more on his plate, so I think it's OK to tell a small lie.

> Are you free tomorrow morning? Grab a quick coffee? Haven't done that in a while.
> M X

I agonise over the kiss then tell myself off for being silly and hit send. I get a message back in seconds.

> I'll add my breaks together and see you at 10

No kiss, then, I notice.

There's a new notification from Countryside Cupids, so I slide it open.

Hi, it's Rusty. Thanks for matching with me. Listen, I know this is supposed to be a rural dates app, but I only recently moved to Birmingham and haven't had a chance to switch to another app. Do you want to meet me here on Sunday night? Dinner and drinks? The German Christmas market is open too. I promise it'll be fun.

Fun? I could do with something fun after the disappointment of Kenneth. Plus, I could combine the trip with a visit to the estate agents, maybe view a couple of properties on the sly? Nobody here has to know, and seeing the places in real life might help me rehearse what it could feel like to actually bite the bullet and get the 'For Sale' signs up.

Let's do it.

I know a nice place in China Town. Meet me outside the hippodrome at seven?

I'll be there. Oh and Rusty? My profile picture is three years old. I no longer colour my hair. OK?

I laugh when I read his reply.

I also no longer colour my hair. P.S. For tradition's sake, I'll be carrying a red rose. Not too weird?

Not weird at all. Just don't carry it between your teeth, or behind your ear?

Got it, R x

I'm enjoying this and already trying to think of something else to type in reply when a message from Patrick stops me. I'm shocked at how guilty I feel, like he's caught me red-handed, cheating or something, which is, of course, totally ridiculous.

Try not to worry about the grotto. We'll work out a Santa rota somehow. Sleep well, P, xx

'OK,' I tell the empty room, running my thumb over the kisses, two of them, no less. 'That's enough getting carried away for one evening.'

I close the app, station my phone in the kitchen overnight as always, and get ready for bed.

I'm smiling in the mirror while I brush my teeth, unsure whether to put it down to the prospect of a city dinner date with lively, funny Rusty or because of my relief that Patrick, my dear friend, is back in touch and the weirdness is over.

Chapter Nine

Friday 8 December: Reels

There are better ways to begin your day than getting a phone call from Izz to say there's a water leak above the cloakroom in the village hall and scrambling down there with mops and towels when you've made the effort to dress up nicely for coffee with a friend. I'd dug out my leather trousers and everything. Worn with a big silvery-grey jumper it doesn't look too try-hard, not that I was overthinking coffee with Patrick at all this morning.

Anyway, I know we definitely aren't off to a good start when I find Izz and Fern in there unceremoniously dragging out cardboard boxes full of clutter from the little cloakroom cupboard while Patrick's legs dangle from a great big hole in the cloakroom ceiling, his T-shirt drenched, sounds of hammering at pipework coming from the dark space.

'Good news is, it's confined to the cloakroom,' Izz tells me as soon as I burst in.

'What caused it?' I call up the ladders.

'Frozen…' – Patrick strains, his arms aloft, stretching to tighten something – 'pipe.' With that, he hands down a length of copper corroded through with green.

'Looks like it's been ready to burst for a while,' I observe expertly.

'There, that should stop it.' Patrick makes his way down the ladder, breathing heavily, his hair both wet and dusty. 'Nobody's been up there since the place was built. There's pigeons roosting under the eaves as well. It's a right mess.'

I should be listening, of course, commiserating with him after his exertions, worrying about the bloody great big hole in the cloakroom ceiling or all the plaster at our feet that the weight of the water brought down, but there's something about Patrick's arms streaming with grimy moisture and the way he's clutching the wrench as he lowers himself back down to ground level that holds my attention far too long.

Luckily, Izz has her common sense switched on and is asking all kinds of sensible questions about the state of the rest of the pipework and whether we need to alert the council, and of course Fern is standing by Izz's side taking in everything through the lens on her phone.

'If we tell the council,' Patrick says, lifting a hand to Fern's phone and politely lowering it, 'there's a good chance they'll come in and shut us down for Christmas.'

This does the trick of waking me up. 'Why would they do that?'

'Well, that bit of pipe you're holding's as old as the rest of it. When they reconnected the power last night and the old boiler fired up, the pressure – and no doubt the ice in the system – was too much for it and, crack, we've got a leak. The council will probably want to rip it all out.'

'Yeah, but not this week. Think how long it took them to order Izz's replacement lollipop; that was months of red tape and budget talks.'

'That's true,' Izz confirms. 'Nobody could agree which budget it should come out of. I told them if I'd known it was going to cause so much of a fuss I'd have ordered one off Amazon.'

'You think they'd shut up the hall?' I ask Patrick.

'Do you want to risk it?'

I picture Mr Scrimengor and his surveyor mates arriving later this morning with their hard hats and their budgetary restraints and slapping tape across the entire place. Condemned until repair works tendered and carried out. 'I doubt they'd be willing to wait until after Christmas to declare the place a health and safety nightmare. Maybe we should keep quiet until Christmas Eve when we're all gingerbreaded out?'

'*Can* you buy lollipops on Amazon?' Fern throws in, but we three are looking up at the hole and then at one another.

'Are you able to patch up this hole?' I ask Patrick.

'Since it's just the cloak cupboard, I could. It was only plasterboard, but it'll take me the best part of the morning, and I'd have to tell Mr Bold why I wasn't at the school.'

'We can help,' I say, hands on hips, looking at all the sopping wet boxes.

Soon Patrick is measuring and cutting, hefting and painting while we sweep up soggy plaster, dry and polish the tiled foyer floor, and rummage through the damp cardboard boxes of accumulated junk that have been shoved inside the cloakroom over the years: mouldy cricket leg pads, decades' worth of lost and never found scarves and gloves, old newspapers, a broken kettle.

'I'll stick it all in the school skip,' says Patrick helpfully.

'What's this?' Fern is picking painfully slowly through her own sagging cardboard box under the watchful bug eyes of the late King's portrait. She's holding up a red plastic disk. 'There's loads of them.'

'Ah!' Izz is on the move, abandoning her pile of rugby boots furred with age. 'I know exactly what that is. Treasure!'

Patrick stops in his work and we all crowd round to examine the find.

'They're cine reels,' Izz clarifies, and of course, Fern's already reaching for her phone to capture the discovery.

'Don't worry, I'm not going live, just filming,' she says, seeing my face fall.

Some of the reels are still in their cases and original cardboard wrappers. Others are loose, just the delicate tape in its round red casing.

'Laurel and Hardy,' Patrick reads, inspecting each in turn. 'Charlie Chaplin.'

Now Izz has her hands in the box. 'We used to come to the hall to watch these.'

'Like a cinema,' I add, and Fern finally gets it. 'That must have been before my time. I don't remember watching films in here.'

'I do,' says Izz. 'They'd hang a sheet over the mural at the far end of the hall and we'd all sit round with our bags of sweets. I'm sure these movies were old long before us kids watched them. Look, there's a few John Waynes too.'

'Country dance competition, seventy-seven.' Fern reads the handwriting on one of the reels. 'Wheaton May Day, nineteen seventy-four.'

Izz says, 'I remember Harry Boulton, the hall manager in the days when there was such a thing, was a cine film enthusiast. These must be his.'

'Do you remember showings of these home movie reels in the hall too?' Patrick asks.

'Not sure, maybe?' Izz is searching her memory. 'If we did, I've forgotten.'

Fern is still pulling out reels, filming each in turn with her phone. 'Wheaton winter dance, sixty-five.'

'What? Let me see that.' Izz takes the reel, then looks at me. 'I was at this dance.'

'You were?' I say with a gasp.

'For sure I was.'

It only takes a few moments to cook up the plan and it begins with me getting very overexcited and saying, 'Dad had a Super 8 projector, you know? Back at the cottage. Doubt it's been used in decades.'

'We can actually *watch* these?' Fern looks like she's about to float off into vintage junk heaven.

'Maybe, unless the film's degraded,' Patrick throws in.

'Will you have time to call in at the cottage before you go to your new job?'

Patrick thinks he'll be able to manage half an hour at fourish, and we all scuttle off to our various occupations: Fern and Izz to the cafe, Patrick back to school, and me to my kitchen and the gingerbreads, except now I'm carrying a sagging box of cine films and worrying someone from the council will sniff out the fresh plasterboard and paint inside the hall coat cupboard, but for now, what they don't know can't hurt anyone – or, more importantly, hurt our grotto – and there's still a lot of work to do.

–

The darkness in the den is cut through by the lights from the Christmas tree and the beam from the projector bulb. Everyone – Patrick, Fern, Lucy, me and Izz – has fallen silent after the excitement of retrieving Dad's projector from the boot room in its cardboard box, gone soft and foxed with age.

There'd been a flurry of coffee making and I'd broken out my mince pies. Lucy threw a fresh log onto the fire where it's smoking now, not yet caught.

The projector whirrs, and two reels spin slowly in the warmth: one – a red spool – feeds the machine with its thin strip of celluloid, the other – a shiny black – smoothly draws the film past the bulb and lens, sending the images bursting in grainy colour onto Dad's rickety silver rollaway screen that took a lot of work to get straight, then spools the viewed frames safely up once more.

After years of familiarity with iPhones and streaming and HD cinema, this old technology should have ceased to surprise us, but as the spools wind and something within the projection box clunks – I have no clue what, but it doesn't seem to be a problem – we all fall under the spell of the wonder of dust motes dancing in the shimmering rays.

The images before us change from a series of jumping black splodges against white to the stuttering words *KODAK film* in two-foot-high type, to a slowly fading-in scene of a smiling man with a hat and cane walking in a street we don't recognise, marks and scratches blooming all around him like black snow, and then he's gone in a blink. Now children in summer clothes run a race on chubby legs on the school's playing fields. There's no time to attempt to identify any of them, they're gone too, and a new scene begins.

A close-up of someone holding a piece of paper with the painted words *Wheaton Winter Dance, 1965* jumps and flickers. The paper's removed to reveal the scene at the village hall.

The men, all wiry in a way that speaks volumes about the working men of my dad's generation, stew- and stout-fed, stocky but fit, are choosing their partners and leading them to the floor, and I find myself remembering the smell of Dad's cigarettes back when he smoked, back when everybody smoked.

'See, that's when the murals covered all four walls,' Izz says, and we peer to make them out, but everything's moving too fast to make them out clearly.

There's a panning shot of the crowd of spectators and I strain my eyes for Mum and Dad, but they're not there, and a heavy longing constricts my chest.

Izz is silent. If she recognises any of the Wheaton folk in their summer clothes pulling faces and waving, or hiding shyly from the lens, or that one man in a suit with baggy trousers making those around him laugh while he mimes a waltz, she doesn't mention it.

Fern's beside Izz on the couch and Lucy's on the floor in front of the fire, all of them clutching mugs, transfixed.

A hot smell rises from the projector. The bulb's getting heated and I worry for the fragile film under tension between the reels. Will it hold out until Izz sees what she came to see?

The screen turns black – only a few white flashes of who knows what interrupt the dark – and Fern turns in her seat to look at me.

'Is that it over already?' she asks.

Suddenly, the den is aglow again, and the scene opens once more, still on the hall, and everyone applauding the end of a dance, their movements somehow accelerated to almost comical speed, all indistinguishable, a sludgy palette of washed-out nostalgia, an artist's brush swirling in water.

'There I am,' Izz says, her voice a breathy gasp, 'and there's my mother.' She points a finger, voice shaking with emotion as the figure, the double of Izz today, slips by on-screen and is gone.

I'm the one who mists up first; Izz is too determined to see the scene unfold to cry yet. She sits forward in her seat and Fern joins her, their necks extended, eyes peeled.

I think how precious each still of this film is, how measured, how economical my parents' generation were with their recordings. Occasions we'd film and photograph every instant of these days – weddings and picnics, holidays and Christmases – had to be captured in moments back then. All of that festivity was, by necessity, distilled into a few treasured seconds on film – all they had to show for their most important days, stored on dangerously perishable film that would have to last them a lifetime.

There's probably more snaps of my mum and dad doing nothing in particular stored in my phone at this very moment than there'll be seconds of footage of them on their own wedding day, and I haven't made the effort to watch any of their films, all jumbled up in the boot room with every old coat, umbrella and walking stick anyone in the Frost family ever owned going back decades, junk and clutter I'll never use but daren't chuck out, thrown in with absolute treasure.

I make a mental note to convert every one of their reels to digital formats for them, feeling guilty about not looking after our memories. All of this rushes through my mind alongside registering that Izz is back on-screen now.

She's tiny and dark, beautiful with her hair tied in a folded headscarf, the knot at the nape of her neck.

'There's little blue flowers on that dress. You can't make them out,' Izz says, motionless.

I get the sense she's specifically talking to Fern, who is now squished up close to her on the sofa.

There's a brownish haze along the outer edges of the images where the film is burning. The heat from the projector is making my spot behind it as warm as if I were in front of the log burner. I daren't stop now in case the film tears and we lose precious frames.

Silence falls, and I sense we're all waiting for the same thing. An electric energy radiates out from Izz on the sofa, a static charge of old emotions building to palpable levels.

When the man appears, it is with a burst, bounding into the shot, a tall streak of fitness and youth. Young Izz already has her hand in his and they're ready to dance. Her face, like a fresh flower, blooms, all rounded cheeks and happy eyes.

'That's Alexi,' she says. 'I remember this part. The contest.'

All the younger couples are dancing this one, the older folks sitting it out around the edges. It's clear even from the seconds of footage who the winners are going to be.

'He was a lovely dancer,' says Izz.

Fern rubs soothing circles on her back, but neither of them can drag their eyes from the screen where the scene cuts to the pair of them, Alexi tall and straight, Izz small by his size, receiving the prize sash and bottle of Asti Spumante from the judge.

All smiles, Alexi stoops as if to kiss Izz on the cheek.

All of us lean in closer to the flickering screen.

The spool ticks with the sound of film working loose. It's the end of the reel. The screen is a blank silver once more.

Izz doesn't move.

'It's over,' she says, barely audible, the words getting lost in shaky sniffs.

'Run it again,' Fern says, soft but urgent, drawing out her phone. 'This time I'll film it.'

Patrick, however, has to get going, so I show him out while the reel runs once more.

He stops inside the door frame and turns. 'Are you going to be OK?' he asks, with a gesture of his head through the den wall. He means Izz.

'Yeah, we'll order a pizza or something, feed her up, crack on with some gingerbreads, then walk her back to her place. She'll be OK, maybe just a bit frazzled from old memories.'

'She ever tell you about Alexi?'

'Just the once,' I say, with a smile.

He nods. He knows Izz and I are close. 'You know, we didn't get our coffee this morning.'

'True.'

'Or our pub meal the other night.'

'Also true.'

'Should we try Sunday? I have the night off from Dunham Gravey. There can't be any strops or leaks stopping us on Sunday, surely?'

'I wasn't having a strop,' I laugh, and my heart lifts until I remember I have plans. 'Actually, I can't do Sunday.'

'What, do you have a hot date?' He says it like it's funny.

'Uh.' I look away.

'Oh! You do?' Patrick stands straighter.

'Kind of. In Birmingham, actually.'

'Right. Well… that's great!'

'Yeah?'

'Yeah, of course! I didn't realise you were seeing anyone, or…'

'It was Lucy's idea. I uh…' I feel my cheeks redden. 'I'm trying a dating app.'

Patrick nods, his lips forming a tight smile.

'You ever use them?' I say.

'Dating apps? No, I prefer real life.'

'That's what I said!' See! He gets it. Though he's obviously in a hurry to get to work as he's stepping away.

'Well, have fun,' he says. 'You should wear those leather trousers on the date.'

I look down at my legs. 'I should?' He's giving me a compliment. It should feel good.

'Yeah, you suit them.' He turns and walks away, leaving me blinking after him. I don't call after him to say thanks, only telling him to drive carefully, the roads will be icy.

When I close the door and walk back into the den, I don't want to examine too closely what this feeling is, like I've crossed a line with Patrick that I hadn't been aware of before. *Have fun*, he said. *That's great*, he said. He really is glad I'm getting out there again, which *of course* he is, he's so nice. That's exactly how a good friend *should* react when you tell them you're recovered enough to date again after being dumped.

Still, something doesn't sit right within me and I'm conscious of the feeling of distance between us. He wanted to grab some dinner but as soon as I told him I was going out with Rusty on Sunday, he didn't then suggest another evening. Why is that?

Patrick's on his way out to Dunham by himself now, working into the night instead of being here with us. There'll be a hell of a lot more distance when I'm living in Birmingham, and I don't want to dwell on that too much right now, but there's a small voice inside me telling me it's for the best.

Lucy, who's been rummaging in the reels while I let Patrick out, greets me by telling me, 'There's a reel in here says gingerbread village. Looks really old.'

'Hah, so it does. I didn't know this existed.' I take the reel from my niece and put it on top of the fridge for safekeeping. If we're watching it with anyone, it'll be with Patrick.

'I think we've had enough reminiscing for one night,' I say. 'Let's get baking.'

–

We all walked Izz back to her cottage in the dark. Izz had protested, saying we were hovering and making her feel like a little old lady, and we'd waved this away as nonsense, we were only making sure she got home safely, but in truth, I've never seen her so tired and despondent.

'Smiling to cover up a secret sadness,' Lucy remarks, I think somewhat dramatically, as we make our way back to ours where Tommy Brash is supposed to be coming to collect his daughter.

We all stand outside stamping our feet under the black sky and wait for him to arrive, and sure enough, he trundles up in a puttering Land Rover, a rusting metal box on wheels with three farm dogs in the back, all stinky, and all delighted to see Fern.

Lucy scratches their heads through the gaps – I mean, I can't technically call them car windows if there's no glass – as Tommy's engine idles.

Brash – a stubbly vision in waxed Barbour – nods to me, flicking fingers to his temple in salute. '*Hmt*,' he grumps.

'Evening,' I say.

Fern's climbing into the passenger seat, but before she puts her seat belt on, she shows him a bit of the film that she's recorded on her phone.

'Do you recognise this bloke, Dad? Alexi Thorne? The one that's dancing with Izz? He was her boyfriend, but because he was already married, he had to leave Wheaton.'

We should head inside, but my feet, like Lucy's it seems, are planted by the vehicle. Lucy's still fussing with those smelly dogs anyway.

Tommy peers at Fern's screen, already lifting his shoulders for a grumpy shrug.

'Nope, never seen him.'

Fern slumps in her seat. 'Grandpa would have known him.'

'Reckon he would have.'

'People don't just disappear,' my niece throws in, and I snap round to face her.

'Don't be getting ideas, you two,' I say, and I'm amazed to hear Brash agreeing.

'Never prod a sleeping dog,' he says.

This is the most I've ever heard him say. Even down The Salutation with his mutts sleeping at his feet he keeps his face in his pint, barely even speaking to the other old-timer farmers.

Fern doesn't have time to say her goodbyes as Brash lets the handbrake off, nearly taking Lucy's dog-patting arm with him as they go.

'So that's Fern's dad?' Lucy says as we watch them sputtering into the darkness, exhaust fumes in the air.

'That old thing definitely wouldn't pass its emissions test,' I say, wafting the stink away.

'Fern's taken a real shine to Izz,' Lucy adds, and we make our way back along the frosty path into the cottage.

'She has, hasn't she? I worry, though.'

'What?' Lucy frowns, and I lock us in for the night. The kitchen is warm and sweet-scented and there are two new gingerbread houses fully decorated on the table.

'I don't know. That all Fern's romanticising will get to Izz, dredge up old feelings she'd gotten over years ago. You saw her crying tonight.'

'Do you ever really get over a badly broken heart?' says Lucy, making me stop in my tracks to the den where the pizza boxes need clearing away.

I turn to my niece, who seems suddenly stricken.

'Lucy?'

She's silent, hanging her head.

'You can talk to me about Craig, you know? You can talk to me about anything.'

'I know,' she says, and I think we're about to hug when she swerves for the pizza boxes and fusses around with them.

Evidently, we're not talking tonight either.

Once she's in bed and I can hear the soft sounds of her scrolling through Instagram reels on her phone behind her closed door, I consider her words.

Do you ever get over a badly broken heart, even if it was decades ago? Are we destined to always carry a candle for that special person we just can't get over? I think of my John – quiet, loyal, patient John. It's not ardent love I feel when I think of him. What's left of him when I really search my feelings? Not much. Only there's a pang of regret for the years we wasted pottering around this cottage together, living with Mum and Dad, and him trying to hide how much he wanted to have kids until it all got too much for him. We weren't exactly unhappy, but we certainly weren't *happy* happy either.

Then there's Don. I definitely have the badly broken heart thing covered with him, but I can't say I'm doing any heavy-duty pining for him. Far from it. Even if I did spend the whole of last Christmas and all of January hiding in front of the telly thinking my life was over. I wouldn't even open the door if he showed up right this second. I've literally nothing I want or need to say to him.

What I'm left with from that escapade is the embarrassment, the feeling of having taken a risk, going against all my inhibitions screaming at me not to, and ending up making a complete fool of myself. That's what smarts the worst. Don was probably my last chance at something lasting.

Now *that* makes me sad, but if I'm pining for anyone at all, it's the old Margi of my fifties. Bold and brave and mouthy. The Margi who took weekends away at the drop of a hat with Izz. Margi the force to be reckoned with. Always dressed to the nines to the extent the village would stare, all heels and tight pants. Chin-up, boobs-out Margi. Now *she* was really something.

I miss her the way Izz probably misses her Alexi.

Chapter Ten

Saturday 9 December: The Older Brother

Wheaton has that 'Christmas is coming' feel about it today, and I'm on top of the world as I carry another gingerbread house (my own little cottage, as it happens) to the village hall.

The wet weather has cleared and today is one of those rare palest-blue-winter-sky days where the sun is dazzlingly bright and low over the frosty rooftops. It's bitterly cold, of course, but I'm wrapped up in my long red wool coat and not minding the chill one bit.

As I pass by, I notice the art gallery is having a pre-Christmas open day. I must remember to tell Lucy to pop in and introduce herself as a sort-of-local artist. Not that she's picked up so much as a biro since she arrived, but I'll keep working on her.

Some of the Wheaton oldies are dashing around running errands. The high street is busy with supermarket delivery vans and overworked couriers leaving parcels on doorsteps.

Patrick's out gritting the school playground, even though it's a Saturday. That headmaster really doesn't deserve him.

'Need help with that?' he calls and comes to meet me at the school gates.

'I've got it, thanks,' I tell him. 'Why are you at school?'

'Bobbie's bootcamp's on again tonight, and there's frost forecast. Can't have them breaking an ankle getting into the building.'

I shake my head. 'Always helping out,' I say, but my brain is harping on in the most annoying, persistent way, telling me, *he shows he cares through acts of service too, just like you!*

'Nobody else is going to do it,' he shrugs. 'How's the exhibit shaping up?'

'We're almost done with the baking, just the school to make, a bit of the churchyard and some bits here and there to finish. Lucy, Fern and Shell have been a big help this year.' I worry he'll think this is a dig, so I add, 'And you and Izz, of course. We're quite the team!'

He doesn't seem to be taking any of this in. I notice his eyes drawn up over my shoulder, and when I turn to see what's making him tense his jaw like that, I almost drop my gingerbread cottage.

There on the pavement is another Patrick, maybe a touch more silvery about his temples, but definitely just as handsome and green-eyed.

'I didn't know you were coming,' Patrick's saying, and I find I'm looking back and forth between the two of them.

'I was passing through on business and thought I'd surprise my little brother. Rather than stay in a hotel, I wondered if I might have the spare room?'

Patrick doesn't say anything.

'Do you think you can knock off, grab a drink?' the man adds, and that's it, I'm a ball of intrigue now.

'I'm heading off to Dunham in a minute,' Patrick says coolly. 'Taken an extra day shift.'

'I thought you said you didn't have a brother?' I pry.

138

Patrick looks stern. Barely hiding the sigh, he tells me, 'This is Charlie.'

'May I help with that?' Charlie's asking me. 'Looks a bit cumbersome.' And the smile he's giving me makes me hand over my house immediately.

'Sure, thank you. I'm only taking it to the hall.' I point down the street in the direction of the exhibit.

'Then you must be Margi,' he tells me, and I turn to glimpse at Patrick once more. He's looking down at his feet.

'Patrick's told me all about you,' Charlie continues. 'You're in charge of the gingerbread grotto.'

'No, I just like roaming the streets showing off my baking skills,' I say, and he actually laughs. It's odd seeing a carbon copy of Patrick but jolly and loud. Patrick's eyes are still upon me now, I can feel them.

'This is going to the village hall?' Charlie adds. 'Allow me. See you later, Patrick. Leave the key under the mat?'

Charlie leads the way down the high street. I'm very aware that Patrick didn't say goodbye, only watching us as we left. Something's definitely up with these two.

'He told you he didn't have a brother, eh?' Charlie's saying in Patrick's voice as we walk, only deeper and a bit smoother. 'Can't blame him.'

'You can't?' I'm not going to pass up an opportunity to mine Charlie for more information about his reticent brother. Something tells me Charlie isn't anything like as word-shy.

'I don't think it's easy being the little brother. Are you a sister, by any chance?'

'I am. Eldest of two.'

'Ah, so maybe you know what it's like being *the chosen one*?'

He says it so dramatically, I laugh.

'Parents aren't supposed to have favourites,' he adds in a theatrical whisper, pulling a guilty face. 'Poor Patrick.'

'Ah!' I say, as it clicks for me. 'I think I know what you're saying. My mum definitely treated me differently to Lydia. Not like I was her *favourite* or anything, but…'

'Only that they had different expectations of you than the baby of the family?' Charlie puts in as we reach the hall steps.

'Yes! Exactly that. Believe me, I wouldn't have spent every Christmas of my life surrounded by gingerbread if I hadn't been singled out for the job.'

'But you're glad your little sister didn't have to take it on?'

I nod. 'She's doing her own thing.' I pull the keys from my coat pocket and let us inside. 'What is it you do, Charlie?'

'I run the family business in Cheltenham. Antiques, restoration, sales, that sort of thing.'

'Patrick did say your dad was an antiques expert.'

'But my brother kept *me* quiet, though,' Charlie says with a wink.

'Through here,' I tell him, opening the doors into the main hall for him. 'You can set my cottage down right there.'

Once it's in its spot, we both stand admiring little Wheaton, Charlie far more enthusiastically than me.

'It'll be better with all of Patrick's bells and whistles added in,' I tell him.

'He always was the handy one. There was nothing he couldn't fix. Mind you, he liked taking things apart just as much.'

'Oh yeah?'

'Yep, like my ZX Spectrum? First computer I had, and he took it to bits to see how it all worked, but he was too young at that point to know how to fix it. Dad was furious!'

'Aww, poor Patrick,' I say.

I understand a little about the unspoken things that go on between siblings. I'm pretty sure Lydia's glad not to have been put through Mum's grotto training, and she definitely didn't want a share in the responsibility for it – she'd have to be mad to – but I've always had an inkling Lydia was sore about the way it bonded me and Mum. I don't think my little sister and Mum were ever as close as we were, and that's got to do something to a younger sibling. I've tried to guard against her feeling excluded, but I still think there's some jealousy there, and it's not made any easier by the fact Lucy and I always got on like a house on fire.

Obviously, I can't replace her mum, but when Lydia left for New Zealand, I was the one helping Lucy with the big things, like helping her move into her flat, and sharing the small things, like taking the picture when she blew out her birthday candles. Lydia and I never spoke about any of that, and there were never any major fall outs either, but still, there's something there.

Charlie's moved on to admiring the hall now, saying it's a wonderful example of mid-century rural civic architecture, and he's gone moon-eyed over the mural. 'Stunning,' he's saying.

I join him in front of the painted orchard, the apples so big and red they make me want to reach out and grab one. 'So… are you staying for long?' I ask.

'Just a few days. I'm doing some valuations in the area, a couple of house clearances. What is it they say? You

141

shouldn't wait for an invitation from family? I think if I was waiting for my little brother to invite me to stay, it'd be one hell of a long wait.'

'I bet he's happy you're here, really,' I say, and Charlie grins a little wickedly. 'It's a shame he's working such long hours. You won't get much of a chance to catch up.'

'He's always been like that. Keeping busy, helping everyone.'

'I'd have been lost without him these last few years,' I confess.

'I'm glad he's got friends here. Whenever I ring him, he's always Margi this and Margi that. I'm just glad I've finally got to meet the marvellous Margi.'

'It really is uncanny,' I tell him. 'How much you look alike.'

'My dad would be pleased to hear that.' Another devilish, silly smile spreads over his lips.

'What, um, what are you doing for dinner tonight?' I appear to be asking. 'Patrick will be working, won't he? Why don't you come to The Salutation with us? Try Lolla's famous cranberry and pork sausage rolls?'

'Us?'

'Me and my niece. She's been staying with me. She's an artist.'

'Like her aunt,' Charlie says, gesturing at the ginger-breads. Very smooth. 'I can see why Patrick likes it around here. Friendly.'

There's something reassuring in the word, coming from him, and as I lead us out once more into the chilly morning, directing Charlie to The Salutation for six tonight, I tell myself I've done the right thing, helping look after a friend's brother when he's visiting and doesn't know anyone. It's a friendly gesture, I tell myself as I make for home and another day's baking.

–

The Salutation smells of good food, mulled wine and green wood burning in the inglenook fireplace. Nothing says 'Christmas in the Cotswolds' quite so much as this place with its lights glowing low under frosted glass shades, horse brasses and farming knick-knacks hung all over the walls, and every surface made of ancient ash polished over the decades into a glossy richness that makes the whole place feel like a hug.

Lucy's behind me, eager to get a glimpse of the man who I, according to her, 'picked up in the street this morning'.

Lolla waves us over to the bar to tell me there's a 'gentleman' in the snug waiting for me.

'Patrick's double,' she says, winking, which I don't appreciate.

I don't have time to protest all over again about how I'm just doing Patrick a favour while he's at work. She's handing me a plastic basket of her fresh sausage rolls and a hastily poured glass of Pinot.

'Better not keep him waiting,' she tells me. 'Lucy, your friends are already here,' and she points out Fern and Shell on the high stools by the dark window.

Shell waves and taps at an empty stool.

Lucy looks torn.

'Go on,' I say. 'I'll be fine. Go and have some fun with your friends that doesn't involve making biscuits.'

Lucy takes three sausage rolls from the basket, bundles them into a napkin, and bites into one before she goes. I think that's her way of telling me she'll be fine too.

Right! Smooth down my top, shake my hair back, deep breath. I make my way to the snug for a not at all meaningful drink with the older brother of one of my dearest friends. What could be more welcoming and charitable?

Charlie stands to meet me and swoops a quick kiss onto my cheek, which I wasn't expecting, but I don't mind; it's still well within the realm of friendly gestures. That's fine.

'You look great,' he tells me, and I bite back the urge to tell him he looks flipping fantastic in a leather jacket that I'm willing to bet Lolla's sausage rolls is a vintage Italian designer number.

Instead, my brain makes me tell him, 'You smell nice,' and I sit down, unimpressed with myself. 'Did Patrick get off to work OK?' I say, gulping at my wine.

Charlie's already got a pint glass of something golden, and he takes a sip then wipes his top lip, exactly the same way Patrick does.

'Sure he did. So, Margi, we've got all night. Tell me all about yourself.' He reaches for a sausage roll, takes a comically big bite, and sits back expectantly with a wild look in his eyes which makes me laugh again.

'Whole life story?' I say.

'Every detail,' he munches.

'I warn you it's mostly gingerbread and bad decisions.'

He laughs warmly, inclining his head at me, and I settle into the cosiness of the evening.

It's some time before I realise the food's gone and my glass is empty and we've shared all the big details about our lives. He knows about John and Don – I think he was pretending not to already know about my second husband. Patrick might have mentioned it in passing – but he still listened politely like it was news to him. He said the usual nice things about how it was Don's loss, and I heard all about his divorce years ago and about his clever daughter off at uni studying architecture. He's not friends with his wife, unfortunately, and it sounds like she made things hard for him in court, but Charlie was magnanimous about it and swept it away with a hand, saying, 'It's all in the past. What matters is the future.'

I tell him I'll get some drinks, and he cheekily tells me to get more of the sausage rolls, which I was going to anyway.

When I'm at the bar, I see a sight that makes my heart swell. Shell, Fern and Lucy are laughing and talking, deeply engaged in each other, like true girlfriends. Like me and Izz when we're battling it out at the pub quiz.

It's loud and getting a bit rowdy in the pub now that all the farmers are a few pints into their evening. I catch Lucy's eye, and she mouths, 'What's he like?' and does a none-too-subtle pointy gesture towards the snug.

I mouth back, 'Not bad.'

She laughs, and I hear it all the way over here at the bar.

'What you havin', love?' asks Ken, Lolla's husband.

The bar staff are seriously earning their tips tonight and the pumps are being worked non-stop. I order the same again, and a scene catches my eye right at the end of the bar that makes me stoop behind one of the boozy farmers so I can get a better look.

It's the superhead. In the pub!

'Surprised to see 'im in here,' says Ken, following my eyeline. 'Thought he'd be 'iding away like usual. He's not like us Wheaton lot.' Ken sets Charlie's pint on the bar and busies himself again. I'm still peeping out from my spying place.

The super Mr Bold is uncharacteristically attempting a smile and is clutching a glass of wine to his chest, and I have to say he is looking a bit less starchy with his blue shirtsleeves rolled back and without the tie knotted at his throat. Less like a sixth-former desperate to be promoted to school captain.

I peer round the farmer's sideburns shielding me to see who's making the superhead quite so wide-eyed and am startled to see Sully Scrimengor, the put-upon young baker who is talking up at him animatedly.

'Ah! That's nice,' I say, making the farmer startle and turn to look at me. 'Sorry,' I say before spinning round to give Lucy an urgent look that says, *There's Sully. Go and invite him over.*

Shell and Fern are engaged in doing something on their phones, so I can gesture and point as much as necessary to get Lucy rolling her eyes and slipping huffily off her stool.

I watch in satisfaction as she approaches the men and invites them to join the girls over in the corner. The superhead clamps his mouth shut, looking panicked, but Sully's made of friendlier stuff, and I watch him dragging Mr Bold by the wrist towards them and Lucy making the introductions. There! Just how it should be. A group of young people being sociable in the local pub.

Ken's taking his time finding my Pinot, long enough for further inspiration to strike. I am *on fire* this evening!

I'm on the move. Lucy's face is a picture of hidden mortification, but I'm not stopping now.

'Evening all,' I begin. Fern and Shell jump to attention. 'Mr Bold! It's nice to see you in your new local. Just wondered if you'd had time to think about the offer we made?'

'*Uh*, what offer was that?' He tries to smile again. He has lovely white teeth. Smiling suits him. He should let his eyes in on it too.

'You know? The gingerbread grotto committee coming into the school to teach the children some icing techniques? So that the little ones can see their own art displayed in the grotto exhibition?'

'Oh, right, that. Well, as I said the other day...' he begins.

'That's a brilliant idea,' interrupts Sully, his eyes bright.

Is this what he's like when he's out from under his grandfather's thumb? Or, and I'm starting to put two and two together now, is it only when he's talking to a handsome head teacher?

'Kids love that sort of thing, don't they?' Sully's saying. 'I know I always did, hanging around the bakery when I was little, putting the buttons on the gingerbread men. It's what made me want to be a baker.'

'And now you are,' I say.

'And now I am,' he smiles.

'Your grandfather makes the best gingerbread men in the Cotswolds,' I tell him, and I'm not lying, even if I am deliberately flattering a teensy bit.

'It's true, you know,' Sully tells Mr Bold, who's looking at me with a raised eyebrow. 'So, when are you going into the school?' Sully directs this at me, and I could kiss him, it's so perfect.

'Well, that's up to Mr Bold.' I smile, turning to look at the flustered man.

'He's just told me he wants to be called Leo,' Sully throws in.

The superhead sniffs a laugh and nods. He knows an ambush when he sees one. I almost feel bad for making use of sweet, innocent Sully, but needs must.

'That's true,' he says to me, accepting his fate. 'Call me Leo. I'm not at work now.'

'So, when are we doing it?' I push. 'We usually bring enough biscuits for sixty kids. Will that cover it?'

Leo Bold looks between me and Sully.

'You know? I can help,' Sully puts in. 'With the icing demo. I can even supply the gingerbread men if you like,' he adds.

'Won't your grandfather mind?' I ask, wanting to hop from foot to foot with happiness, this is going so well. It's obvious Sully knows nothing about the Great Gingerbread Spat of 1982 that set our two houses warring.

'I doubt it. He's knocking off earlier and earlier these days now that I'm there to clean and lock up. I can put aside sixty gingerbread men, no problem, bring them to the school, say two o'clock-ish?'

'That sounds great,' I say, smiling up at the poor, beleaguered teacher. He knows when his number's up.

'All right,' Leo says, his shoulders dropping. 'Friday, two p.m. sharp. That gives you an hour and a half, but you'll need to help clear up, Mrs…?'

'Ms,' I reply, 'but you can call me Margi. Thank you so much,' I tell him, and I really do mean it. 'The kids will be so happy. And thank you, Sully. I just knew you were going to be a lovely addition to the Wheaton community. That's neighbourliness, isn't it?' I say, turning pointedly to Lucy, who's sucking her cheeks into a half-amused, half-outraged pout. 'Well.' I deliver my parting shot with a big smile. 'Have a lovely evening, you five.'

148

Pleased with my work, I make my way back to the bar then onwards into the snug where Charlie's looking delightedly between me and the sausage rolls and rubbing his hands together hungrily, and it almost feels like there's nothing missing from my evening.

'To friends and more,' he says, as we clink our glasses together.

'I'll drink to that.'

—

It's late, and I'm rattling around the kitchen doing some last-minute candy decorations inventory when I hear the sniffing from Lucy's bedroom. Not being one to interfere, I listen at her door, count to twenty, take some deep breaths and, when I'm convinced she simply must need her auntie, I knock.

'Luce, darling? It's me.'

I get no reply, so I peep round the door, and there she is, a sorry shape under the duvet and two dark-circled eyes peeping back at me.

'Auntie Margi,' she says, and it's so pitiful I fly to hug her.

It takes a lot of rocking and shushing like Lydia used to do to her when she was tiny to comfort her. Eventually, I feel Lucy slumping in my arms. I can feel the exhaustion in her whole body.

'Luce, it's a frosty night in the middle of winter, the exhibition is nearly ready, you don't have to get up for work in the morning. I figure we've nothing to do. Why don't we just… chat? About Craig and maybe… why you're here and not living it up in Birmingham with your mates? Not that I don't want you here. I really do.' I say it as softly as I can, giving her a gentle squeeze to cajole a response from her, and, very slowly, it happens. Her sorry, sleepy eyes lift to mine and she starts to say it all out loud.

'It was the pub that did it. At first it was just me, Fern and Shell, and even though they're kind of young, it was kind of nice too. And then you roped in poor Leo and Sully as well, and at first it was nice, but then after a while, and a few drinks, it struck me.'

'What did?'

'Sully and Leo were flirting all night. It was like watching a golden retriever trying to get a saluki to run after a stick, Leo's so...'

'Stand-offish?' I suggest.

'Refined, self-contained,' she corrects. 'But they were kind of perfect together, in spite of their differences. Sully couldn't have been nicer about Leo's Ofsted worries, he really let him talk, you know? Then there's Fern and Shell acting like some kind of power couple. They're basically made for each other, aren't they?'

I nod. 'I know.'

'And I was the odd one out. I was lonely in a pub full of people.'

'You've done so well to make new friends, Luce. That's a bit miraculous if you think about it.'

She doesn't let this sink in. 'But it's just... I sat there with everyone coupled up, and I kept thinking, is this it? Have I missed out forever? Was Craig it?'

'*Pfft!* I only met him that one time at your place and I can tell you with my hand on my heart, Craig wasn't anything, let alone *it*!'

She nods slowly, thinking. 'All that time I was with him, it was a waste. And Reese before him? He ghosted me after practically moving in for four months, and there were the others, all nice enough, but nothing permanent. There's something wrong with me.'

'There's not,' I say. 'You are perfect.'

She passes this off with an eye-roll. 'You always say that.'

'Because I'm old and wise, like an oracle. Trust me. It's true.'

Lucy laughs, thank goodness, and I hug her closer.

'It's not you,' I repeat. 'And it's probably not those dopey lads either.'

'Well, what is it, then?' she sighs.

'Oh, I don't know. It's the times, maybe?'

She tips her head again, waiting for me to say something helpful and I'm not sure I've got anything to impart, but I still hear myself talking. 'It's just very, *very* hard to meet people once you're out of college, isn't it? And dating's hard work, even with the algorithms. And it doesn't help that nobody's got any money and everyone's working all hours and we're pulled in a million different directions at once, and we're all so *tired*, and frankly, we're all a bit antisocial. And can you blame us, really? After everything we've all been through these last few years?'

'So how are you supposed to meet people?' Lucy pleads. 'And not just people who'll do for a while, I mean really special, nice people?'

'You wait until it happens?' I say. 'Someone will just walk into your life. You've plenty time.'

She lowers her eyes in a way that speaks volumes. She can see I'm an old fraud. I can talk the talk but what about my love life?

'I mean, I don't exactly have all the answers, do I?' I throw in. 'I'm single again at sixty-five, and maybe that's it for me now, but you're young. It'll happen when you're least expecting it.'

She's quiet for a long time before she says, 'Last night, when Leo and Sully were getting to know each other, I could see it happening.'

'They were falling for each other?'

'Yeah. It was like they'd known each other all their lives and they were talking and laughing and just beaming at each other.'

'Hmm, that's lovely,' I say, cosying up to her again.

'It is, but Sully's younger than me and I can already say for sure he's going to be with that head teacher forever.'

'Forever?' This feels like quite a jump to me, but I let it go.

'Yes, definitely. And Fern and Shell are something like eighteen and twenty years old, for God's sake, and I can already imagine those two rattling around up at Brambledown Farm together when they're little old ladies.'

'Fern already is a little old lady,' I joke, but Lucy's spiralling now.

'Maybe you're right,' she says. 'Maybe it's a generational thing. Maybe I've missed my chance. I'll be renting a flat in Birmingham and clinging to crappy zero-hours contracts and messing around with dating apps and never actually liking anyone forever, until I give up!'

'No, don't think like that,' I tell her.

'You just said you were giving up.'

'I didn't say I was giving up, only that I'm not expecting anything to happen now. If it does, it does. Anyway, it's different for me. I've been married and, as far as I can see, it's not all it's cracked up to be.'

'I'm just so tired, Auntie Margi. It's all so exhausting.' She pulls the duvet around her all the more. 'Something's got to change,' she whimpers.

'OK,' I say softly, deciding to nip this in the bud. 'I'm giving you eight hours to wallow in your bed, OK? Then we'll get up, cook some food and watch some Christmas telly, and we can put the finishing touches to Olsen's bike shop, if you can face baking. We still have each other, and it's Christmas, and just because I'm a grump doesn't mean I'll let you disappear under your duvet all December.'

'OK,' she mutters through the thirty-tog, half-asleep already, and I stay with her, keeping her wrapped in my arms until morning, and for the first time in a long time I sleep all the way through the night without waking.

Chapter Eleven

After a pleasant evening in the pub keeping Charlie company, the prospect of my second dating app date (this time in Birmingham) has been a little less daunting. I even considered wearing my leather trousers but the fact Patrick suggested I wear them for some bloke I've never even met before put me off somehow.

When Rusty spotted me walking towards the Hippodrome under the Christmas lights, he immediately clamped the rose between his teeth in a silly grin, which he could absolutely pull off, being model handsome – as in M&S tailoring or Saga-cruise-brochure-cover attractive.

I burst into a loud laugh which seemed to delight rather than scare him, and that set the tone for the rest of the evening so far. Fun, just like he'd promised.

His eyes are blue, his voice deep and confident, but there's nothing cocky about him, though by rights, he could afford to be cocky – he must have his pick of women on the apps. He'd already booked the China Rose Garden, telling me it wasn't at all touristy, it is in fact where loads of Chinese families eat – 'the best dim sum in Brum' he'd joked, but it turns out he was absolutely accurate.

He pulled my red chair out for me in the red dining room but not in a showy way, and he let me order for myself, which is always a relief, but he insisted we get 'a bottle of fizz, since it's Christmas', and by the time dessert arrived, I was definitely charmed.

'Are you a Christmas markets girl?' he wants to know, and I'm enjoying myself so much that I say, 'Yes, I am.' Anyone else, and I'd have pulled a face and said, 'I'm not very Christmassy these days', but Rusty is so easy to be with, so alive and cheerful, I forget I'm a lady Grinch.

'I'll just pop to the loo,' I say, and I leave my money for dinner on the table.

When I said we should go Dutch, he'd not made a fuss. Only saying the one time that he'd like to pay but giving up as soon as I reached for my purse, which I take as another good sign, him not being rigid about the whole gender roles thing, which has always given me the ick. I hear him call politely for the waiter as the bathroom door closes. Being nice to the waiting staff is another big tick in Rusty's favour.

I reapply my lipstick – 'devil red' because I've been thinking of the old Margi since spending the evening with Charlie and feeling like he saw the real me, and now *I* can see her. She's smiling.

I take a minute to fix my eye make-up, sticking with the new technique Lucy showed me this afternoon before she drove me to the station, lining thinly with shadow under my lower lashes instead of applying a black sweep along my waterline, which is 'a bit outdated', apparently. That had been news to me.

I touch it up now and have to agree it's a softer look and opens my eye up. I don't have to do much to my hair, but I smoosh it a bit in the mirror. I'm surprised to see my silvery strands actually sparkling in amongst the ash-brown. They're positively gleaming, reflecting the strip light over the glass, and they're honestly a bit breath-taking.

I angle my head to admire them. Fairy strands of gossamer steel, metallic and blingy, and all mine. Natural. The way I wanted it when I told Jill at the Wheaton hair salon a couple of years back that I couldn't face dyeing my hair any more, and she'd rung me later at home to ask if I was having some sort of breakdown and should she call my mum.

I'd been resolute. Covering up these shiny signs of survival seemed absurd to me somehow, and for the life of me, I couldn't remember why I'd ever wanted anything other than my shoulder-length waves in grey, ash and silver. I love it.

Once I made the change to grey, I looked more like me than I had in years, if you see what I mean? Soft, virgin hair, untreated and allowed to shine, felt absolutely right for my new chapter – my sixties – and it certainly worked in attracting Don. Even though Don barely made it to the end of my new chapter's first page, my lovely locks are still with me, and Rusty out there doesn't seem to mind them either.

Every time I make him laugh, he rakes a hand through his near-white hair, all thick and shiny, and I can tell he's doing it in a flirty way, and I don't mind one bit.

Soon, we're making our way through the thronging streets, busy with Christmas shoppers, and even if my feet hurt because I squeezed into my knee-high boots with pointy heels that must have thought I'd died long ago, I'm still feeling happy with how this is going.

'Grab hold,' Rusty offers, crooking his elbow, and I grip onto the arm of his smart grey coat. He's made an effort too: a good suit, a crisp shirt. No ring – or indentation where a ring should be. I checked. Lucy would be proud.

His shoes clack on the tarmac as he walks me beneath the street lights and illuminated candy canes lining our route, dodging the crowds down twisty alleyways and backstreets until we're in amongst the clamour of the Christmas market.

'You know the city like the back of your hand,' I say. 'I thought you only just moved here?'

He taps his temple and says he's amazing with maps. 'It's like The Knowledge in here,' he says, laughing.

We look at each stall and take our time, commenting on the pretty iced biscuits – this is when I tell him about my gingerbread grotto. It takes a while – long enough to have to take a break to buy glühwein in pretty cups that Rusty says we should keep 'as a souvenir of a lovely evening'.

'Wow,' he says when I'm done talking, the steam from the fragrant booze drifting in swirls around his face. 'And you're doing all that on your own? Amazing.'

'Not quite on my own,' I say, not going into detail about Izz and Patrick, only wanting to focus on this lovely buzz we've got going between us.

'And you've no kids?' I ask as we examine some Christmas tree baubles and the stall-holder's looking expectantly at us like we're a couple choosing decorations for our tree.

'Never wanted any,' he says, his eyes narrowing a bit like he's making a confession.

'I get it,' I say. 'I never wanted the whole babies thing either.'

'Really? Not everybody understands,' he says, and he doesn't follow any of this up with the question that literally everybody, apart from Patrick, has asked when we stumble onto the topic of my childlessness. *And you haven't regretted it?* A question which, no matter how much a person inclines their head and does the frowny touchy-feely face while they ask it, is an absolute intrusion into a person's privacy, not to mention their gynaecological history. Doesn't stop them asking, though.

'Well, I'm not everybody,' I say, feeling like a girl in a movie who might say that sort of thing. It must be the glühwein. I should definitely buy a bottle of this stuff to take home with me.

'No, you're not, Margi.' He beams back at me, the breeze shifting his hair around in the most appealing way. I can hear old Margi yelling at me. *Kiss him, kiss, kiss, kiss!* There's still enough of the new, sensible, hold-your-horses Margi telling me not to. I listen to her and am glad I do because a second later a text pops up on my phone. It's the estate agent I spent the morning with visiting properties.

'Excuse me a sec,' I tell Rusty and wander over to the lights of a big wooden windmill display with jolly elves frozen in a dance all around it while a busty fibreglass girl in lederhosen hangs from a window proffering two steins of frothy beer, just in case you'd forgotten you were at a touristy German market.

> The Daisy Road terrace vendors have said they're willing to reduce their asking price by 30K if you agree purchase today.

I read it twice to make sure I'm not hallucinating.

Daisy Road was my favourite of the lot, the one with the potagerie, which even in December was leafy with sprouts and curly greens. There was a 'suntrap' patio, two spare bedrooms, big enough to host both Izz and Patrick and of course, best of all, it was only four streets away from Lucy's place.

I'd wandered around inside trying to imagine myself living there; not all that easy somehow, so I resorted to pretending I was some other kind of woman, a city girl, playing a part for the benefit of the estate agent who told me he was knocking off after he'd shown me the properties on my list so I hadn't wanted to keep him longer than strictly necessary.

I liked the modern, square rooms and the big windows. Nothing creaked or ran squint – unlike every line and surface at my cottage which is warped and slumping with age.

The roof tiles were all new and wouldn't need replacing for at least my lifetime, unlike my cottage's slates which come loose in the mildest wind and shatter on the path and are expensive to replace. It was warm too. Plus, there was no wood burner to sweep out and reset every single day in winter. 'Eight rad system,' the agent had thrown out as he guided me from white room to white room. 'Cosy.'

I'd thought at the time that cosy wasn't quite the right word. My cottage is cosy; this place was functional, warm, bright, all those good things, but no, not cosy as such. With thirty grand knocked off the asking price, however, it is even more attractive now.

My phone pings again and the estate agent's listing appears, just in case I've forgotten the place. He's seriously pushing me for a response but this isn't the right moment, not with Rusty over there waving to me from the fudge stall. I need time to think, to see if I really can picture myself there, baking in that kitchen, and for myself, not for a thankless, exhausting gingerbread grotto that demands so much of my life.

What would it be like sleeping in that white bedroom with no cobwebby oak beams slanting above my head, and fresh grey carpets on the floor instead of cold flagstones and Mum's old rugs?

Another message pings and I get a flush of heat up the back of my head. Only it's not the pushy estate agent; it's Fern. I forgot I'd given her my number so we can coordinate gingerbread efforts.

> What name am I using for the Insta and TikTok accounts?

I reply with a question mark. What's that girl up to? A reply flies back quicker than anyone ought to be able to type into a phone.

> For the fundraising accounts. I can't use mine. Is 'The Gingerbread Christmas Village' all right?

I send back three words: *Whatever you think.*

I've got to get back to this date. Why must my every waking minute be dominated by chuffing gingerbread?

But I'm distracted now the messages have yanked me out of my lovely evening. I make my way towards Rusty. All I need to do is have fun with him and then head home before I turn back into a pumpkin. Easy. Old Margi wouldn't have agonised over any of this. She'd take the evening as it came, surrender to the fun of it all.

'Problem?' Rusty asks when I rejoin him. He hands me a candy cane tied with a red bow that he's just bought for me. I think of the box of two hundred such canes still in their wrappers on top of my wardrobe. I bought them at the cash and carry to hand out to the grotto visitors.

'No,' I tell him, trying to shake off the bewildering prospect of the Daisy Road property and smile like a normal person.

'You've got an emergency and have to go?' he asks, doing the same sheepish, sweet look he did when he'd confessed to not having wanted kids, like he was afraid of what I'd say, but he's robust enough to risk asking anyway.

'Oh my God, no! A get-out text? I hadn't even considered it, honestly.'

Rusty laughs.

I think of Kenneth bolting on me. 'I'd never do that to you.'

My phone buzzes again.

Two other interested buyers. Need an answer quick to secure Daisy Road.

Rusty's talking once more. 'Listen, it's a long way for you to go back to your village...' He's pulling something from his coat pocket and I'm not quite present enough to register what it is. There's loud polka music playing from a stage over there and it's making it hard to think.

'Sorry,' I say, shoving away my mobile. 'I'm getting sidetracked and that's not fair on you. Only, that was an estate agent texting me about a property that's reduced in Birmingham. I'm thinking of moving here.'

'But you're from the Cotswolds, aren't you? Miles from Brum?' He says this while stepping back an inch, enough that I notice, and it sets a little engine revving in my head. It sounds conspicuously like Don's Harley speeding away from me.

'Yeah,' I say, 'but I like it here, and I've often thought I might move here if I got the chance...'

'Listen,' he says, spreading his hands like he's defending himself from attack.

I have time to think how quickly a person's face can change. All the fun has drained from his.

'Listen,' he says again, catching his breath. 'I've met some lovely ladies on the apps, but God's sakes, you're all the same, one date and you're too keen. I understand the pool's shallow but...'

'I'm not moving here for you, Rusty. I don't even know your surname, you numpty.'

That's when I register he's pinching a hotel key in his right hand. I can make out the purple of a Premier Inn logo. This completely throws me off defending myself against his accusation of bunny boiling.

'Is that what you were about to ask me?' I say. 'Were you going to invite me to a hotel?'

'Well...' He shrugs it off, his eyes lifting to the sky like it's all just one big laugh. A bit of fun.

'Don't you live nearby?'

'Uh, not so near.'

'But you live in the city, and yet you pick up dates and take them not to your place but to a budget hotel?'

He's silent, shrugging and spreading his palms.

I step closer so I can lower my voice. It's gone a bit growly. 'Did you really move to Birmingham recently?

Where exactly in the countryside did you say you lived when you registered for the dating app?'

He attempts another laugh, brushing off my detective skills with a sweeping hand.

'I see.' The penny drops. He'd only just been remarking how far it would be for me to get home tonight, like he had the solution. 'How many out-of-towners are you showing a good time to? How many of us lonely rural women do you lure to the city, give us a petrol station flower, let us split the bill with you, and romance us a bit? Then it's back to your crappy hotel room? *Ugh*, I'm an idiot!' I shove the empty wine mug and the red rose into his hands.

He doesn't even watch me go as I stride towards the train station, my ill-advised boots seriously pinching now.

As soon as I've checked the next train heading remotely close to home, Moreton-in-Marsh will do, and texted Lucy asking if she'll pick me up from there, I fire up Countryside Cupids. I resist the urge to leave an unkind review for handsome, gregarious Rusty who was only after a shag in a budget hotel with a country bumpkin from some backwater where the dating pool is shallow, a yokel blinded by the bright lights of Birmingham. He's not looking for romance or a relationship at all, and, as he's just proven, he scares really easily at the first (imagined) signs that a woman actually wants something from him.

I hit *Delete app*, watching my very last chance at finding love online disappearing before my eyes.

Chapter Twelve

It's here. The deadline that has regulated my entire life for years. It's the third Thursday in December and the exhibition opens tomorrow at half-three, as soon as the school bell rings for the holidays. Mum's already Face-Timed twice to tell me not to be nervous, which has only served to make me nervous.

'You don't seem as… invested as previous years, Margi,' Mum observed during the second call, her face so close to the screen as she examined me for signs of gingerbread fatigue that all I could see was her eyebrows.

I didn't want to tell her the main thing I'm feeling is relief that it's almost over and I won't have to do it again, even if it's been lovely having Lucy's help this year, and Fern and Shell have promised to come along to the help with the final layout.

'It's a lot of work,' I said. 'Not like the old days when you had all those women helping. Plus, I always have to make the exhibit bigger and better than it was the year before. There's an expectation.'

'From who?' Mum wanted to know.

'Well… I…'

I didn't know how to answer that. The truth is the pressure is coming from myself. I decided to pin the blame a little further from home.

'That's just how Christmas is, isn't it? Always grander and more expensive year on year, always one-upping itself, with presents and food and decorations…'

Mum interrupted. 'When I started, it was all about the village, about the people.'

'I don't think the people are all that interested nowadays.'

Mum took a moment to compose herself. I watched as her nostrils flared on a big in-breath. 'Margi, darling. Nobody's making you do the grotto. If you feel like it's getting too much, you can hand it over. I wouldn't be disappointed.'

That was a first. We'd never spoken about me stopping. I assumed she'd be happy for me to just go on forever, baking and icing myself into the grave.

'Who do I pass it on to? Everybody's got their own lives.'

'Your young helpers?'

'They're kids. They're not going to stick around in Wheaton.'

I'm not lumbering my niece with this – anyway, Lucy and I will be swanning round the Bullring by next Christmas, so she's ruled out. The best bet might be Sully, but what kind of a poisoned chalice would I be handing him? He's just so young. Even if he didn't mind doing it, who'd help him? Sully and Patrick might make a good team, but no, it's too much for them, and will Patrick want to so much as look at another piece of gingerbread once I've moved away? I doubt it.

I made a good show of pulling myself together, for Mum's sake, and she wished me luck and told me not to stay up too late fiddling with the small details.

'All that folks want to see are some funny little buildings and to have a chance to meet their friends and
have a catch-up with their neighbours before Christmas.
Remember that. Once the village is set out, there's no
need to add extra little bits and bobs. You have to know
when to stop or you'll exhaust yourself.'

Too late for that, I didn't reply. Instead, I gave her a kiss
through the screen and hung up.

That familiar old sense of flatness followed me all the
way down the high street, alleviated only by the sight of
Patrick loading a bag into a strange car outside the school
gates. Just knowing he's here makes my heart lift. But
when I call his name and hurry closer, I realise the man
turning and grinning back at me isn't Patrick at all. It's
Charlie.

These were the thoughts that hit me at that exact
moment.

One: he looks gorgeous, so like Patrick.

Two: I wonder if he's going to ask me out on a real
date this time?

Three: I'll have to decline if he asks. *Dammit!* For
Patrick's sake. For the brothers' friendship, and for ours.
Charlie told me Patrick has lived in his shadow all his life,
and I don't ever want Patrick to feel that he comes second
to Charlie in my eyes.

Four: *Dammit*, again Patrick! Why aren't you just a little
older? A little more available? Why don't you look me over
in the hungry way Charlie does? Like he wants to pounce
on me in the street!

'Morning, beautiful,' Charlie greets me, and I come to
a stop. 'Glad I bumped into you,' he adds.

His bags are in the back seat of the car.

'You're not leaving, are you? Right now?'

166

'Those antiques don't value themselves.'

'That's a shame,' I say, and I really mean it. 'Patrick will miss you too.'

'*Hmm.*' That wry smile again. 'I'm not so sure.'

'You didn't have a falling out, did you?' I scan the street behind Charlie, wondering where Patrick is and why he's not coming to wave his brother off.

'Not since the last time,' he says, whatever that means.

'Why don't you come and see the exhibit getting set up? We're nearly done, and I know Patrick will love showing you the finished village. Get his big brother's seal of approval.'

Charlie takes a step towards me on the pavement. 'I don't think he'd love that. In fact, I don't think he'd be very happy I'm still around, talking with you.'

'With me? Why?'

Charlie sniffs a laugh and shakes his head in an amused way. 'I can't keep doing my little brother's work for him. Why don't you ask him yourself?'

'Huh?'

Another wry smile and Charlie's backing away, getting into his car. He shakes his head. 'I can see why he doesn't want to lose you. You are something else, Margi Frost,' and with that, he wishes me a 'Merry Christmas', and he's yanked his door shut and started the engine.

I wave after him as he pulls away, my head still cocked, wondering what on earth he meant. '*Lose* me?' I say to myself. 'Patrick doesn't want to lose me?'

–

The display tables are covered in white fabric which I've swagged around the table legs the way Mum taught me years ago so there's no risk of someone tripping and landing head first in Brambledown Farm.

Lucy's helping Shell stick down a few squinty tombstones in the snowy gingerbread churchyard with some last-minute emergency icing bags Izz brought with her. This isn't Izz's first rodeo.

She's in the foyer setting up the urn for the mulled wine and unwrapping stacks of paper cups. Fern is, of course, filming our preparations, having had moderate interest in the video she posted to The Gingerbread Christmas Village's new social media channels showing the empty hall and the mural on the day we set about cleaning the place up.

I asked her if she thought it would help sell tickets and she pointed out the few lovehearts and comments the video received were from people all over the world, not Cotswold locals, so probably not. I didn't say, 'What's the point of it, then?' like I wanted to. It's best if she just carries on doing her own Fern thing while the rest of us see to the last details. So we've let her carry on filming.

I'm keeping Patrick company while he runs tiny LED lights on copper wire through the display. He wants them to be invisible so there's been some pretty hairy moments drilling through gingerbread and then threading the lights inside before icing over the gaps so it's neat again and the walls don't crumble.

'So, you'll be seeing my brother again?' he asks after a long time concentrating in silence on an especially fiddly-looking bit of miniature electrical work.

'Am I?' Doesn't he know Charlie's gone already? Patrick's eyes are dark and his expression tense. I don't know how to break this to him.

'It's just Charlie was waiting up for me the other night,' he says. 'Said you two had fun. He was full of it, actually.'

'Full of what?' I feel uncharitable, digging for details, but I still do it.

'Admiration, for you.'

'Oh.' I brighten. 'That's nice. He was good company.'

Patrick revs his drill into nothing like he's thinking hard before carrying on with his task.

'Would you… mind if I was seeing him, properly, I mean?'

There's more silence while he reaches for his soldering iron and does some intricate work fusing a bulb and a bit of metal flex together. I watch his nimble fingers moving and his eyes narrow with a furrow down his brow.

'I might,' he says eventually.

'Why's that, then?' I push, totally unable to turn back now.

Again, he gets lost in his task, but as a twist of smoke rises from the solder and he fixes two bits of wire together in a molten clump, he lifts his eyes to mine. 'You can do better than Charlie. He's not the best partner a woman could have.'

'Why?' I'm genuinely confused now. 'He seemed friendly and attentive, and he was, you know… open.'

Patrick sniffs a wry laugh. 'He was definitely open to my last girlfriend.'

'What?'

'It was years ago now, but, yeah, we were getting to know each other, nothing serious like, but still, we liked each other, I think.'

'And he stole her?'

'That's not how either of them saw it. Bold as brass, she told me she'd had a better offer, and off they went. This time of year as well. Ruined Christmas dinner at Mum and Dad's, sitting there watching them pawing at each other.'

'No!'

'True,' he says with a firm nod. 'He has a habit of taking what he wants, and it's never his fault when it goes wrong. I suppose he told you about Tina?'

'Tina?'

'His ex-wife? She caught him messing around in some country club kitchen with one of his friend's wives. Bet he didn't tell you that.'

'He didn't! Why did you let me go to the pub with him?'

'I didn't know you were.'

'Or you'd have stood in his way?'

Patrick lowers himself to the table's edge again, crouching and working the wire along to the next gingerbread build in the row. 'Might have done,' he says, eyes fixed on his work.

'Patrick,' I begin, as softly as I can. 'I just saw him getting into his car.'

'Gone, has he?'

I nod.

'And he, uh, didn't ask for your number?'

'Nope.'

'And you're not... upset about that?'

'Not especially. Not if it would bother you?'

Patrick nods like he's reassuring himself. 'OK.'

'You should call him, though. Say goodbye properly.'

'I might,' he says, and things go quiet for an awkward moment.

'Did you tell your brother to stay away from me?' I ask, but I don't add 'because you don't want to lose me,' like Charlie said.

170

He can't meet my eye. He changes drill bits instead, acting occupied. Eventually, because I'm just standing over him refusing to give up now it feels like we might actually be talking about something important for once, he says, 'I can't tell anyone who to date, or who not to date, but…' he sighs like he's giving up an internal battle. 'I told him not to go hurting you… after everything you've been through lately.'

Oh God, that is so like Patrick. Why must he be so nice?

I smile when he flits his eyes to mine. He's searching for signs I'm disappointed or offended, maybe?

'If your brother had asked me out, I wouldn't have said yes anyway.'

'OK,' he says again, looking a tiny bit relieved.

'In fact, I am romanticising my own life,' I add, grandly.

'What does that mean?' He looks sceptical.

'It means I've had enough with random Kenneths and Rustys and Charlies.'

He throws me another quick glance then sets to work once more. I have to raise my voice to speak over the sound of his drill.

'I deleted my dating app,' I tell him. 'Won't be doing that again in a hurry.'

Suddenly, Patrick stops and straightens up, hands on his tool belt. 'Right,' he says. 'Good to know. Sensible.'

There's another quiet moment where I don't know what to think or how to act. Have I said the wrong thing? Thankfully, Patrick fixes things with an abrupt change of subject, pointing out that our exhibit looks underpopulated.

'Is this some kind of commentary on second-home ownership in the Cotswolds or something?'

'Hadn't thought of that,' I laugh weakly, catching my breath after the awkwardness. 'The school kids will be bringing their own crowds of gingerbread people tomorrow, after Sully and me—'

'And me!' cuts in Lucy, who I hadn't realised was eavesdropping all this time. Did she hear that whole weird thing about Charlie, and Patrick telling him to leave me alone? I won't hear the end of it if she did.

'Yes, you too, Luce, after we've had our icing party at the school.'

'So Mr Bold softened then?' Patrick looks impressed.

'Like month-old gingerbread,' I say, proudly.

'I think Sullivan Scrimengor had something to do with it,' Lucy adds, and I hear Fern mumble her agreement from behind her phone screen where she's typing away busily.

'I heard they were going out for dinner in Broadway tonight,' Lucy adds.

'So romantic,' Shell says, now that she's got the church-yard finished.

'It is,' Lucy says, then adds in an oddly exaggerated manner, 'Christmas is a time for asking people out on romantic dates.'

Izz wanders in from the foyer bringing the smell of cinnamon and oranges studded with cloves all prepped for tomorrow's mulled wine. 'Who's asking who on a romantic date?' she says, innocently enough. I notice her lips are pink. She's had a snifter of red wine while setting up the refreshments stand. All the young ones exchange glances and smile.

'What's this?' Patrick asks, as confused as I am.

'Oh! I see,' Izz says, a little less innocently, looking from the giggling Fern to me then back again. 'Well, asking someone out on a romantic date is the only way out of the… the, um, the, um, what did you call it, Fern dear?'

'The friend zone?' Fern replies.

Izz brings her hands together. 'That's the one. See, Margi. You're not the only one who's been getting an education this winter. Fern's told me all about it. It's when one or the other of you is so afraid of losing a friendship you risk losing each other anyway. You, Patrick Wootton,' she slurs a little, 'have been friend-zoned. Now, where's me biggest ladle?' As Shell follows after her in her search, we all hear Izz confide, 'That wine's got a kick to it. Better add some juice to it tomorrow or we'll all be sloshed.'

Fern and Lucy are still trying to stifle giggles.

'Right, well,' Patrick flusters. 'Electrics are done. Shall we try the lights?'

As he stoops to hurriedly clear away his tools, I mime a cutting motion under my chin at Lucy.

'What?' she mouths at me over Patrick's back, amused with herself.

—

'Three, two, one, switch on!' we all chorus.

Everywhere is blackness. I don't move for fear of knocking into one of the displays which are still worryingly unilluminated.

'Patrick?' I say into the silence. 'It can't be not working?' Not when he's spent the day on his knees, under tables, drilling, glue-gunning, screwing in bulbs, threading coils of wire-thin lights, surely? Patrick can make anything light up. He's good at everything.

'Just a sec,' he says, and after a moment's flickering hesitation our display bursts into light.

'Patrick!' I turn on the spot, trying to take it all in, not knowing what to look at first. There's a small ripple of applause from the gang as they crowd closer to inspect it.

'It still needs finessing,' he says, joining me by my side, admiring our Gingerbread Christmas Village brought to life. Every little house is aglow from the inside with Patrick's clever lights. 'Wait, wait,' he says, making for the spot in the room where the grotto will be. 'There's more.'

There's a panel of controls and plugs by his feet, though he's taken care hiding every flex and cable under the heavy black matting he keeps for the exhibit. He flicks another switch and above our heads the suspended sleigh and reindeer are illuminated, the reindeer bobbing softly up and down in flight with the magic of some kind of clever hydraulics and pulley thing I knew nothing about.

'Surprise!' he says.

I gasp, lost in admiration.

'Beautiful,' Izz tells him. 'A lovely addition.'

'I'm not done yet,' he says, getting caught up in the moment. 'By order of your chairwoman, there's also… this…' He lifts a white bottle from beneath one of the tablecloths and, after pulling on thick gloves, walks around the miniature village adding drops of liquid down the chimneys here and there. 'I put these liquid chambers inside so we can have…'

'Dry ice!' says Shell, applauding as little puffs of white rise above the cottages. 'Nice one!'

I admit it's very clever. Izz hits play on the old CD player we drag in here every year and the usual carols spill out. Fern's live streaming so she's whispering a commentary to her followers.

I've never seen the display so beautifully lit or with so much movement and colour. This has to be it, my crowning moment. My big finale? Only, there's something missing and I can't quite account for it.

I give Lucy the nod before she wheels in the trolley with my little surprise for Patrick.

'This is for you, as a thank you, Patrick,' I tell him. 'Since, apart from Fern, you're the only one of us who never got to see it when Mum was in charge. I haven't even watched this myself yet.'

Lucy's quickly got the mains connected up and there's a whirring sound as Dad's old cine projector starts up.

On the longest of the hall's blank white walls a shimmery scene appears. It's shadowy with age but there's no doubt what we're looking at.

Two rows of tables meeting in a horseshoe shape, and the dark shapes of people admiring gingerbread houses. The builds appear smaller than ours, and all that really stands out on the grainy footage is their white iced roofs and the stubby candles between each of the cottages and the few fairy lights around the hall, nowhere near as many as I remembered there being. From the hall rafters there hangs garlands and sparkly waterfall lanterns all made from that metallic foil so typical of Christmas decorations when I was a kid, and, of course, there's lots of tinsel draped everywhere, but there's no sight of Mum or Dad, and nobody I could identify with any accuracy, but for a moment I feel like I'm there, being jostled by the crowds, holding on to the lead of whichever beloved childhood dachshund we had at the time, and everyone's remarking on how clever Mum is and how kind, and there's jokes and laughter and everyone in high spirits and the sense that after a long year's waiting, Santa's finally coming to town. Then out of nowhere, and for the first time in forever, I picture myself bursting with excitement, unwrapping my little red and yellow play kitchen on Christmas morning and Great Aunt Margaret saying I was a chip off the old Frost baking block. And I'm not even in the hall any more when the film flickers to an end and the place fills with silver light from the noisy projector.

Patrick's the first person I become aware of again. He's asking me if I'm OK, and Fern's hovering around me, saying, 'she's probably just tired', but as the dry ice is clearing around our exhibit, I'm thinking how I don't actually feel like a chip off the old block, or all that proud of what I've achieved this year, or even relieved. Instead, I'm left cold and a bit confused, wondering why my latest gingerbread village doesn't feel a bit like that candlelit one of Mum's.

'Something's not right,' I say, and I'm aware of everyone looking at me worriedly.

'Let's tidy up, then I'll give her a lift back with the projector stuff,' Patrick says, and I'm left standing in the middle of our exhibit feeling like a time traveller who's made it back to their own time only to discover they made some slip-up back in the past and without knowing it, changing some tiny aspect of the course of history and everything's just a little bit strange now.

The exhibit looks like Wheaton, or thereabouts, and it smells just like it, sweet and spiced, and the village hall setting's just the same as it always was, but something's out of kilter, and I can only conclude it must be me. This was supposed to be the big finish, a fond farewell to the villages of my past, but no matter how hard we've worked, the essence of it is missing, and I'm the only person who knows it.

–

It's almost midnight by the time Patrick swings open my garden gate for me. He's letting Lucy fetch the projector from the boot herself, possibly as punishment for teasing us earlier.

I get the feeling she's taking her time on purpose.

Patrick looks like he's debating whether to just turn and go. The muscles in his jaw work and it's a good twenty seconds before he can lift his eyes to mine. When he does, he blurts the words out.

'Listen, I'm not on the Dunham rota for Saturday night, and Shell said you'd roped her in to playing Santa Claus at the grotto's opening weekend. I think you should come with me to Dunham Gravey to see what all the fuss is about.'

'Is this about what Izz said? The friend zone thing? Because you know she'd been...' I mime Izz knocking back the mulled wine and going cross-eyed, but he won't be consoled.

'No, it's not that...'

'There's no need,' I say in my friendliest, lightest voice. 'We're fine, Patrick. We're friends. All right? I get it. There's no need to prove anything.'

'What? I'm not... Look, I haven't seen you properly in ages, and we should spend an afternoon together doing something... fun.'

I think of Rusty and his definition of fun. Rusty couldn't be further from loyal, solid Patrick.

'I mean,' Patrick says, still rushing his words, his hands stubbornly jammed in his pockets. 'You have this irrational dislike of the Dunham lights; why don't you come see them for yourself? Maybe you'll pick up some tips for when the gingerbread exhibit kicks off again next year?'

'First off, my dislike of that place is totally rational,' I say. 'Secondly, Patrick, my gingerbread grotto days are over. I've been feeling it for a while now and watching that film of Mum's exhibit really underlines that. This is my last year here… on the committee,' I add hurriedly.

The concern in his eyes fades away. He probably thinks I'm just overtired too.

'Maybe you just need some time away from Wheaton? And gingerbread?'

I lift my eyes in surprise. 'You think I should get away from here too?'

'Course I do. Come with me to Dunham. A few hours away will cheer you up.'

'Oh, yes, of course. A few hours. Well then, sure.' I shrug, accepting his offer.

'Good,' he smiles. 'I'll pick you up at four. Wear something warm, OK?'

'Can I bring Lucy?'

'Uh…' He's blinking at me, not sure what to say. He had no intention of taking both of us. I can hear Izz's voice ringing in my ears. *You, Patrick Wootton, have been friend zoned.*

'Sorry. Just me. That's fine,' I tell him.

His shoulders drop a fraction. 'Four o'clock, Saturday,' he says, backing away, bringing his hands together in a clap like he's catching a baseball in a mitt, pleased with himself. 'Warm clothes,' he shouts as he passes Lucy carrying the projector down the path.

'I'll be Arctic-expedition ready,' I reply stupidly.

We both watch him drive away.

'Old-school date, is it?' Lucy smirks by my shoulder.

'What? No.' I wave away the suggestion and immediately busy myself with my keys. 'It's not a date,' I repeat as I let us both inside, but that's not what my traitorous body is telling me. My heart's pounding and the back of my neck's gone all hot.

'Sure it's not. Try telling Izz that when she's had half a cup of mulled wine.' Her voice is droll and amused.

'Don't just stand there,' I tell her. 'Make the cocoa.'

She sniffs a laugh at my stubbornness and sets the projector down, and in spite of myself, I find I want to laugh too.

Chapter Thirteen

Overnight

I barely slept, and not just because of the rain lashing at the windows like ice pellets.

That niggling feeling I'd had when watching scenes from Mum's grotto just wouldn't leave me alone and I couldn't put my finger on what exactly was wrong.

I've come to the conclusion that it may have been down to the fact there were all of those people in the hall at the time, which I'm just not used to during set-up. I normally indulge in a few moments of quiet reminiscing, and Izz and Patrick give me time by myself, but yesterday everyone was so excitable and there was all that dry ice and hydraulics dragging my attention away, not to mention all that stuff with Patrick and his brother and how awkward it all felt.

Maybe I feel like this because I didn't get a chance to just enjoy seeing everything laid out and ready? Or to say goodbye to this part of my life?

So that's why I'm up at five o'clock and in my warmest clobber, battling my way down the high street in the rain, just to be sure. If I can have a few quiet moments to look over everything by myself, I'll make it back to bed by half past with this niggling feeling of dissatisfaction sent packing.

Whipping wind and rain lift my hair. Dodging puddles, I'm almost there. A car sloshes by, followed by a van with flashy orange lights, and then another. We don't get much traffic through Wheaton overnight, so they don't go unnoticed.

I must be sleep-deprived because it doesn't hit me, not until I'm almost at the Wheaton Village Hall steps and there are suddenly voices and a man in a hard hat with a torch and he's unrolling white tape across the pavement in front of me.

Roadworks? In the middle of the night? Right outside the hall? Not on the exhibit's opening day, surely! Wait until I have a word with that bloody Scrimengor. This will be his doing. I pull the hall keys from my pocket and stoop to go under the tape.

'Can't go any further, love,' a gruff voice says.

That's when I really wake up.

I'm close to the foot of the hall steps, and the hall doors are wide open. Both sets of them are propped open, in fact, and I can see right inside through into my exhibition, and it's only when the police car pulls up alongside me with its blues flashing, lighting up the interior, that I see what's going on.

'Roof's down,' the same man in the hard hat tells me. 'Stay behind the tape, please.'

Then he's motioning for me to get back, telling me the police need to get past. From where I'm standing, hair soaked, rain running down my face, staring inside where our folding tables lie under cracked plaster and fallen tiles and there's slushy water streaming down from the ceiling into the middle of the hall, exactly where Patrick had rigged up my flying Father Christmas. The whole display is in ruins.

Izz arrives first, still in her nightie, with her winter coat and wellies on top. Then the early birds appear, dog walkers and workmen, even the milkman, and we all stop to gape.

I'd long since made the decision not to call and wake Patrick; he needs his sleep.

We stand behind the tape and listen to the surveyor (I know he's the surveyor because that's what's written across the back of his high-vis, and he's in a hastily thrown-on suit and not yellow council overalls like everyone else). He fills us in. Nobody was inside at the time of the collapse. He thinks it looks like an accumulation of water, possibly over many days' duration, that's brought the attics down, and we should all get out of the rain; there's nothing to see and nobody's getting inside.

Mr Scrimengor arrives, accompanied by Sully with sticky-up hair and a drawn look on his young face, and I watch through the sheeting rain from under Izz's umbrella as the elder baker has a word with the surveyor and shakes his hand grimly. He takes a look inside the doors but doesn't go in. One of the workmen hands a large object out the door. It's the painting of the bug-eyed King.

'Not worth a thing,' I hear Scrimengor remark. 'Frame's worth saving, though. Good thinking,' and he hands the picture to Sully, telling him to 'stick it in the car before it gets wet'. Then I see him speaking closely to the surveyor while scanning the crowd, then pointing his finger towards me.

The surveyor approaches me with a hand outstretched. Weirdly, for a second, I think he's going to shake my hand.

'I hear you have a set of keys,' he says, and I surrender them without protest.

Sully's already taxiing Scrimengor away but I'm staying until someone tells me what exactly is going to happen to the hall.

There are more of them now, swarming in, a sea of neon yellow with the torch beams from their hard hats crisscrossing and dancing everywhere. Someone's shouting about how they can't get a person on the roof until the weather clears. 'That's the water turned off at the main, boss,' someone else cries.

Finally, the doors of the hall are pulled shut upon us. I take one last look at the exhibit tables, crushed under piles of wet rubble.

The small crowd clears as the late winter dawn breaks. I stay put with Izz.

The surveyor is the last to leave the site, but not before he's taped up the doors and attached a notice on the lamppost.

I already know what the laminated paper says before we approach it. Izz reads it aloud.

> Building condemned by order of Wheaton and District Council. No entry other than authorised council personnel. Trespassers will be prosecuted.

That's when Izz begins to cry after holding it together for so long, and I walk her home through the rain thinking how *of course* the roof has fallen in, and *of course* the exhibit's ruined, and *of course* this was always how I was going to retire from Wheaton life. It all feels grimly inevitable and appropriate after everything else I've touched going so wrong lately.

Chapter Fourteen

Friday 15 December: Cronies

The hours that follow are bleak ones. I don't know what to do first, so I don't do anything other than lying on Izz's sofa in front of her electric fire unable to stop shivering.

When the doorbell rings, I don't respond until I hear Izz saying, 'She's through there, isn't speaking or anything. I don't know what to do with her,' and I wonder who she's referring to until Patrick strides into Izz's living room, his face all concern, and I realise it's me they're worried for.

'Margi, hey,' he says, sitting me upright as he slots in beside me on the sofa. 'Come here.'

He pulls me to him, tight in his arms. The closeness overwhelms me completely. It's so long since anyone's held me, and he's so big and warm and safe.

I let all my tears fall, for our gingerbread grotto and all our hard work, and for our village hall, and for Mum and Dad and the legacy they handed me, now crushed under rubble.

I hear him saying to Izz, 'We should have said something about the cloakroom leak, got a real plumber in. If they find out I fixed that first leak, we could be held responsible for the roof coming down.'

When I try to speak and tell him it's not his fault, I find my voice won't work properly, and he shushes me gently, telling me to rest.

He rocks me, his steady hands stroking my hair, and I close my eyes and sink into him.

–

Having had four hours' sleep on Izz's sofa and woken up with Patrick gone and a splitting headache that took three espressos to shift, I find myself wondering if the term 'emergency meeting' isn't a little over the top, actually.

'We need some answers,' Izz insisted, and I was so over-caffeinated and still wrapped in the sensation of having been rocked to sleep in Patrick's arms that I found myself going along with anything she said.

I wasn't fully sold on the idea of a meeting, not until we went back to look at the village hall taped off in the cold afternoon light. I suppose it did spark a little fire in my belly. It's not like I can leave Wheaton while the fate of the building is uncertain, can I?

Mum would be hopping mad about all this, not with me, but with the council for just blockading the place, for not organising a big community clean-up like it's the blitz, and especially for not offering any kind of sympathy for the loss of our exhibit.

I daren't ring her, though. She'd have a few motivational words for me, no doubt. She'd want me to kick up a fuss, to call the *Midlands Today* newsroom, alert the papers, rally some support. Only, we tried all those things last year, and the year before that, and nobody bothered to turn up. To give it its due, the *Wheaton Parish Newsletter* did run a feature about the opening of the display last year – it said *Newlyweds' Sweet Sensation* and there was a picture of me and Don in our wedding clothes cutting the ribbon across the hall entrance and a crowd of schoolkids and their mums waiting to get in – but that was as far as we ever got with attention-grabbing headlines.

'There's local interest pieces and then there's very, very local stuff,' the BBC intern on the line had told me years ago now.

If they didn't send any reporters out to see our glorious gingerbread grotto in all its sparkly splendour, they're hardly going to send a camera crew to look at it when it's been flattened.

Anyway, the meeting had taken Izz all morning to arrange. She was the one who phoned round everybody.

When Lucy said she was up for causing a bit of a ruckus, there was no backing out for me, so here we are, occupying the school gymnasium.

The unfortunately named Mrs Slaughter, the school receptionist, was easy to inveigle. I knew she would be. We've always got on – and dropping in a big box of chocolate seashells and a decent bottle of wine every December in return for the school letting us use the car park has not been forgotten, it seems.

She even dug out the council regulations – she's their secretary too; quite our woman on the inside – and has set the book on a desk open at the page that states that any member of any established local interest group or committee is entitled to call an extraordinary meeting of the relevant members of the council, and at short notice too, should there be any of the following: natural disaster affecting the community; evidence of crime, corruption or a safeguarding issue; or if the council is deemed to be in breach of its commitment to local groups as outlined in their 'community cohesion framework', section 12, part C.

'But will they come?' I ask her, and my voice echoes through the school gym.

'They have to,' Mrs Slaughter says. 'Rodney Carruthers is going to join us by Zoom because he's at his second home in Salcombe for the winter.'

I reckon she's secretly enjoying this. Mrs Slaughter is cheesed off with Leo for what he's done to Patrick and, let's just say, she's no fan of Scrimengor's either, and I know she'll be a stickler for the rules, firm but fair, and not one member of the council would dare test her knowledge of the rule book.

A glance at the clock tells me it's six p.m. Still nobody's here. We turn at the sound of soft footsteps, my heart lifting.

'Oh, it's you, Bobbie,' Mrs S says, as my heart sinks at the sight of the muscly boot-camp instructor in neck-to-knee Lycra.

'I'm just setting up,' they say. 'What's all this?' They point at the eight chairs laid out in front of the desk on the little raised area which the school ambitiously calls its stage.

'Council meeting,' I say.

Bobbie bites their top lip, not even pretending they're fine with this. 'I've paid for the hall from half-six till eight.'

'We won't be long, I promise,' I say, and Bobbie harrumphs at me.

'They're coming!' Lucy calls from the hall's swing doors where she's been keeping watch.

'Is Patrick there?' I say. I want to thank him for this morning, for being a friend when I needed comforting. For having such strong arms and being so good at holding me in them, but of course, he'll be at work. Probably for the best, in case I actually did say all those daft things and make everything awkward yet again.

Before Lucy can answer, she's propelled into the hall by both doors flying wide open and a very annoyed Mr Scrimengor, accompanied by the guy in the suit who pinned the notice on the lamppost early this morning, and behind them, Sully Scrimengor in a white bakers' overall, leaving a light trail of flour from his boots. Following all of them is Leo Bold with his jaw fixed hard and his tie knot loosened.

'Right, let's get this started,' Scrimengor says, taking a chair from the row and placing it on the stage facing us plebs.

Izz immediately takes a bag of rhubarb-and-custard boiled sweets from her coat pocket and hands them around like we're at the cinema.

Sully is fiddling about with a power cable, setting up a council-issue laptop in front of his grandad.

'Wholly unnecessary,' Mr Scrimengor grumps as a connection is made and we all enjoy the sight of coun- cilman Rodney Carruthers's nostrils as he struggles with his camera angles all the way down in Devon. His lips are working but there's no sound at all.

'You're on mute, Rodney,' tolls Mrs Slaughter, pulling a chair up onto the stage and instructing Leo (politely, mind) to please bring her a table of her own so she can keep minutes, and to his credit, he springs to his feet in an obliging manner, hefting a table for her. Young Sully stands up equally as fast to assist him. The men nod to each other once they set it down and, for the very briefest of seconds, I think they hesitate under the other's gaze, but it's over before I know it, and they retreat to opposite ends of our row in the cheap seats.

A quick glance at Lucy tells me she saw the spark too, and I smile at her. I wish I hadn't teased her about fancying Sully that day we went to the cash and carry, but a spell of being single might be just what she needs. Even with all the drama today, she looks better rested than the day she arrived here and there's some pink returning to her cheeks at last. She's sucking one of Izz's boiled sweets. I refrain because I'll have to speak.

'You're still muted, Rodney,' the secretary says. 'Have you got your mic switched on? Check your settings.'

We all watch the screen as Carruthers gets up from his spot in front of his computer, revealing to everyone present he's wearing bright Bermuda shorts beneath a hastily thrown-on, I imagine, shirt and tie. Izz splutters a laugh, Lucy hangs her head out of respect, and I catch Mrs Slaughter's wickedly twinkling eyes. When he's down The Salutation, he's forever banging on about his Devonshire holiday home with its Jacuzzi and sauna room. No prizes for guessing where he was when he got the agenda sent through.

'Any apologies?' the secretary asks the room, the picture of professional integrity.

Izz's eyes are upon me when she says, 'Patrick Wootton of the gingerbread grotto committee sends his apologies. He's working tonight.'

Izz told me he'd set off for work once I was soundly asleep, still blaming himself for not reporting the leaked pipe above the cloakroom. He'll be at Dunham Gravey now, probably feeling rotten about this whole thing.

'Can we get on with it, please?' Mr Scrimengor complains. 'And for the benefit of the minutes, let the record show Mr Collins, the council buildings surveyor, is in attendance as our guest expert.'

Mrs Slaughter makes a note. I stare along the row at the hard-hat and suit-wearing Collins, but he keeps his eyes on the front, a survival strategy learned at planning meetings over the years, I suppose, to avoid irate NIMBYs at war over unruly conifers and boundary disputes. The fight over who's responsible for the back alley behind Izz's cafe has been raging for years now, and I've seen how heated these things can get. One time, a few years back, Errol Burford launched a chair across the meeting room swept up in a rage about Mr and Mrs Sadler's Leylandii being an eyesore, despite repeated pleas they cut the thing to a respectable height, and he hasn't lived it down since.

'Why am I here and not sorting my delivery men's pay packets, as I should be right now?' Scrimengor barks.

Sully looks sheepish and keeps his head down like he doesn't want people to think he's with the angry old bloke.

'Ah! This must be my cue,' I say. I feel moved to stand up, only I've no idea if that's what you're meant to do at one of these things, I've only been to two or three, but I'm on my feet and everyone's looking at me, so here goes.

'I called for this emergency meeting because the community needs to know the council's plans for the hall. If it's condemned, does that mean it's finally getting the extensive programme of renovations and repair it deserves?'

I direct this to the side of Mr Collins's face, and when he doesn't look at me, I turn to Scrimengor himself.

Izz stands too and asks, 'We just need to know, please, if the hall's ever going to reopen, either as our exhibition space or as a properly restored heritage and leisure attraction for Wheaton.'

'And, um, we also wondered,' I add, thinking of the hasty repair job we did on the cloakroom leak, 'if somebody could shed any more light on what actually brought the roof down, um, please.'

We drop into our seats again. Izz pats my hand proudly.

As I'm catching my breath, the door gusts open and in drifts Fern in a charming kind of Victorian doll nightie, lace-up boots, and a long crocheted cardigan belted with brown leather. She looks more like a flower fairy every time I see her, and the sight of her tiptoeing, pink-cheeked, into a chair on the end of the row warms my heart. The girl really does care about us and our ginger-bread venture. You have to give her that.

'Perhaps my colleague can help answer your questions,' Mr Scrimengor says, drawing his face into what I think passes for a smile for him. Whatever it is, it's disconcerting.

His words activate something within Mr Collins who immediately turns in his seat to address me.

'After concluding a full structural survey this morning, we, as you know, saw fit to condemn the hall,' he says in a thick Brummie accent. 'It was found that load-bearing attic beams were badly rotted. We're fortunate it happened overnight and not when the hall was full of locals.'

I feel Izz's shoulders drop and I sag with relief. It wasn't us. We're not to blame for the roof fall. I want to text Patrick but don't want to appear suspicious.

'And will it reopen?' Izz pushes.

Mr Collins looks to Scrimengor who gives him a nod.

'The building requires extensive repairs,' he begins. 'Obviously, a new roof is required; all the old wood will need replacing. It'll be under scaffold for a long time. The council has concluded it will need a full electrical overhaul and new plumbing to bring it into line with new building regulations.'

'Two birds, one stone,' Mr Scrimengor puts in, his lips contorting once again into an odd smile.

'That doesn't sound too bad,' Izz says, but I'm less certain.

'Even after these initial repairs,' Mr Collins carries on, 'it's uncertain whether the hall will become a functioning community venue again.'

'The council,' Scrimengor takes over, 'conducted a cost-benefit audit over the past year and found the building was only in use for eighty days.'

'Because it's freezing most of the time,' Izz puts in. 'You just said yourself the heating needs replacing.' Nobody reacts to this.

'Then there's the problem of restoring the mural,' Scrimengor says. 'Not an easy or a cheap thing to do. We'd need specialist conservators in.'

'OK, and can we not do all that and reopen as a community venue?' comes a voice and, to my amazement, it's Sully.

Mr Scrimengor is unrolling a large sheet of paper taken from somewhere under his desk and using the still-muted Rodney's laptop to hold it flat on the table. At the moment, the screen's showing an extreme close-up of Carruthers's neck, flushed red with annoyance, as he fiddles with cables and settings.

'The roof fall is perhaps… timely.' Scrimengor says, then clears his throat.

'Timely? How?' I want to know.

'Councilman Carruthers, myself, and other members of the council had already begun a consultation with an architect to work out the cost and benefits to the community of turning the village hall into a dwelling.'

'A house!' My mouth shouts before my brain knows what it's doing.

Mr Carruthers is still very close to the camera. I can see he's speaking too, but there's still no sound coming out.

'What Carruthers is trying to say,' Scrimengor begins, 'is that the shell of the building, apart from the roof, is in good condition. Isn't that correct, Mr Collins?' The hard hat bobs in accord. 'And perhaps, the only option is, sadly, gutting the place to create units.'

He doesn't look sad.

'To sell?' I say.

'Of course, to sell.'

'How many properties?' I press.

'Well… perhaps, one?'

'One?' Izz butts in. 'The building's easily big enough for three or four *units*, if making homes for local people really is your aim here.'

'Mr Collins has assured me he will have the plans ready for public consultation on Monday.'

'So a community hall that belongs to a whole village can become one big palace for one person?' I say. 'And a rich one at that? Not even flats for the young people who have to leave because they can't afford a property here, what with all the holiday homes and the surge in property prices?'

Izz is on her feet now. 'I love…' she begins before checking herself. 'We, the people of Wheaton, love our village hall. We'd use it year round if it was warmer.'

'Put that in the minutes,' I tell Mrs Slaughter, and she obliges.

Izz plops into her seat again. This is all water off a duck's oily back to Scrimengor. He's a picture of calm. 'I think you'll find,' he says, 'there'll be more community support for turning a condemned, barely-used building into a watertight, functioning home than you anticipate, Miss Frost.'

The 'Miss' is said so sharply I hear everything it implies. You, Miss Frost, twice divorced and single again, are meddling, and no number of little misses can save the hall now.

I'm winded, I admit. While I'm gathering my strength for a second assault, Izz slips me a conciliatory boiled sweet, and Fern timidly raises her index finger.

We all look at her, amazed, and Leo Bold's teacherly instincts kick in and he gives her permission to speak. 'Go ahead,' he urges.

Fern's voice quivers but it's loud enough to reach the stage if not, perhaps, Carruthers's speakers. He's given up and sat back in his chair with his arms folded like a man who's washed his hands of the whole thing already.

'People *are* interested in the village hall, actually. My followers are interested,' announces Fern.

Mr Scrimengor lifts his cuff to look at his watch.

'Oh yes? Can you tell us about that?' Mrs Slaughter says, breaking protocol entirely, and Mr Scrimengor gives her a sharp look.

'I shared a video tour of the hall, and then some cine footage of the gingerbread exhibit in the olden days, and today I made a quick post about the damage to the roof and how all our gingerbreads got spoiled, and my followers cared.'

'*Pfft!* Social media? What about in the real world?' Scrimengor says with a bitter laugh.

'Between those posts, they got forty-five thousand likes,' Fern says gently.

That's enough to get me on my feet again. 'See? Forty-five thousand people care. That's loads.'

'And there are about two and a half thousand comments,' Fern adds, allowing her phone to be passed around.

Sully keeps a hold of it, clearly interested. After a moment's scrolling, he pipes up, 'Grandad, that's a lot of engagement for a few videos about a village hall in the middle of the countryside.'

'It's meaningless,' Scrimengor says. 'Any fool can watch a video and give it a thumbs up.'

'Some of these people are asking where they can donate to the repair fund,' Sully says, refusing to be cowed by his haughty grandfather.

'They are?' I splutter, almost spitting the shards of my rhubarb and custard.

Sully passes the phone to me. Playing on a loop onscreen is a video, rather well edited, I have to say, showing pictures of the hall in the past cut with some of the footage Fern filmed that day at my cottage as we watched the cine film. It's spliced together with pictures of all of us making the gingerbread houses, and of Shell with icing sugar on her nose in the Brambledown kitchen, then there's all of us admiring the completed exhibit last night. It feels like a long time ago now, and my throat turns thick and I have to gulp a few times to stop myself crying. Fern's recorded a commentary over the images explaining our 'sixty-year-old tradition'. Then there's a bleak scene shot from outside the hall and a glimpse at the big hole in the roof and a couple of council workers erecting scaffolding. Sure enough, there are comments underneath, lots of them.

'Quite a few of them are asking how to donate,' I confirm.

'Yeah,' Fern says, doe eyes sparkling. 'Does the hall have a JustGiving page or something?'

'Do we?' I turn to Izz, letting her take hold of the phone so she can have a look too.

'We stick any money we raise from the gingerbread grotto into a bank account,' Izz announces, looking out of her depth. 'The money from tickets, donations, and the mulled wine stall all ends up in there.'

That grabbed Scrimengor's attention. 'And this is your fund? What, may I enquire, is the balance?'

I don't know if he looks hopeful it's a high figure or if that's what he's dreading. Does he want us to save the hall with our fundraising or not?

'Well,' I begin, already feeling wretched because, of course, it's not a high total. 'We made our last fundraising deposits on December the first, and it came to…' I look to Izz for confirmation and we both end up saying it at the same time.

'Fifteen pounds fifty-two pee.' Our voices trail off at exactly the same time too, as the hopelessness hits us. Any savings we had from last year were wiped out buying the baking ingredients this year.

'I can vouch for their bookkeeping, Mr Scrimengor. Exemplary,' says Mrs Slaughter, who acts as treasurer for all the community groups: us, the fireworks committee, the village fete, and all the rest of them.

'Are we allowed to set up a JustGiving page to accept donations from the gingerbread grotto's TikTok and Insta accounts followers?' Sully asks, his face all eagerness and eyebrows rising like a Labrador's.

196

Mr Scrimengor starts mumbling something about there being strict fundraising rules for social enterprise projects, and I see Mrs Slaughter looking as though she wants to set him straight, flipping through the big book of regulations on the desk, and we're all surprised when it's Leo who replies.

'Actually,' the head teacher says, his eyes lighting on Sully, 'I think you make a good point. Anyone can fundraise for any cause if they want to. You don't need to be a registered charity or anything. You can fundraise as an individual if you like. A cousin of mine in Arkansas did a GoFundMe to help pay for his emergency appendectomy.'

This makes an interested rumble rise in the room, and we're all glancing around at this surprising turn of events (everyone except Sully and Leo, who are looking at each other in a way I can only describe as electric).

This is when Mrs Slaughter arrives triumphantly at a page in the big book of rules. She lifts the book towards me, and I stand to grab it.

'Paragraph two,' she says.

I read it aloud. 'All Wheaton parish community fundraisers have as much of a stake in planning and renovation process consideration as council bodies.'

'What does that mean?' I say, looking at the words, none the wiser.

'It means if you want to save the hall through your own fundraising efforts, you can try. Only, you have until the end of Mr Scrimengor's planning proposal period to do it.'

'And how long's that?' I say.

'I'd say until the end of next quarter,' Scrimengor says, his lips curling.

'Spring?' Izz spits, forgetting about the reels playing noisily from Fern's phone and looking round the room like a spooked meerkat.

'Best say end of Feb, just to be on the safe side,' Mr Collins pitches in. 'Sometimes planning proposals fly through.'

'Not if the community objects,' Leo Bold says, still looking at Sully, and there's something bright and alive in his eyes that wasn't there before.

'As per regulations,' Mrs Slaughter adds, 'all planning applications will need to go through the regular channels and public consultations.'

'Oh, they will,' Scrimengor says assuredly, like this is a game of poker and he knows he has the winning cards up his sleeve.

'It's nevertheless hard to argue a condemned building should lie unused and unfunded, becoming a danger to others and attracting thieves after lead pipework,' Collins says before he's cut off.

'Excuse me,' interrupts Bobbie, making us all turn in our chairs. They've two kettle weights gripped to their chest and rolled yoga mats under their arms. 'You're on my time now.'

'Ah, there we are! It's working!' Rodney Carruthers chimes down the line from Devon, where someone – it looks like his daughter – has finally sorted his sound issues.

'Meeting adjourned,' tolls Scrimengor, snapping the laptop closed upon his colleague, shooting me a challenging glance as he departs. 'Come along, Sullivan,' he calls behind him. 'You've the bread trays to wash down.'

Before he runs after his grandfather, Sully makes sure to say good night to everyone, and he doesn't forget to direct a nod at Leo, who, even amidst all the fuss of

Bobbie plunging us into full light and the chairs being noisily moved aside, hurls himself across the room to hold open the door for Sully. They exchange smiles only to be separated by the arrival of a gabbling group of village mums pouring through the doors in their exercise gear and clutching oversized water bottles.

Bobbie pointedly hits play on the sound system, blasting out what's probably supposed to be motivational techno music but to me sounds like a torture soundtrack. I'm going home before I get roped into doing squats.

'Fern, what exactly is a GoFundMe?' I ask her as the last of us file outside into the playground.

Izz walks a pace or two behind. She was the last one to get a hold of Fern's phone and is looking over our new social media accounts that caused so much consternation amongst the councillors tonight.

Fern's explaining how it all works, how all we really need is an appeal page explaining who we are and why we need donations when Izz jolts to a stop near the school gates.

'What's this?' she says. I can hear dreamy music coming from Fern's phone.

'Did you know about this?' Izz asks me, a strange look on her face as she shows me something on one of the Gingerbread Christmas Village's pages.

I shake my head. I've not had time to look at reels, not for days.

There are delicate, sad strings playing over a shot of the village hall in its Saturday-night-dancing heyday and words in bold type fading in and then out again.

ONCE UPON A TIME, it reads, *IN OUR BEAU-TIFUL OLD VILLAGE HALL.* This cuts to a close-up of young Izz from the cine film, almost receiving a kiss from her Alexi. *NEXT-DOOR NEIGHBOURS DANCED THEIR WAY TO LOVE.*

'Oh no!' I say, realising what I'm looking at.

Then comes the shot I just knew would be next: Alexi and Izz dancing together. *THEIR ROMANCE WAS FORBIDDEN. ALEXI MOVED TO MALTA. THEY NEVER MET AGAIN. WHAT HAPPENED TO ALEXI THORNE?*

As the words fade away, Izz and Alexi bloom into life on the screen again. It's the still image of them from the foyer of the village hall, where they'd been secretly holding hands, all in black and white.

'When did you post this?' I demand.

'First thing,' Fern whispers. 'Don't you like it?'

The view counter is ticking over every few seconds, climbing higher and higher. 'Over seven thousand likes?'

'I know, it's doing really well,' she says, looking between a stony-faced Izz then me like she doesn't understand what's wrong.

I scroll through the comments.

Fern has posted the first one. It says: *Reunite Alexi and Izz so they can dance together once more when the Wheaton Village Hall is restored.*

'Oh no,' I say, glancing up at her. She looks afraid.

My heart sinks at the endless thread of gushing support below this: hearts and crying faces, a torrent of love and enthusiasm mixed with the odd few incredulous people to whom the love story *Seems Fake;* but overwhelmingly, it's positive. Then there's the inevitable speculation. One comment, I notice, reads: *My great aunt was from the Cotswolds. I'll ask her.* Another makes the claim: *This is where I went to school. Will try to find out.*

As I scroll further, the comments turn to hashtags *#FindAlexiThorne* and *#SaveWheatonHall*. There are hundreds of them.

'I asked if you minded me using some of the cine footage for the fundraising pages,' Fern says to Izz, whose eyes are fixed on the phone. She's saying nothing.

'Did she agree to you using this particular *angle*?' I press. 'This is really personal stuff.'

I can already see Fern's distraught with panic. Her eyes dart from her film to Izz's face.

Izz pins her with a glare. I've never actually seen her glare. It's extremely disconcerting, and I'm not even the one on the receiving end.

'Why would you force open a can of worms like this?' she says at last. 'I have no idea where Alexi is or what he's doing. What if he reunited with his wife? What if he has a family of his own? What will they think of this? What if he never forgave me for spoiling his marriage? Or for his mother chasing him out of Wheaton? He could hate me all the more for this. What if he's… what if he's…' Izz tails off, and I can see she's fighting back tears.

'I can delete it,' Fern tells us. 'Only, there'll already have been loads of shares, and remixes, and reaction videos, and we won't ever know how many screen grabs and downloads.'

Both Izz and I stare blankly at her.

She goes on. 'I'm saying that even if we delete the original, it's already out there. Copied.'

The meaning of this revelation falls around us and we both gape and gasp, not knowing what to do.

'I'm going home now,' Izz says. 'Please just let me be.'

That's how the longest, saddest, most fraught day of my life ends, with Izz shuffling off home in a state, leaving me to comfort Fern in tears by the school gates while a planning application to take away our village hall for good is no doubt being rushed through whichever processes lie in Scrimengor and Carruthers's way. There's nothing for it but to make my way home to bed and hope that the catalogue of Christmas disasters that is my life lately is closing.

Chapter Fifteen

Saturday 16 December: The Spectacular

Welcome to Dunham Gravey Christmas announces the huge digital billboard as we make the turn for the car park.

I'd been surprised Patrick still wanted to go through with this, given everything that's happened, and I gave him an 'out' by saying I was so tired, I didn't mind just staying home and taking a long bath, but he was having none of it and arrived at my door at four on the dot.

A young lad with a high-vis jacket and walkie-talkie waves us straight through without taking any money.

'Ooh, am I getting the VIP treatment?' I say, wishing I wasn't so unnecessarily nervous.

It's only Patrick, I remind myself. I wasn't nearly this giddy for my Countryside Cupid dates, not even when Rusty the Rural Lady Romancer was flirting so convincingly over the dim sum. I'll need to keep this in check in case I make an even bigger fool of myself than I did in Birmingham. Getting giddy always leads to trouble for me.

'It's all free for us if that's what you're asking,' jokes Patrick. 'But I have arranged a few added extras that the general public won't get, yes.'

We park in an unlit bay: an area designated *Staff Only*. I wait in the car while he nips into a Portakabin where there are lots of green gilet people on breaks clinging to steaming mugs.

This is the first of me fully realising what it means for Patrick spending his evenings outside in the wintry cold. Another reminder of how selfish I've been, thinking only of the grotto losing its Santa when he's busy working two difficult jobs. It hardly matters now the grotto's kaput, but still, when he gets back to the car, I'll apologise again.

Except, when he pulls my car door open, he's carrying something that makes me forget all about sorrys.

'For you,' he tells me, and I stumble out of the car. He presents me with a fresh posy of wintry blooms.

'They're glorious,' I say, shoving my nose in amongst the waxy greenery.

'They're all cut from the Dunham Gravey estate.'

'Are you supposed to pick the plants?'

He shrugs. 'Most of them are wildflowers. Look, there's holly. It was *not* easy finding some that still had red berries on; I had to fight the blackbirds for that sprig. There's early witch hazel, some winter flowering jasmine.' He points to the little cluster of yellow stars. 'And these pink ones? They're my favourite.' He smiles as I sniff the blushing cluster appreciatively. 'They're viburnum.'

'And that's mistletoe?' I ask, even though I know full well that the little bracts of silvery green leaves and milky berries are definitely mistletoe.

He suddenly looks like he doesn't know what to do with himself. It's subtle, but I see the shift in him.

'Thank you for these,' I hurry. 'I can honestly say they're the nicest flowers anyone's ever given me.'

He's happy with this. 'Do you want to leave them in the car, or...?'

'I think I'll carry them.'

'All right, then.' There's a proud little hitch at the corner of his mouth. 'Shall we?'

I jam my bobble hat down – a nice cashmere job I've been keeping for best and then never wearing; how silly is that? And we walk, side by side, through a shortcut, Patrick lighting our way with a torch, because of course the man carries a torch on him, through a dark patch of trees towards the sounds of Christmas.

We emerge into a courtyard, all high brick walls and more brick underfoot. Every inch of the place is sparkling with frost. I see Patrick give a nod to another Dunham employee working at an old-fashioned street food cart. The cold's creeping in through my boots (I'm back in my super-soft Doc Martens today – now that I've decided to hang up my hot date heels forever). I wore my leather trousers too. I clocked Patrick's eyes sweep down my legs when he called to pick me up, and I think I spotted a flickering smile of realisation I'd taken him up on his advice to wear them on a date.

'What is that lovely smell?' I ask. I recognise it from long ago. A smell of Christmas. The vendor's already making his way towards us with the answer and leaving a long queue of visitors wondering where he's off to.

'How do, Patrick?' he says, holding out a pink paper cone for me. 'Enjoy.' As soon as I take it, he's gone again, back to work.

'Roasted chestnuts!' The glorious sweet steam rises right into my face. 'I haven't had these since I was little. Mum and Dad would roast them in a special pan over the open top of the wood burner. Ah! That smell.'

I feel eight years old again as Patrick takes the cone and my posy from me so I can slip my gloves off, pick a chestnut and peel the glossy dark skin away.

'Mind, they're really hot,' says Patrick.

Once I've freed the creamy insides from the shell, I lift the chestnut to Patrick's lips.

'You first,' I insist.

He obliges with a smile before opening his mouth. There's a fraction of a second where my eyes fix at the point where my fingers brush his bottom lip, and everything else falls out of focus.

I'm aware of a big swirl of white breathy vapour clouding the space between us – I've exhaled so hard at the sight of him taking in the chestnut – and I have to look away.

'It's good,' he tells me, not seeming to notice me getting carried away, thank goodness.

I have to check myself. *What is this, Margi? One posy of winter blooms and a bag of nuts and your brain goes haywire? Sort yourself out.*

'Come on,' he says, 'there's lots to see.'

I focus on peeling the chestnuts, one for me, one for Patrick, and I'm far more sensible about feeding them to him from now on. He's still carrying my flowers. We make our way out of the courtyard, past the pizza van queue, past the mulled wine stall, and the picnic benches where families huddle over their food, and there's lots of happy chatter mingling with the odd howling toddler for whom it's all got too much, and I try not to think how they paid thirty quid for that kid to cry through the whole thing because that would be truly Grinch-like and not at all festive of me.

We leave the courtyard through a gate where a woman is scanning tickets.

'All set up for you,' she says as we pass by. 'Have a nice evening.'

'What exactly have you set up?' I ask Patrick, but he only smiles and guides me down a path lined with low star-shaped lanterns. There's a bit of a bottleneck here so we end up walking slowly, polishing off the last of the chestnuts.

'Have you ever been here during the daytime?' he asks.

'Oh yes. Lots of times when I was younger, in the summer. I remember the fountains on the big lake, and me and my parents and Lydia having our sandwiches on the lawns. But I haven't been for ages. You know how it is. You visit places miles away and forget about the beauty right on your own doorstep. So, you're enjoying working here?'

'It's fine. The people are nice, but it's kind of a long day after six hours at school.'

'I know. I'm sorry about that. You shouldn't have to take another job. That superhead's got a lot to answer for, even if he did promise we could ice gingerbread men with the kids, and he didn't *have* to come to the council meeting. I do think he's getting more involved in Wheaton life, don't you think?

'Or one particular aspect of Wheaton life?' Patrick glances at me, his lips curling sweetly.

'A lovely young baker?' I hazard.

'I think so. I'd had Sully picked out for your Lucy. Shows what I know. How is she?'

I shake my head. 'Sad, I think.' I like that Patrick had been thinking of ways to make Lucy happier. We'd reached for exactly the same solution: Sullivan Scrimengor and a holiday romance. Shows what we *both* know.

Patrick blows out a hard exhale. 'That's a shame. You're really close, you two, aren't you?'

'We were, once. She's opening up slowly, though.'

I'd feel a lot less happy about leaving her back at the cottage alone if I hadn't seen her at the kitchen table turning to the first page in her sketchbook and opening up the little palette of paints I bought her. I'd left them out for her to discover this morning when she woke. Things have felt so bleak and Lucy's looked even more lost since the exhibition was destroyed and she has nothing to do. I didn't want to wait any longer to give them to her.

She didn't dip her brush, at least not while I was there getting ready for my afternoon out, but she was contemplating it, I think. There's nowhere for her to hide away now, pretending everything's fine, keeping busy with my failed projects (the grotto and even the online dating). Maybe now she'll focus on herself and her own interests. Might that make her happier? I hope so.

I scrunch the empty paper cone in my hands and reach once more for my posy. Their sweet honey scent hits me, and I bring it to my chest. 'Winter flowers definitely have the edge over summer ones,' I say, wanting to try and focus on this moment and not let my mind be dragged back to Wheaton.

We're reaching the end of the path and Patrick gently guides me by the elbow, the touch lasting only a second. 'This way,' he says. The route breaks off into four smaller paths. We take the one leading off to the farthest left. 'More people turn right for some reason, some kind of human preference; it'll be quieter along here.'

'I've read about that, I think. Something to do with right-handedness?'

'Ah, well, I'm left-handed,' he says as we break away. 'Maybe that's why I always end up on my own.' He realises he's made a joke and it sounded sorrier than he intended so he laughs to chase away any hints of self-pity, but I felt a little shift in the air too. There was some truth in what he said. I think of Charlie taking over the family business, taking his girlfriend, being the favourite of the two.

'Do you get lonely, living alone?' he asks, like we've both been thinking the same thing.

'Um, yeah, of course I do. I've lived with other people more than I've lived by myself, and it's still strange waking up on my own in an empty house.'

Patrick takes this in, nodding in agreement. 'I've never lived with anyone. I don't know if it's the late-night drives home from this place and letting myself in to a dark house that's doing it, but I wish I had someone waiting for me.'

I keep my eyes on the bark chips underfoot as I tread. 'I know exactly what that feels like.'

'Don't let your Mum know, or she'll ship one of her strays straight to your door.'

I'm grateful he made the joke, so we can relax again. I tell him he's right; Mum doesn't need any encouragement.

'I don't like to think of you being lonely, though,' I add once the silence settles around us again, and Patrick doesn't reply.

The gardens grow quieter the deeper we go down the path and under the tree line. We seem to be walking away from the blaze of changing colours lighting up the mist in the air where, over on our left, even though I can't see it from here, Dunham Gravey House is situated, a grand Victorian home made of light Cotswold stone, all turrets and towers.

'Is this really part of the lights walk?' I ask as we're forced to walk closer together by the increasingly narrow path.

'See that glow up ahead?' he says, and sure enough, there's a peachy colour rippling through the rustling beech hedges. 'We have to head towards it.'

Passing through a gap between the brown hedges, we find ourselves inside the skeleton framework of a parterre garden, all bare branches and low box topiary. We're sheltered a little from the cold of the late afternoon by the towering horse chestnut trees over our heads. There's a grey statue of a sylphlike woman lifting a basket above her head in the middle of the space, which has the intimacy of an outdoor room.

It's a moment before I register them, but all around us in the bare flower beds are the tiniest pinpricks of coloured light at the heads of black stalks.

'Hah,' I gasp, seeing their soft glow, and as if by magic, each little light bursts into a bloom of hot pink before fading again. 'What was that?' I ask, and again the lights explode, into teal green this time, brighter and lasting longer than the pink, before dying away again.

'They're voice-activated,' Patrick whispers, and the lights shimmer tiny and white.

'They are?' A burst of yellow heats up the night, then disappears just as fast. 'Oh, I love them!' Those words are translated into a thousand blushing red bursts.

'This bit of the display's made by a local artist,' Patrick tells me. 'To turn sounds into light. There are hidden sensors in the trees.' As he speaks, all around us, there's a brief riot of rainbow colours. My laugh sets a small cluster of lights glowing a low orange.

'It's not just voices it translates,' says Patrick. 'The sensors can hear the trees rustling, and they pick up bird-song. You should have seen the place at sunset last week when a flock of starlings came for my sandwich crumbs.'

He's smiling in a flush of blue and indigo lights, and I picture him here alone, eating his sandwiches before his shift begins, not even having time to go home after the school day. He works so hard and he doesn't complain about anything.

'Try moving around,' he says.

I have to think for a second what he means but when I shift my boots against the crispy conifer chips that mulch the footpath there's a scuffing sound that brings the colours back.

Laughing, I dance along the path, which is fine because there's nobody else here; they all took the three busy, brightly lit paths to the right, just as Patrick predicted.

I've reached a hand out to him before I can tell myself that's a dangerous thing to do, and he's smiling and moving towards me, and within seconds we're running together around the little parterres. Patrick twirls me under his arm and we're laughing quietly, our boots making all the noise, swinging our free arms about, my posy of berries and waxy flowers up in the air above my head, our bodies activating every light in our little private world, red then vibrant green, and so many shades of purple and the occasional burst of gold.

When we come to a halt, we're in the corner of the parterre at the point furthest from the gap in the beeches where we came in. I'm out of puff and holding in the last bubbles of laughter. Patrick's eyes shine in the dying lights before we're left in the silent darkness.

I daren't move. Patrick's breathing settles long before mine.

I feel him shifting closer until I can make out the outline of him against the tree trunks that enclose this magical place.

In the shadows, his hand reaches for mine.

'Margi,' he says, and there's a soft glow of lavender colour at our feet.

My name, when he says it, sets off electrical impulses in me too. I try, and completely fail, to ignore them.

'Patrick,' I begin, so scared of what I'll say next, but in the white glow I find I have no words of protest whatsoever.

My hand in his feels absolutely right. Him this close to me and getting closer is exactly what I want.

I swallow hard. He's breathing close to my ear.

'Let me,' he says, and his voice is so low only the darkness hears it.

I only hesitate for a second before I let my eyes close and I lean into him.

His lips find mine softly and slowly and with so much deliberate self-control that my mind falls dark and silent like the garden where we're hiding, afraid to move too much, and I don't know anything else but this kiss.

I pull him nearer, letting him wrap me up in his arms. When I let my hands roam through his hair, a thick moan escapes his throat, like he can't help himself, I lose it completely and gasp out a sound I've never made for anyone, and it only makes his kiss wilder. He gathers me up in his arms so I'm pressed tight against him. Our hitching, gasped breaths released in low, ragged sounds send a thousand sparks of coloured light racing around us.

I'm barely aware of them, but they surround us where we stand, pulsing and dying, burning and lilting as we melt together, getting as close as we possibly can through layers and thick coats, and we light up the winter darkness.

'That was not planned, I promise,' I tell him untold moments later – what is time when you're being kissed like that? – after we heard a noisy family approaching and we slipped out of the colour garden, scurrying down a dark path to rejoin the crowds.

Ahead of us, a slow stream of people are gazing up in wonder at the entrance to a broad tunnel of silvery lights.

Patrick doesn't say anything, and when I look at him, there's a curl at the edges of his rosy, kissed mouth and a look of abandon in his eyes that say it might have been part of *his* plan.

We're inside the tunnel now, drifting along with the crowd. I'm floating.

'Should we...' I begin, feeling all kinds of elated and brain-numbed from the kiss – it was such a good, *good* kiss. He has the side of his thumb raised to the point below his lips like he's feeling the same way. 'Should we talk about it?'

He pulls me to a stop at the end of the tunnel just before we emerge onto a wide path between lawns lit with big red toadstool installations.

'What is it?' I panic, thinking he's going to call the rest of the night off. 'What are we stopping for?' I don't want to stop.

He only smiles and shows me his phone. 'Everybody else is taking selfies. Look.'

He's right. Literally every adult behind us in the light tunnel is either filming themselves or snapping photos of loved ones. 'Oh, OK,' I say, quickly straightening my bobble hat. It hadn't occurred to me to document this moment at all. It's not like I'll be able to forget it, is it?

He gets ready to tap the button, but not before he puts his arm around my shoulder.

'Is this OK?' he asks before he pulls me back into the sweet, warm nook of his body, which feels oddly gentlemanly after the way he just set my entire nervous system on fire back there.

'Yes, it's OK.' I can't help laughing, and he joins in.

The picture, when he shows it to me, has caught something lovely. My nose and cheeks are pink, the same as Patrick's. My eyes are crinkled, our faces are turned towards each other, and we're wrapped in a big arc of blazing light all around us like it's us that's emitting it. Like we're glowing.

'I'll send it to you,' he tells me, typing already, and I feel the picture's arrival buzzing in my coat pocket.

'Where next?' I ask, trying to fight off the dazed sensations that are making me feel wide-eyed and light as a feather. *This can't be right*, I tell myself. *You're getting carried away*, but the rebel in me wants to see what's going to happen next.

What happens is Patrick takes my hand and doesn't let it go the whole time we're wandering through the land of illuminated toadstools, then a world of giant flower structures that droop high over our heads and press up against the path so we feel like tiny things.

'It's like we've fallen down Alice's rabbit hole,' I say, and he greets that with a starry-eyed nod.

'Me too, though we haven't had anything to eat or drink yet.'

'No magic potions,' I say.

'Let's fix that.'

I don't pry into his plans. It's enough to have my hand held and to see him looking so proud and happy. I'd hate to spoil it for him by trying to take control, but I'm curious as we break away from the wide path entirely, striding onto the lawns, past signs warning us, *Do not walk on the grass.*

'Ignore those,' he says.

He's leading us up a steep bank. It gets so steep, in fact, my boots are slipping.

'Little help here?' I squeak, just as I'm about to slide all the way back down.

With a sure arm, he pulls me with him, up and over the peak, away from the slippery, frosted lawns and onto a dark wooded plateau and a path that's chained over.

'That sign says no entry,' I say as we step over the chain.

'Except for staff. Probably,' he says casually, his arms still around me, bundling me along. I can feel his excitement.

'Where are we going?'

His eyes are fixed on a point in the distance a little way along the path, and he reaches into his pocket for his torch, flashes it up ahead once, then twice, only for our light to be greeted by two flashes in reply. Shadows shift, leaves rustle, and then all sense that someone else was up here before us dies away.

We're quite alone as we make the slightest turn in the path, revealing a rounded arbour with a conical roof, wide enough for a bench to sit on and two fat tree stumps for tables. The little hideaway is wide open at the front, and when we sit down, we can see the entire Dunham Gravey estate stretched out down below us.

Patrick's opening a wicker basket, saying, 'Well, look what we have here.' Inside are glass lanterns and matches to light the candles.

I've no words in me, it seems. Then he produces two rolled blankets. One he folds and, motioning for me to lift my bottom again, he lies it along the bench under us.

Once seated again, he places the second blanket across our legs. I notice the price tag still attached. They're from the Dunham Gravey gift shop.

'Did you buy these specially?'

'More like… liberated?' he says with a laugh, and I don't know if he's joking. I don't really care at this point. I'm loving this side of Patrick.

'I've never seen you quite like this,' I tell him.

'*Hmm?*'

He's busy opening a bottle so I reach inside the basket for the two tall glasses nestled beside neatly wrapped packages of food.

'Happy, like this,' I say, as the cork escapes the bottle and flies down over the slope below us.

'*Argh!*' Patrick ventriloquises an injured man down below, and I blurt a laugh.

'You've gone all giddy,' I tell him.

I hold the glasses for him to fill. He takes his time so the fizz doesn't spill over.

'I reckon you're right,' he says eventually, his eyes sparkling in the lantern light. He clinks his bubbling glass to mine. 'Merry Christmas, Margi. I'm sorry it isn't quite the holiday you planned. I really am.'

'It's OK,' I tell him, but my mind's already reliving that first awful glimpse through the doors of the village hall and the collapsed tables, running water and piled rubble and broken beams. I throw back the first gulp from my glass to chase the memory away, swallowing hard.

Wordlessly, we look out at the view below, where the dark lawns lead off to the series of wondrously lit gardens, all melding into a blur of shifting colours. The high walls of Dunham House itself are illuminated by some kind of giant projector. Across its stonework, snowflakes dance to the piped festive music. The snowflakes melt into a scene of trooping nutcrackers before they fade out, and in their place, a fairy flies to the top of a Christmas tree, waving a wand in a sparkling swirl.

The monster oaks and ash trees which mark the perimeter of the estate are also lit from below so they tower like red, purple and blue giants, beautiful in their winter nakedness.

I don't know how long we're quiet for, at least the time it takes to drink half a glass of this very, very gluggable bubbly.

I tell myself to slow down. I'm getting dizzy.

'Let's eat,' Patrick says, his voice low. It makes me wonder what he's been thinking of. 'Here.' From the basket he brings the foiled packages, fat and round. A seriously good aroma lifts with them.

'Pulled pork and apple. Hope that's OK?'

I take one, telling him that's definitely OK, and I rip into the package, taking a big bite. He does the same, like a ravenous man.

I shouldn't love watching him bite into his food like this, but he's watching me the whole time and it's really quite mesmerising.

I swallow and ask, 'Did your Christmas elf friends deliver these?' I glance around in the direction the invisible helpers must have fled.

'You're closer to the truth than you think,' he says before taking another bite.

A cold wintry wind hits us, making the bracken on the wooded floor rustle. 'Shift closer,' he says through his food. 'Keep warm.'

I close the gap between us on the bench and we fall to eating contentedly. We've grabbed pub lunches together and shared coffee and cake at Izz's cafe a hundred times before and it's never felt loaded with meaning like this, like we're so far out of the friend zone we might not be able to find our way back.

I tell myself I've been leaving breadcrumbs of common sense to follow that'll lead me back to safety come the morning when this lovely escapade's over; only a niggling thought insists that I might never find my way back to that old version of myself. Margi, the gingerbread lady, the retiree, the divorcee, the Wheatonite everyone whispers about, the pain in the backside of the council. I don't know if that's who I am at all any more. I'm on the cusp of starting a new life as someone else, aren't I?

I take another long drink. Don't spoil this, I tell myself. Why not just enjoy it, just for an hour or two?

We eat, and he refills my glass, reminding me he can't have any more – he's driving.

He checks that I'm happy and I think I'm telling the truth when I say I am, even though it's turning chillier up here now.

'Good.' He smiles, and his eyes crinkle at the corners the way they always do. I don't even try and drag my gaze away.

When we've finished eating, he asks if I fancy dessert. 'We need to walk if we're going to find something sweet.'

'Silly question. Only I don't want to leave here just yet. Let's stay, at least until Greg Lake comes on again. You know, the "I Believe in Father Christmas" one?' The event's piped music is playing on a loop, maybe seven or eight songs at most on repeat. 'Does it drive you demented? The same songs over and over?' I add.

'Usually, yeah, a little bit. I haven't minded it tonight, though,' he says.

Soon enough, the jaunty, hippiefied orchestral opening of Greg Lake floods the estate from hidden speakers and we both turn and grin at each other.

'This song's from when I was a teenager,' I say. 'Hard to believe.'

'I know, it sounds more recent,' Patrick says. 'But then again, it's been playing every Christmas for as long as I can remember.'

I don't say anything. There's a breadcrumb of common sense. It's telling me to stop this, quick.

'What is it?' he says. 'Your face fell. Did I say something?'

'Of course not. I'm having a lovely time.'

'But…' he leads.

I hold my breath then let it go in a big rush. 'But, it's always there, bothering me.'

'What is?' He genuinely looks like he has no clue. Can he really not be aware?

'How much younger you are than me, for a start.'

'What does that matter? I've two jobs, a car, a home. I own power tools. I have a life insurance policy. I kiss like this.'

Before I can forge ahead with dismantling the fairy-tale atmosphere he's worked so hard to make for us tonight, he's done it again, brought his lips to mine and swiped away all my objections. I have to clasp the stem of my glass to stop it spilling, but still, I kiss him back.

It's Greg Lake who brings me round. He's singing about how you get the Christmas you deserve. I pull away, blinking, trying to get my eyes to focus. It's not easy.

'You're going to have to stop doing that,' I tell him. 'It makes me forget things.'

Patrick screws his nose in the nicest way. 'Forget what?' He thinks I'm trying to be cute.

I'm trying to be sensible. I want to put a stop to all the giddiness before it hurts both of us, but I also stupidly, annoyingly feel like saying *to hell with it, let's get lost in the woods forever.*

'This is dangerous,' I tell him.

He smiles back. 'I don't think it is.'

'Jesus!' I lift my eyes in appeal. '*You're* dangerous,' I say, but I get the feeling anything I use as a protest will fall flat right now. It's so cosy and warm and nice up here under our blanket. I decide to spoil it good and proper. 'It's easy to want me when there's music playing and it's Christmas and you're half-cut on champagne,' I say.

'I've had one glass.'

'But when the cold light of day hits, you'll regret this.'

'Doubt it.' He's so sure, it's exasperating.

'I went on a date this month with a geezer who was horrified by my grey hair. And then another date with a bloke who'd, in essence, set himself up as a one-man charity, delivering shags to lonesome elderly ladies who live out in the sticks.'

'What? A sort of feels on wheels kind of thing?' he says, wickedness sparkling in his eyes.

I bump his arm with my own. 'I'm not joking. I'm saying I've gotten too old for dating, and I'm definitely…' I put my glass down, 'too old for you.'

'Can't I decide that for myself?' he says, serious now.

'No, you can't,' I grump, folding my arms.

'I'm sorry those guys were shitty.'

'Thanks. They really were.' I picture Charlie's self-assured grin. I think how it was actually nothing like Patrick's. How could I have thought it was?

'But that's not me,' he's saying. Then he waits for my reaction.

I don't know what else to say. I'm back to being tired all of a sudden. 'Come on,' he says, making to move. 'One last stop?'

We blow out the candles and leave them alongside the basket and blankets. I assume the elves are coming back for them. I cling to my winter posy and try to walk like someone who hasn't just drunk two glasses of bubbly and been kissed until her knees went weak.

He doesn't reach for my hand this time as he leads the way down a long flight of stone steps between the lawns where the frost glints, reflecting the coloured lights. There's no moon or stars, just low cloud and colours in the air, and there's no words either. Maybe my warning worked. Maybe we're heading back to the friend zone and this is what reacclimatising feels like. I hate it.

Once we arrive among the crowds again, it's clear how much the temperature's fallen. Every shivering leaf and blade of grass is touched by a hard frost.

I feel a bit stricken, but still, it was the right thing to do.

We don't talk as we walk through what I'm guessing in autumn is an orchard alive with ripe fruit and buzzing bees; now the trees are bare and decorated with sequined lanterns in the shape of oversized red apples. It's me who draws out my phone this time and I ask Patrick to stand in amongst them while I snap a shot. He folds his arms and tips his head a little, lifting his eyes to me as I count down from three.

'Good one?' he asks, and looking at my screen, I have to stop myself saying it's perfect.

'Yep.' I shove my phone in my pocket.

He says there's a shortcut to skip the crowds if we go through a gate in a drystone wall which to me looks like the outer perimeter of the estate gardens, but when we pass through the *Staff Only* exit I realise we're at the back of what was once the gardener's cottage where the Dunham Gravey staff must take their coffee breaks in better weather. There are picnic benches, big bins and a designated smoking area under an awning.

'Through here,' Patrick says, walking just ahead of me round the side of the darkened cottage with the words *Estate Office* on the bolted door.

We come out into another public area floodlit with very tall, conical trees entirely made of lights. There must be twenty of them at least. That's not what holds my attention, though. What I'm interested in is the fact that the entire place is absolutely teeming with costumed elves.

'Ready?' asks the approaching man with rouged circles on his smiling cheeks and wearing a green and red stripy outfit with a bell on his hat.

Patrick says, 'We are, I think?' looking at me, unsure, before we're whisked through a curtain by the elf to wait inside what I think is an open-ended garden shed.

'Patrick?' I say, disorientated. 'What's this?'

He looks apologetic and like he's about to say we should head back to the car.

'*Ho ho ho,*' a voice booms from through the curtain, and Patrick holds it open to reveal, of course, a grotto. 'Ah, welcome!' a very jolly Father Christmas says. 'It's little Margi, isn't it? And Patrick Wootton. Lovely to see you again.'

I have to laugh. 'You don't want me to sit on your knee, do you?'

'*Ho ho ho.*' Santa shakes his round belly. 'That would be against the estate's safeguarding rules, *ho ho ho.*'

He does, however, pat a cushioned seat beside him. I make my way across the grotto, all sumptuously swagged red velvet disguising the fact this is probably just a tarpaulin-covered gazebo – clever that they don't let you see it – and there are plush rugs on the floor and a real tree decorated with red baubles.

'Tell me, what do you want for Christmas, Margi?'

Got to hand it to him, he's doing a good job of keeping up the act.

'Well,' I say. 'Well…' Only, I can't think of any special thing I'd like, nothing you could buy in shops anyway. 'There's only one thing, actually.' Thinking about it makes me aware I might be on the verge of crying and I don't know what to do about that.

'Go on, Santa's listening.'

I know it's only make-believe, of course, and I have to remind myself I've absolutely lost all of my Christmas spirit this year, but after tonight and all the lights and the kisses and the warmth, I feel it all the more: the loss of my entire reason for being.

'What I want is…' I begin, knowing I won't finish the sentence without tears coming, and sure enough, they're already sneaking down my face. 'I want my gingerbread grotto.'

The Santa glances ever so quickly at Patrick with a hint of panic in his eyes.

There's a moment's awful silence before Patrick intervenes and comes to me, taking my hand.

'That's what we all wanted,' he soothes. 'I'm so sorry it's gone.'

I turn to face him, wiping my cheek with my glove. 'I thought I was dreading it, all that work and effort and a whole fortnight of selling tickets in a freezing hall, pouring mulled wine, listening to carols, and, worst of all, you weren't going to be there, and you're such a good Santa, the best, really. Oh, sorry. No offence.' The Dunham Gravey Mr Claus nods this away. The guy's clearly regretting doing Patrick this favour. 'But now it's all been taken away from me, I just want it all back, and I want the smell of gingerbread all month long, and for the ovens to be on eight hours a day while I bake, and I want icing sugar in my hair like always and… I want my purpose in life back.'

That's when I really cry, and Patrick holds me until I stop feeling sorry for myself and drowning in thwarted Christmas nostalgia.

'Let's get you home,' Patrick says. 'Cheers, Kev.' He pats Santa on the shoulder.

I hear the sounds of excited kids scrambling into the shed waiting room behind the curtain, ready for their encounter with the big man.

On the walk back to the car I barely stop apologising, even when we stop to collect a cup of tea and a banana Nutella crepe at a van beside a beautiful dancing horse carousel – 'All on the house,' the woman says through her hatch, winking at Patrick, not knowing I've got all emotional and spoiled the night out that he'd planned so nicely.

There's an announcement over an unseen tannoy that the musical fountain spectacular on the lake will begin in thirty minutes. Patrick knows I've had enough and don't want to see it.

I spend the drive home eating the sweet pancakes and feeding little folded chocolatey bites to Patrick as he navigates the back roads to Wheaton. We don't say much, only I continue to apologise and thank him umpteen times for a beautiful evening.

When we pull up at my cottage door, I unclip my belt. He cuts the engine.

'What do we do tomorrow?' he asks me, turning in his seat, all earnestness.

It really matters what I say now, so I need to hold my resolve.

'Nothing. You do your Christmas and I'll do mine, whatever that's going to look like. We go back to how it was before.'

'How's that supposed to work, then?' Patrick says, and I see his lip hitch at the side in the persistent, wicked way it did earlier. 'And what would Izz say, huh? She told us to sort ourselves out, and I thought we had. You can't let her down now. You're her best friend in the world.'

'*You're* my best friend too,' I say.

'I could be an even better friend.' This is said so pointedly I feel it in my stomach. My mind tells me to pull him by his coat, haul him across the gearstick, kiss him so hard we both turn faint.

'Margi? Are you listening?'

'Hmm?' I snap out of the vision.

'You were thinking about kissing me. You were looking at my mouth.' He's smiling broadly now, and if he wasn't so genuine and kind, I'd think he was toying with me.

'Who is this person?' I say, trying anything to break the tension. 'What happened to Patrick? I can't cope with you smiling and being all sure of yourself like this. Seriously, it's throwing me.' He tries to straighten his lips, looking chastened. 'We need to act normal or else,' I warn.

'Or else people will think I like you?' he says.

'Yes.'

'And they'll think you like me?' he goes on.

'Maybe.'

'And don't we?' There's so much sincerity in his eyes I can't look at him.

'That's neither here nor there, is it?' I reply.

'Stop that.' His voice is firm.

This draws me up short.

'Just stop,' he says again.

He reaches for my free hand and presses it flat against his chest.

'Let's not throw this away like it's nothing,' he says, and he's not joking around now.

I wish he was. I wish he would turn back into the giddy, excited Patrick of earlier, because this is exactly what I'm afraid of. This is what happens when things get too real and there are feelings involved.

'Patrick, please…'

A tap at the passenger window makes me shriek. The shadow outside jumps about a foot into the air. Patrick drops my hand and we all look back and forth at each other. The face at the glass is joined by another, and I roll the window down.

'I scared you?' says Sully Scrimengor. 'Sorry.'

'Sorry to interrupt,' Leo Bold adds with an apologetic wave from over Sully's shoulder.

'You weren't interrupting anything,' I say, rearranging my face so I look like a respectable member of the community who hasn't been kissing in a magical forest with an achingly attractive handyman fifteen years her junior.

'OK,' Sully says, doubtfully, and I catch him throwing a glance at Leo who's now back to being as serious as the day I first met him, only he looks a bit bee-stung around the mouth too – as does Sully, come to think of it.

'We've been thinking, and the thing is…' Sully goes on, 'we've come up with a solution.'

'To your grotto problems,' Leo adds, already finishing Sully's sentences like a proper couple. 'The school board have agreed that you can have the gymnasium for a new gingerbread grotto. I've already done the risk assessment.' He holds up an A4 file as proof.

I stare back at the men.

'You want to use the gymnasium to host a display of gingerbread biscuits?' I say, incredulous.

'A model gingerbread village,' Leo Bold replies. 'A historic community event.'

Sully echoes his words encouragingly, nodding and smiling, suggesting these were originally Sully's words, his sales pitch to convince Leo to help us.

'So, technically,' Leo goes on, 'it's educational, if you really think about it. And that's what I'm planning on telling the Ofsted inspector if he turns up, but mainly, I think, it's good to do things to make the children happy, especially at Christmas.'

'But…' I look between their faces and Patrick's. 'Everything got flattened, and soaked, remember? There is no gingerbread and no grotto either.'

'That's not strictly true,' Patrick puts in. 'My costume and beard are hanging in my wardrobe at home and the grotto stuff is in my store room at school.'

'We've nothing to exhibit,' I say again.

'Not if you don't get baking, and sharpish!' says Sully.

'Even baking around the clock it would take a fortnight to recreate Wheaton.'

'School breaks up on Wednesday,' notes Leo. 'Can't we be ready for the kids' last day? And then the exhibit could run until Christmas Eve, like it usually does, or longer, only in our gymnasium?'

'Wednesday?' I repeat. 'But... how can I be ready by then?'

I realise there are three sets of eyes on me, waiting for me to catch on.

'I'm a baker,' Sully coaxes. 'With a great big bakery?'

'You'll help? But what about your grandad? He'd rather drown in golden syrup before he helped one of the Frost women ice a gingerbread house.'

'It's just as well we signed the paperwork this morning then, isn't it? Making me an equal partner in the business. I think he's relieved, actually. That was always the plan, and the reason I came back, only he was reluctant to go through with it at first. Maybe he thought I'd not stick around. But I promised him I was serious, and I'm not going anywhere.'

Another goofy smile passes between the young couple.

'He's practically retired as it is,' Sully continues. 'Besides, if I want to help out some friends with some extra ingredients and some manpower, why can't I?'

'But... but... what about Bobbie and their spandex punishment room?' I say, scrabbling for impediments.

'She means the boot camp thing,' Patrick clarifies.

'I got that,' Leo says, another smile blooming. 'Bobbie's going to move their class into the art room. It's a bit small, but I threw in access to the covered Astroturf at the back and they agreed instantly.'

'Nothing like doing star jumps on plastic grass in the freezing cold to help you drop a dress size for Christmas,' I say, my heart beginning to lift.

'Well, quite,' Leo says, and Sully grins at him.

'So, that's it? We're back on?' Patrick asks.

'I'll need the committee to teach me how it's done, all the gingerbread building work and stuff,' Sully insists. 'We'll need everyone joining in, a team effort.'

'Well,' I say, slumping into my seat. 'I can't believe this is happening.'

'Believe it!' Sully cries. 'So, what do you say?'

I move to open the door, making the boys jump back.

Out under the dark Wheaton sky I hug Sully, then Leo, totally overwhelmed by all of this.

'You're right. We will need all hands on pins,' I warn. 'The school kiddies too.'

'OK.' Leo says it like it's nothing.

'OK?' I echo.

'We're doing this?' says Patrick, joining us on the pavement.

Then we all take turns saying it – *We're doing this. We are! We're doing this!* – through rising laughter and adrenalin and much jumping and clapping and hugging as it sinks in for all of us that we have four days to rebuild a whole world.

Chapter Sixteen

Sunday 17 December: The Recipe

The next morning, under the strip lights in the Scrimengor and Grandson's Bakery, there's me and Lucy, Izz and Patrick, Leo and Sully standing in white coats and hairnets.

We're looking down at a single sheet of paper, inscribed with green felt tip years ago, the recipe handwritten by my mum and gifted to me, and – because the measurements aren't counted in pounds and ounces or grams, or even in cups, but in Mum's trusty old glass pudding bowl which she'd use to scoop up ingredients and level them off with a spatula like she was making sandcastles instead of biscuits – I've brought along the very pudding bowl she always used.

Everyone assembled has been warned that both the scrap of paper and the glass bowl are priceless so they're standing with their hands by their sides peering down at them on the stainless steel workstation like wise men around the manger.

The bakery, in spite of being little more than an industrial unit – all glass, white tile and steel – is warm from the morning's loaf baking. The delivery men have long since filled their vans and left on their rounds, and the ovens are waiting.

I read Mum's recipe aloud and it feels like I'm incanting a spell.

Large Batch Gingerbread

For my darling Margi, carrying on the tradition

This is sufficient to make three of the larger Wheaton cottages, or one school and the church.

Remember to make enough gingerbread men, stars, hearts, etc., with the remainder after cutting-out for Grotto visitors to eat.

Ingredients

12 bowls of plain flour
2 bowls of demerara
2 packs of butter, unsalted
4 bowls of golden syrup
Quarter bowl made up of equal amounts ground ginger and ground cinnamon (it ought to be fiery)
Pinch of ground cloves or nutmeg (you want it to smell wonderful)
Salt, half a tablespoon
3 tablespoons of sodium bicarbonate

Instructions

Heat the butter, sugar and syrup until liquid

Mix all dry ingredients in your largest bowl

Pour wet over dry and mix thoroughly until you have a firm dough

Get your hands in and add a splash of water if it won't bind

Refrigerate, covered tightly with clean cloth

Make a cup of tea and put your feet up (and have a decent sherry in your pantry for when you have company baking)

Heat the ovens. 180 degrees.

Knead then roll between two sheets of parchment using Dad's spacers to achieve the right thickness

Lay the gingerbread slab on top of your template and begin cutting

Transfer cut-outs to baking parchment on your largest trays

Thirteen minutes in the oven should be long enough. Use your nose.

You may have to turn larger structures midway if they're catching at the back, but be fast and allow extra time in the oven to make up for heat lost.

Out onto racks and cool completely, ideally overnight.

Ice, decorating with angelica, cinnamon sticks, chocolate buttons, star anise, candied orange, silver sugar balls, gumdrops or whatever you and the village helpers can afford

'That's it?' says Leo. 'Where's the icing instructions? How do we stick the buildings together?'

'You just sort of glue them with icing and hope for the best,' says Izz.

'There's wooden blocks and dowelling to support verticals,' I say, gesturing to the box of equipment by my feet that I brought from home. 'And I've got all the paper templates for cutting to.'

Patrick rubs his hands together. 'Shall we get measuring, then?'

I lift Mum's pudding bowl with both hands and convey it to Sully who accepts it like a king at his coronation receiving the golden orb.

'I reckon we can quadruple that mixture,' Sully tells us, and we all stand round the huge mixer and count together as the dry ingredients go in.

I break away with Izz to work the big burner, heating the sweet ingredients with the butter.

'This is the biggest vat I've ever seen,' I marvel, while Izz empties industrial quantities of golden syrup from squeezy bottles into the pan and I drop in a block of butter the size of a house brick.

'How was it?' Izz asks me in a surreptitious way as she climbs a stepping stool to stir the melting mixture. 'Your date with Patrick?'

I glance around. Patrick's busy across the room sorting through the paper templates. 'It wasn't a date…' I begin, but this is met with a lifted eyebrow. I relent immediately. 'It was nice,' I sigh. 'Too nice.'

'No such thing,' Izz tuts. 'Did he make you happy?'

'Yes.'

'There we are, then. Hold on to happiness where you find it.'

'It's hardly as simple as that,' I say, and Izz falls quiet. 'Keep stirring.' She already knows all my objections. I bet she's sick of them. I know I am. 'And what about you?' I say while I have the chance to change the subject. 'Have you heard anything?'

She knows I mean has she heard anything about Alexi, and she's trying to remain placid, but there's a tiny glint of that fearfulness in her eyes that makes her look about five years old.

'Nothing at all,' she says. 'I think it's already blown over.'

'Old news already?' I say. 'Like yesterday's newspapers are today's chip wrappers.'

Except even we know enough to understand that *digital* content never dies. That stuff lives on forever, is impossible to escape. Lucy was telling me only the other night that she once knew a girl at uni who was caught on film being obnoxious to a barman. Apparently, she's twenty-nine now and the video's still doing the rounds. Even I've seen it and knew instantly what Lucy was talking about. I decide not to share this with Izz.

The good, familiar smell of melted butter and sugary syrup on the edge of turning opaque drifts into the air. Izz is quiet, thinking, if that frown is anything to go by.

'I'm sorry if I made things awkward with Patrick,' Izz says eventually, and her voice reverberates inside the big vat as she stirs.

I check again that he's nowhere near to overhear. 'It's all right. We'll be OK,' I reassure her, even if I can't know this for certain.

'And I frightened little Fern.'

'She'll live,' I say, but I know we're both quietly wondering where she is. 'Has anyone phoned up to Brambledown Farm to check on her?'

'I did,' Lucy puts in from across the room – listening in as usual, just like I used to when Mum gossiped with her gingerbread helpers. She's been preparing vast sheets of greaseproof paper on oven trays four times the size of my ones at home. 'No answer,' she tolls.

Izz hasn't seen her either. 'Didn't turn up for her shift at the cafe yesterday.'

'She'll be fine,' I say again. 'She's got Shell, remember?'

We nod, comforted at this recollection.

'Ready with the butter and sugar mix?' Sully calls across the room.

With a good deal of skill, and aided by Patrick, the vat of bubbling, cloudy liquid gold is run into the spiced bed of flour inside the machine and Sully lowers in the mixing arm.

I take a picture of this to send to Mum. 'She's not going to believe this.'

Even though we're in a great big bakery with noisy machines and clanking ovens there's something about the scent of glossy spiced dough coming together that transports me right back to Mum's kitchen.

I can't help thinking of her adding a pinch more ginger or a sprinkling of water flicked in with busy fingertips and surrounded by a rising cloud of flour.

'It's good,' Leo says, taking a deep sniff, and I look around at the faces of my very own gingerbread gang murmuring their agreement.

'Right,' Sully says with an authoritative clap. 'Let's get to work on the next batch.'

–

Leo had to leave a while ago – even with his new chilled-out approach to head teaching there's still weekend admin to do – and so missed me and Izz giving our masterclass in cutting out from raw refrigerated and rolled dough.

Patrick proved to be quite the draughtsman by scaling up our old templates to make every building a quarter as large again – I figured Mum would have made hers massive too had she had the oven space – and we made excellent progress lifting the big slabs of cottage walls, gable ends and roof onto the trays and onward into the huge ovens.

I check them off on a list. 'That's Izz's cottage, the old post office cottage, numbers three and five high street and Sully's bakery done already.'

Sully smiles again at the inclusion of his grandad's business in the diorama for the very first time – Mum (and me) knew how to hold a grudge just as well as Mr Scrimengor. In the end, it was the easiest of the lot to cut out; just four big squares for the walls with a long strip of window and a flat roof.

'These would have taken me, Margi and Patrick at least three days to do,' Izz remarks, wiping her hands on her apron, looking at the trays slotted into the oven racks.

Lucy produces a tray of teas while we wait for the gingerbreads to bake and we all take a mug.

'And there was no running around the village to use three different ovens,' I say.

Patrick laughs. 'True,' he says, shaking his head at our old, inefficient ways of doing things.

I regret not befriending Scrimengor, or at least trying to. Instead of rocking up every December the first to antagonise him with a poster for the grotto exhibit, knowing he'd say he wasn't going to display it in his windows, I should have asked if he'd reconsider his old offer. We could have been working together for years. He might have softened earlier. Though when I picture his sour, pinched face and the glee he took in telling me he'd as good as signed off on refurbing the village hall into a fancy pad for a Cotswold millionaire, I'm not convinced it'd have worked. I can only hope Sully's easy-going influence will change the old duffer. I wish it could be enough to get him to drop the planning application altogether, but I know that's unrealistic.

'We'll have half of Wheaton high street done by three, I reckon,' says Sully through my thoughts.

He's keeping an eye on the ovens but I tell him it's OK, he doesn't have to worry. 'We'll know when it's ready.'

Izz agrees. 'You can smell when it's properly baked.'

'That's what Grandad always says,' adds Sully. 'Trust your nose, not the timer.'

Thirteen minutes is all it takes and the trays are delivered onto the cooling racks, great slabs of sugary construction material, exactly the same colour as Wheaton's lovely golden stonework.

'I'll make a start on the windows,' I say, and I set to explaining how to melt boiled sweets to make coloured glass panes that we'll pour into the empty window apertures so when they set hard they'll glisten and hold firm like thin glass.

There's a rattle at the bakery door.

'Someone after a loaf,' says Sully, breaking away from my demo to speak to the customer. Opening the door, he cries, 'Fern!'

We all stop what we're doing to gape at her, probably scaring her out of her wits.

'You're all right?' asks Izz, shuffling to greet her.

'Where have you been?' says Lucy, drawing her away from the door and into the heat of the bakery.

Fern's eyes dart around, seeing the gingerbreads, registering what we're all up to.

'I got your messages,' she says quietly. 'I'm sorry I wasn't around.'

Nobody's saying anything in case we spook her right out the door again.

'I was keeping an eye on this,' she says, turning the phone to show us a fundraising totaliser. 'I made it after the meeting at the school.'

Izz cautiously takes the phone from Fern. She studies the screen for a moment. 'Eighty?' she says under her breath, and I crane my neck to look too.

'Eighty?' I repeat, looking at all those noughts. 'Eighty thousand pounds? In donations?'

Fern only nods. She looks like she's going to pass out on the floor.

'Bloody hell!' Izz blurts, and I catch Patrick smirking at – by Izz's standards – the sweary outburst. 'You've raised eighty thousand pounds for the hall repairs? By posting some videos?'

'Shell made a website too,' Fern says, like the success isn't down to her at all. 'With the hall's history written up and some of the old pictures from the foyer wall that I photographed. And Dad had some photos in an album at home too. The site's had a few hits.'

'Fern,' says Izz, looking at the girl in amazement. 'You clever, clever thing. You didn't delete the video, did you? The one about me?' she asks suddenly.

Fern shakes her head. 'I didn't know what to do, not when it had already been seen by so many people, and they were really reacting to it.'

Izz nods, thinking.

'It's because they talk about everything,' I blurt. 'Nothing's secret with these kids. It's how they've been brought up. They're not ashamed of hurting. They don't keep it in, choking down pain for years, suffering alone. They just... talk about stuff out loud and in public. Right?' I offer, hoping Fern has the gumption to grasp the end of the olive branch I've thrown and run with it. I catch Patrick narrowing his eyes the tiniest fraction at this.

I've no idea what he's thinking. We've been too busy since last night's visit to Dunham Gravey to talk properly and frankly, that's working for me. The longer I can keep this up, the better.

'I s'pose,' she says softly.

'It's true,' Sully jumps in. 'Look at Grandad. He's what, nearly seventy, and he's eaten up with anger about how Gran left him and that was, like, fifty years ago? It's toxic, keeping things in.'

'That's right!' I jump in. 'These kids, they don't like the toxic stuff. They want it out. They're always banging on about it, *this is toxic, that's toxic...*' I don't know why I'm working so hard to defend Fern, especially when she's been intrusive and naive, though I know for certain her meddling came from a good place.

My mind flits between Izz and Fern and on to Lucy and the way they're all stuck with their own habits. Izz and Lucy never talking about anything hasn't actually done either of them any good. And Fern doesn't know how to keep things to herself.

'We *can* still stop the video if you want to,' Fern says.

'No,' Izz says, shaking but resolute. 'How can you delete it when it's working? It's making money for the hall.'

'I'm sorry I messed up,' Fern says in her smallest voice. 'I feel bad about sharing the video of you and Alexi without showing you first to check it was OK. I'll just have to sit with these feelings, and I promise I won't do it again. I've learned from it and I'll do better in the future. But… I thought you should know about this.'

She flicks to the video of the dancing couple that caused all the drama in the first place. 'You should see this,' she says. 'The top comment. It appeared this morning.'

'"We've got to get these two reunited"', reads Izz, struggling to make out the tiny words.

I join in by her side. 'Wow! You've really caught these people's imaginations,' I say. 'Hashtag reunite the Wheaton sweethearts?'

Izz pulls a pained face.

'No, not those ones. Above that.' Fern scrolls up until we see it: a comment 'liked' by precisely 4,343 people and exciting enough to garner many hundreds of replies in turn. Izz clamps her hand over her mouth as we read the words.

@carlie7bts2006 Alexi Thorne is my grandad

Chapter Seventeen

Tuesday 19 December: The New Venue

The school gymnasium smells of fresh floor polish. Patrick's work, of course. He came in early this morning to do it.

He's also hefted in new rolls of white cloth that we're using to cover the tables but there's enough here to turn absolutely every surface in the school hall into a wintry wonderland. They're all piled up in fat rolls on the low stage. I see he's brought in the big folding screens we use to make his Santa grotto too. Thankfully, they weren't set out under the hall roof when it collapsed but in Patrick's school storage room. They're still decorated from last year with their *This Way for Lapland* signs and my cut-out penguins.

The heating's on full blast so the first thing we'll need to do is turn the radiators down or our icing will melt and we'll have a natural disaster scene rendered in collapsed slabs of biscuit instead of a picturesque gingerbread miniature village.

'You've been avoiding me,' the voice says behind me and my shoulders jump.

'How can I have avoided you when we were baking in the same room for two whole days? Well, until you had to leave for your Dunham shifts.'

'You know what I mean,' Patrick says, not slowing in his work, manoeuvring double desks into a big oval just like we'd set out the village hall tables. 'Thirty enough?'

'Should be.' The school tables are smaller than the hall ones and lower too. 'I'd say thirty's a good guestimate. See how we get on?'

'Can always add more,' he says, and I'm relieved we've moved into safer territory until he says, 'So, are we doing it again? Dinner, maybe? Indoors this time?'

'Patrick, you have to let it go. I can't…'

'I heard you needed some muscle,' interrupts a voice from the hall doors and in comes Bobbie, looking oddly overdressed (compared to their usual layer of Lycra) in white trainers and a pastel tracksuit with a ski jacket over it.

'I didn't recognise you for a second,' I say. 'You're here to help?'

'Certainly am.' Bobbie grins. 'After I saw that viral video about Izz and her boyfriend, I knew I wanted to help.'

Suddenly, there's Izz in my mind's eye at her cottage doorstep last night as I walked her home from the bakery, not a car on the road and all the lights on the high street long since out, the whole village asleep.

'Check one more time,' she'd asked me.

When I showed her the app there was nothing new from @carlie7bts2006 even in response to Fern's request she message the Gingerbread Christmas Village page. A handful of comments below asked for more details too. Strangers wanting to know if it was true and had he been in touch. *Has Alexi been found!!!!* one user asked, their profile picture a greyed-out avatar and their handle just a stream of numbers.

'People are looking for him,' I said, not sure if that was going to comfort Izz or unsettle her even more. 'Is that what you want? For him to be found?'

Izz lifted her eyes to the starry black sky and inhaled deeply.

'It's been a long time, not knowing,' she told me. 'Always wondering where he was, what he was feeling. Always missing him. If I knew, one way or the other... maybe it would help?'

She didn't try to plaster on her usual smile as we said good night. I think we're past pretending now. After nearly sixty years of smiling through pain, as Lucy put it, I reckon Izz should be allowed some respite.

'Bobbie?' I say gently. 'We're not going to mention Alexi to Izz today if that's OK? It's been a lot.'

Bobbie crosses their heart and says they get it.

'Right, well, I've got forty metres of white cloth to fix over these tables and Patrick will be making a start on covering the windows, the walls and the gym equipment with black drape. Are you handy with a staple gun?'

Bobbie mimes lifting guns from invisible holsters and firing staples at me, so I take that as an enthusiastic yes. 'There are other helpers waiting outside,' says the boot camp teacher. 'Mrs Slaughter's getting them all signed in with school visitor badges.'

'There are?' I say, looking between Bobbie and Patrick, confused. 'Who is it?' I say, but before Bobbie can fill me in, the hall doors open and in spills Fern with her dad Tommy – thankfully, he's left the farm mutts at home – some of The Salutation regulars and Lolla the landlady, Lucy and Izz, a few of the mums from the PTA, a school dinner lady on her day off, and two of Sully's bakery delivery drivers, every one of them apparently keen to take part.

'Don't tell me, you've all seen Fern's fundraising videos online?' I ask, and there's a murmur of agreement. Fern doesn't know whether to be proud or sheepish. 'Right! Well, let's get started, shall we?'

I set up a construction station on the low stage where the bakery lads, the dinner lady and one of the mums set to work constructing cottages following Patrick's template plans.

At another cluster of tables, Lucy and Izz direct Tommy Brash, Landlady Lolla, and the others who are roped in as decorators, putting the finishing touches to completed builds.

I spend a good hour mixing different colours of icing and loading them into piping bags – kindly supplied by Sully who's back at the bakery completing the last of the village builds by himself – until there's a pile of bags ready for the icers to wield, and no danger of them running out any time this morning.

That's when one of the teachers brings the reception kids in and the noise increases by about a hundred decibels.

They're delighted when I produce the spare tubs of dolly mixtures, gumdrops and candy canes that I picked up from the cash and carry back at the start of December when I had a very different image in my head of how this year's exhibition would look.

I demonstrate the 'flooding' icing technique Mum showed me so long ago, perfect for gingerbread men. They all crowd round while I show them. I forgot how closely little kids can concentrate on things like this. They all watch my hands as I ice the outline around the edge of the gingerbread biscuit. 'You'll need to make sure there are no gaps in your outline,' I tell them. 'Like this. Then, get your coloured icing, these ones are runnier.' They ooh and ahh as I let the pale yellow icing run into the middle of the biscuit. 'Now you can drag the runny stuff right up to the edges of your outline if you want to, but I prefer to do this.'

I gently shake the gingerbread man, keeping him level, and the yellow icing spreads itself smoothly right up to the outline.

The kids react like I've done a magic trick.

'Now it's your turn,' I say, setting them working in pairs, one responsible for the outline, their partner flooding the shape with icing.

I notice Patrick watching me as I move amongst the pairs helping to wipe away spills from overzealous shaking. He's looking at me with admiration. He's never seen me in my Home Ec teaching comfort zone, and it turns out it's like riding a bike. I remember how much I enjoyed this. I wish there was more of this in my life.

Izz, meanwhile, shows the adults how to fill the gaps between the roof panels with twists and wisps of piped icing to resemble gathered drifts of snow, and Lucy, getting into her art teacher stride, suggests new ways of achieving brick effects and pretty gates and ivy-clad gables, and the icing team soon falls into deep concentration, working away.

Fern and Shell roll up their sleeves and muck in with setting up a stall to sell the gingerbread hearts we made yesterday – wrapping biscuits in cellophane bags, again courtesy of Sully – and decorating each with a red ribbon tie.

Very soon there's a happy assembly line bringing together our village in miniature, the children's happy chatter punctuated by the crunch of Patrick and Bobbie's staple guns as they transform the gym into a black box backdrop.

By noon the kids have left their wonderfully decorated gingerbread men to set and are led back to their classrooms, all beyond excited to see the finished exhibit with their handiwork on display, and it's grown so dark in the gym with the drapes across the walls we need to have the ceiling lights on and, if you don't look up at the standard issue school ceiling tiles, you could be forgiven for mistaking this place for a rather theatrical Bedouin tent in the Sahara.

Every now and then we hear the bell ring or the sound of children making their way around the school. There are bursts of giggly laughter and excitement beyond the hall doors as well as a few words of calm from teachers when things get too lairy, all accompanied by the rising aroma of Christmas lunch drifting in from the dining room.

'Turkey and all the trimmings for the volunteers?' Leo – or should I say Mr Bold since he's in head teacher mode – announces at half-one after the bell has rung for afternoon classes. 'I've asked the kitchens to keep you some.'

Downing tools, the whole team follow him out of the hall. Only Patrick and I hang back to look at the completed builds ready to be lifted into place. They look wonderful, far better than our usual efforts. It just shows what a big creative team can do when it's all just a jolly novelty and not an annual slog to the finish line for a few weary volunteers.

'How many's that left to do?' Patrick asks.

'There's still the schoolhouse and church to put together.'

'It feels like it was a lot longer than a couple of weeks ago we were making them the first time round,' Patrick says. 'A lot's changed since then.'

He's not just talking about the hall roof falling in. He sees me struggling, not knowing what to say.

'It's OK,' he tells me. 'Let's just go eat. I don't want you feeling uncomfortable around me. Come on.' He walks away, heading for the door, and I follow.

Everything has changed, Patrick's right. I'll never be able to go back to being the person I was before we kissed, and I know now that I can't just switch off this feeling of wanting more and how difficult it is, knowing I can't have him.

—

After the crackers have been cracked and the terrible jokes told, and the roast turkey, pigs in blankets and delicious roasties washed down with orange squash, we're back in the gym and everyone is standing around me peering at the images I printed out at home eleven months ago when I was first planning this year's event. I'd pasted them into a notebook for inspiration.

'It's possible I was being a teeny bit too ambitious, trying to emulate the famous Pepperkakebyen,' I say. 'But this was what I was thinking.'

Tommy Brash and one of the mums had to get back to work, but everyone else is inspecting the images. Patrick and Izz hang back. They've already seen them.

'Pepper-coke-u-bee-in?' Shell echoes back at me.

'That's the one,' I say. 'The Pepperkakebyen is a historic Norwegian gingerbread exhibit in Bergen. All the locals help out and it's a huge deal every winter. They have loads of bakers contributing, a true community event.'

'It's magical,' Fern coos, bending closer to the images of the many hundreds of buildings and landmarks all laid out amidst train tracks and working Ferris wheels and cruise ships.

'Impressive,' says Lolla. 'It's the lighting that makes it,' she adds.

Everything in the images is softly washed with a blue wintry glow reminiscent of the northern lights. It makes the glittery icing shimmery. It sets a cool, otherworldly mood.

My mind's ticking over, and when I look to Patrick, I see he's thinking hard too, absently rubbing his fingers over his chin.

'You weren't *in love* with the electric lighting on this year's first exhibit, were you, Margi?' he asks me.

I don't like to admit it, not when he worked so hard to make all the buildings glow.

I pull a hidden-lipped smile of apology. 'It's not that it wasn't beautiful,' I reply, aware everyone's listening. 'It was *so* beautiful!'

'But it didn't have the right feel?' he coaxes.

'No,' I admit. 'Something didn't feel quite right.'

'And all the dry ice and whirring motors and hydraulics?' he adds. It's not really a question. He draws a deep breath and exhales. 'I reckon… our new venue's gingerbread grotto would feel cosier by candlelight,' he says, now addressing the helpers. 'The way Margi's mum always did it.'

I want to gasp and say, *That's it. That's what was wrong the other night at the hall.* All the lights and smoke and hydraulics weren't necessary. I want to hug him, the relief is so strong, but I don't.

Instead, I say, 'Mum did tell me to keep it simple, that's what people want. Patrick, do you know where to get, like, two hundred candles?'

He looks at his watch then nods assuredly.

'I'll be back in a while,' he says, striding away.

'So we're going back to basics?' Izz asks, excitement in her voice.

'I think so,' I tell her, closing the notebook. 'Something more heartfelt.'

'Doing it for the 'gram?' one of the mums asks as she ties on her apron.

'Actually, no,' I say gently. 'Let's do it for us. For Wheaton. And our beautiful hall. And for my mum, and all the kiddies,' I say.

'All right, then. You heard the boss,' says Izz. 'But it's half-two already and there's still hours of work ahead of us. Even on a normal year it could take us twenty-four hours or longer to assemble the whole display.'

'And we have...?' asks Fern.

'Until bedtime,' I tell her. 'But we've got our images from Bergen as inspiration, we've got the people power, we're...'

I'm halted in delivering the end of my inspirational pep talk by the arrival of Sully. He's carefully ferrying his own creations made this morning at the bakery.

'I'll unpack them over here,' he says, finding a spot in the corner.

'Well, you all know what to do,' I say, giving up with a grin. 'Action stations.'

We've been working for a good hour and the school bell's rung and all the kids have screeched and laughed their way off school grounds. Tomorrow's their last day of term and you can feel the anticipation in their retreating chatter.

The traffic noise dies away too. I only notice it when it's gone and we're left with the total silence of us shuffling gingerbread builds into place and tearing off hunks of white fluffy stuff from a roll to make the snowy landscapes around them.

Patrick returns with a big box of battery-operated tealights and sets to work again on building the grotto area.

It's dark outside when Mrs Slaughter appears at the hall doors. At first, I think she's going to ask us to leave so she can lock up, which makes my heart pound, we're nowhere near finished. But instead, she summons me, Patrick and Izz out of the gym's fire doors and into the car park. 'Delivery for you,' she says. 'These all need signing for.'

There, by the school gates, is a red Royal Mail van, and piled by its open doors are umpteen boxes of all shapes and sizes, and all of them, it turns out, are addressed to The Gingerbread Christmas Village, Wheaton. A few of them say they're for Izz in particular. All of them are marked *Fragile*.

Once we get them inside, the little crowd of volunteers gathers once more to watch us ripping the tape on the first box, Sully perching beside me on the ground.

I lift out a letter from the top of a bubble-wrapped package. I read the note aloud. 'For the Wheaton ginger-bread grotto. We hope this arrives in one piece, with best wishes, from the Wheaton bakery, Nebraska!'

'No way!' Shell's eyes goggle. Fern reaches for the letter, checking it over.

'That's one of Wheaton's twinned villages,' Izz informs us, and I cut short the expressions of amazement by gently removing the bubble wrap from the Nebraskan bakery's traditional candy-covered house with a ginger-bread animal leaning against its beautifully iced front panel.

Lolla gasps. 'Is that a moose?'

'It's some kind of deer,' I say, peering closely. 'With a little white tail. Isn't it beautiful?'

Patrick takes the build in silent astonishment and carries it to a display table, and then we all fall to opening the other boxes.

'Just like Christmas morning!' one of Sully's delivery men remarks.

In minutes we've revealed gingerbread creations from all across the globe, from libraries, baking clubs, book groups, societies and sororities. I keep every letter and postcard so they can be displayed with their creation. Every one is lifted onto a table in the exhibit. At first, Lucy directs their placement, separating the builds out into roughly themed areas.

She says, 'The waterfall-and-rocks scene from Cork should sit there on the wild table with the Nebraska house and all those reindeer biscuits on their little stands from the Cairngorms.'

Sully takes the multi-coloured IKEA building that made us all laugh in delight when we pulled it from the box – sent from a Swedish school after the kids voted for the subject matter, according to their teacher's letter – and he places it with an Eiffel Tower and an understated, not-at-all-to-scale-with-everything-else Little Mermaid from

Copenhagen. And it doesn't matter one bit that increasingly, there's little rhyme or reason to their placement.

'Think of the Pepperkakebyen,' I say. 'People from all over Norway send in their builds to Bergen. It hardly matters if they're not all the same size or style, does it? It's how it feels that's important.'

There's a huge box from a school in Edinburgh with a delicately wrapped gingerbread building representing a gold-domed Ukrainian church, according to their note, and the whole thing is absolutely covered in yellow and blue iced loveheart biscuits with a child's name on each one.

This stops us in our tracks while we gaze at it and Patrick says there's nothing stopping us putting it right at the end of Wheaton high street where our own little world ends, and so we do. And next to that, Fern places a wonderfully bonkers garden of gingerbread flowers with cat faces peeping out from green biscuit shrubberies that arrived with no letter or clue as to who sent it whatsoever.

'I think a pretty jumble might be the way forward,' Lucy agrees, as the tables begin to get full.

We're all so high with the excitement of setting out our display by now, adding in Sully's Wheaton Village Hall (complete with gaping hole in the ceiling), which ends up beside a windmill from Amsterdam with sails that actually spin.

Lolla had slipped out. I only realise when she comes bursting back in just after six o'clock with her husband. She's carrying a crate of Coke cans, and he's got a big, flat, dusty box under his arm and little Ben holding on to his dad's trouser leg.

'Train set,' the landlord says, setting it on the stage by the grotto.

'And vintage too, by the look of it,' adds Fern happily.

'Like the peppery bee caken, or however you say it?' Lolla adds. 'They had a train set in those pictures.'

Patrick's on it like a shot, saying he's got just the spot for it, and he and The Salutation lot unpack it and pretty soon there's a steam train running smoothly around a big gingerbread Taj Mahal made by schoolkids in Small Heath.

Shell appears to point out that a Taj Mahal seems like a good nod to the 'whole history of spices and colonialism', and most of the workers stop and listen as she goes on to explain, 'It's not like you could ever have cute gingerbread houses all covered in snow here in England without bloody massacres and oppression overseas during Britain's colonialist invasions and violent takeover of the spice routes.' She stops for a big breath, looking very serious.

'Uh, right,' I say. 'Yes, well, I suppose that's true. I hadn't thought about it quite like that. Er, well done.'

Fern is by Shell's side and squeezes her arm proudly, and with everyone looking at our exhibit in a newer light, we fall back to work.

A small delegation turns to helping Patrick add the finishing touches to Santa's grotto behind it's big screens, placing the same old red velveteen drapes over a couple of chairs that we always use. Once some fairy lights are strung up in there, it's not that bad, nothing like as pretty as the Dunham Gravey grotto, but then again, this isn't the Dunham Gravey grotto; it's unmistakeably a Wheaton effort.

Still, I whisper to Lucy to drive along to my cottage and bring the Christmas tree from the den and grabbing a can of cola, she leaves, kissing me on the cheek first.

I think she's happy. This is what she's good at. Being creative, being in a school, getting stuck into a project. Maybe it'll be enough to encourage her back to work in January? I've no idea.

By the time we've taken a break to drink our sodas, Lucy's back with the tree, a little more bedraggled now it's been heaved in and out of the back of her little car, but Fern quickly fixes it up, and it looks wonderful peeping out of the grotto area.

Once the donated builds are positioned on the tables along with our Wheaton cottages there are only a few spaces left unfilled. I have a feeling we'll be taking delivery of more gingerbread creations in the morning if today's surprise arrivals are anything to go by. I fight back a tug at my heart that wants me to stop and have a little overwhelmed cry about all this. What a day!

There are volunteers all over the place, flopped on the floor wherever they've been working, saying they're done in and ready for bed.

I see Fern and Izz talking quietly by the doors before Izz leaves for the night. I wonder if she's giving Fern her cards for missing shifts and being late and generally airy-fairy in her approach to employment, but their conversation ends in a hug, so I think she'll hang on to make another lot of fried breakfasts.

I smile at Izz's soft-heartedness. Maybe the village is taking Fern to their hearts. She has, after all, mobilised all these people and all these bakers from across the planet, intent on keeping our gingerbread exhibit on the road.

As soon as Izz leaves, Fern's on her phone again, but this time before she lifts her camera she makes sure to check no one has any objections to being filmed, and we're all so tired we don't object but let her pan around, talking into her camera as she updates our followers on what she's calling the 'installation' so far.

–

I'm so tired I can hardly move the broom. The others left hours ago, once they were satisfied the very last gumdrop was iced down, and every roof that needed it was appropriately dusted with an icing sugar and edible glitter snow flurry. There'd been a brief moment of hysterics when the east wing of the Tower of London caved in, but Lucy bodged it back together with an icing 'tree' and to be fair, it wasn't awful, and we were all too exhausted to do any more anyway, so it'll have to do. They'll all be asleep by now, I reckon.

It's nearing twelve. I'm grubby, I'm hungry and close to overdosing on cinnamon and ginger – I swear, I've absorbed the stuff through my pores – and Patrick takes the broom from my hands, leans it out of sight under a black swag and asks, 'Shall we see what it's like with the candles lit?'

Wheaton church bells ring out for midnight as Patrick stations me right in the middle of the room, surrounded by exhibit tables, and tells me to close my eyes.

His jumper was discarded long ago and his brown shirtsleeves are rolled up, smudges of sugar and coloured icing up his arms. He's tired too, hasn't stopped all day, but he still looks handsome and put together in a way I'm sure I don't.

I get my last glimpse of him under the gym's harsh strip lights as the last bell chimes from the church tower and he flips a switch and plunges us into darkness.

There isn't a crack of light in the place.

Nevertheless, he tells me to close my eyes again, and I listen as he makes his way around the room. I could keep my tired eyes closed like this forever, just knowing he's nearby.

Soon a dawning awareness of his proximity reaches me, and his pinkie finger touches then curls around mine.

'OK, have a look,' he says, dropping my pinkie. I have a second to register how much I miss the touch of him before I open my eyes, instantly forgetting all the sad, tired, conflicted mess of the last few days.

On every white cloth-draped table our gloriously raggle-taggle gingerbread buildings and the soft, snowy spaces around them are lit subtly by tea lights, the little melted boiled sweet stained-glass windows reflecting their glow.

Above it all, invisibly suspended from the ceiling, hangs a foil paper moon, Lucy's idea, so simple and so pretty catching the candlelight.

'It's perfect,' I say, my voice croaky.

'Uh-huh,' he says, jamming his hands into his pockets, something I'm noticing him doing more and more when he's around me.

Before they left for the day, the volunteers had helped string metres of white lights on black flex over the drapes hiding the walls, disguising the fact this is a gymnasium, and now each little bulb is gleaming against the black like stars in a winter sky.

'It doesn't look a bit like Mum's exhibit,' I say. 'But it feels more like it than any gingerbread village I ever made in the past.'

'It's got heart,' Patrick says.

'And simplicity,' I add.

'Oh, and it's got a little train,' Patrick says, remembering, and leaping forward to turn a switch under the engine. The steam train powers along its track, drawing my eye to its own little light in its cabin where a tiny driver traffics open wagons behind him, which Lucy had the bright idea of filling with sweets, turning it into the 'Candy Express', as she called it.

'The kids will love it. All of it,' I say.

Eventually, after taking it all in, I sit down on the edge of the low stage by the entrance to the grotto where the Santa suit hangs ready for its first outing of the year. Tomorrow the schoolkids will get a sneak preview of the exhibit on their very last day of term.

Leo Bold, the superhead who didn't believe in nativities, or grottos, or even in Wheaton village, having experienced a Christmas miracle of his own, has offered to wear the suit in the morning for his pupils. The presents are waiting in the grotto for them: the usual chocolate coins – I'd already bought them so they're having them – and sack loads of teddy bears, donated by Dunham Gravey management at Patrick's request, every one of them wearing a little green branded fleecy jumper.

'We should get going,' says Patrick, but he still sits down beside me, lowering himself slowly. 'Ooft! It won't be easy waking for work tomorrow,' he says.

'Another epic shift?' I ask.

'Yep, the school day then Dunham till midnight,' he says, and my chest aches at the thought of everything this man sacrifices to help me out.

'Thank you for doing all of this,' I say.

'It's my pleasure.'

Even with a day's stubble showing, his skin's pretty in this light. I hope I look a tenth as pretty.

'I owe you an apology,' he says out of nowhere.

'You do? What for?'

'For pursuing you when it's abundantly clear you're not interested.'

'That's not true.' My sleepy brain is suddenly flooded with adrenalin at the abrupt straying into the danger zone.

He looks at me wordlessly.

'It's not that I'm not interested. I'd have to be crazy not to be.'

'It's the age thing? Still?'

'That and other stuff,' I say, not wanting to go over it all again but realising it's time Patrick heard it all out loud, so he can grasp it once and for all, the reasons why we shouldn't be together. 'You could have a young girlfriend. Someone in their thirties, even,' I say, and I feel a bit sick and, frankly, jealous of the imaginary thirty-year-old he's besotted with. 'I've stopped a man from having kids before, you know? John. My first husband. For a long time he kept it hidden, but in the end, the need was too strong in him. He wanted to be a father, and now he has two kids of his own, grown-ups by now, I should think.'

Patrick fixes me with his eyes. 'I want *you*, though. I don't need kids.'

I'm not going to insist he'll change his mind one day when he meets the right person. It always grated when people said it to me.

'Why do you want me?' I plead. 'I really, really don't get it.'

'I don't know,' he states plainly, and that takes me aback. 'No, no,' he adds hurriedly. 'I just like *everything* about you. Your style, your body, your smile, your eyes. The way you fight and fight for the community, even when you're on the back foot. You never give up. And I just like being with you. Isn't all that enough?'

The words make me dizzy on top of my tiredness. I want to sink into him right now, to make no objections. I want to give in.

'I'm in my sixties. You're in your forties. That means something.'

'I'll be fifty soon enough. Will it matter then? And I beg to differ. Look,' he says, pointing to where his eyelids meet his temples. 'If I'm such a child, what do you call these?'

He means the little kisses at the corners of his eyes. I can't tell him that I call them that. I say nothing at all.

'Margi, you don't get to tell me how to feel about ageing. I've been going silver for years and barely even thought about it, but you leaving your hair uncoloured is supposed to be some kind of affront to society?'

'Yes. To all the Kenneths,' I joke.

'But that's bullshit. The difference in standards is crazy. You're no older than Jamie Lee Curtis or Sharon Stone or Michelle Pfeiffer, and they're all hot as hell.'

I scoff at this, but it's hollow sounding. There's so little resolve left in me.

'Look at Catherine Zeta-Jones and Michael Douglas,' he says. 'There's like twenty-five years between them, isn't there?'

I cast my mind back to when *OK!* and *Hello!* went bonkers for their wedding and all the salacious, unkind jokes made about them in the press. That must be two decades ago at least.

'They've been together for ages, haven't they?' he says.

'They have,' I agree.

'So, did their age gap matter, really?'

'Not fair!' I protest weakly, wanting to close my eyes and slump into a sleepy pile on the stage but making myself fight like I can really win this. 'Age-gap millionaires are nothing like normal age-gappers! I can't afford to get things lifted or filled for a start.'

'I'd hate it if you did.'

'You say that now, but give it twenty years and I'll literally look like Michael Douglas! Then what?'

He laughs, and there are those eye kisses again, sending starlight in lines across his temples.

'I think you're running out of excuses not to want me,' he says.

'Wanting you was never the problem.'

'I won't hurt you. I won't leave you. I won't humiliate you. I'm not fickle. I'm not Don. And I don't care about village tattletales, and neither should you. Not when there's this thing between us.'

And that's how my resolve snaps. Blinking at him in the glowing light in the silence of the empty school after midnight, I have nothing left to throw at him.

His eyes are searching my face as I lift myself towards him, and he lets me draw my leg over his, straddling him. He doesn't touch me yet.

'Let me?' I ask before – as slowly as I can so I know that he's certain – I kiss him, and the electrical connection between us buzzes back into life.

His hands rise up over my thighs and wrap around me to the base of my spine. He straightens his body, pulls me hard towards him, and we're goners, kissing uncontrollably in the glow of the little world we've made for ourselves, forgetting everything and everyone outside.

Chapter Eighteen

Wednesday 20 December: Dawning

I'm dreaming on a soft bed with a heartbeat at my ear. Warm. I can go back to sleep. With my eyes closed I still see Patrick's lips. Patrick's chest. Hmmm, tiredness in my whole body. I stretch out.

It's so dark. There's no morning alarm for a while yet. How I love a deep winter's sleep. I let myself dream again.

Voices penetrate the haze. Funny, that sounds like Sully. He's saying, 'I made one more gingerbread house.'

There's his Leo too. 'It's cute, Sull, but I don't recognise it. Is it a Wheaton cottage?'

Soft. Soft. Pulling the covers over me. No need to get up yet.

'I thought that might be our house,' Dream Sully is saying to Leo.

Sweet Sully. Sounds like he's blushing. There's laughter. A kiss.

Oh, I don't want to get out of bed. It's still early.

There are children laughing. Getting louder. Footsteps…

Footsteps?

I jolt awake the second the school bell rings.

'Oh no! Oh no!' My heart's pounding. I cover my ears. Was I drinking last night? Was I…?

'Oh shit!' Patrick says, springing awake beside me.

We've slept the night away on the floor of the grotto, wrapped in metres of red velvet drape and our winter coats.

Patrick's bleary-eyed but on his feet already, buttoning his shirt.

'Shh!' I pull him towards me. I jab my finger in the direction of our exhibit. 'Out there behind the screens, I think I heard Sully and Leo. They can't know we're here,' I whisper.

The sound of children chattering gets louder and my tired eyes bulge.

'We have a very special surprise for you, Year One,' says a teacher just outside the hall doors.

Oh my God! The kids are coming in here!

Patrick rushes over to where we chucked off our shoes and bundles them up in his arms.

'Handbag, handbag,' I hiss, and he has to run back to locate it.

'This way.' He yanks me towards the side fire exit, keys in a code, presses the bar lock down, and we're outside in the icy chill of Wednesday morning.

I hear the kids filing into the exhibition, still beautifully lit from the night before. They're gasping and shrieking at the transformation in their gymnasium just as Patrick eases the door closed behind us.

We pull on our boots and outer layers in the bitter cold. It's only just growing light out here behind the school by the big bins.

'I was only going to close my eyes for a minute,' I say.

'Me too,' he laughs. 'How is it eight forty-five? Come here.' He leads me further round the back of the school and into a padlocked shed he has the keys for.

'I can make you coffee?' he says once we're inside. There's barely room to move for piled logs, tools and stacks of papers, but I see a kettle and a mini fridge.

'I should get back. Lucy won't know where I am.' I check my phone. No messages. No missed calls.

Patrick notices and says with a smile. 'I reckon she has a pretty good idea where you are. Or at least who you're with.'

'Oh God,' I laugh, my face in my hands. 'You should get to work. Leo... Mr Bold will be wondering where you are.'

'Not yet,' he says, firing up the heater at my feet and straightening up before me, taking my hands in his. 'Come here.' He pulls me into a hug.

'I feel like we were at a party and we drank a bottle of vodka,' I say.

'Me too,' he says, still holding on. 'It's the exhaustion. I can't believe we've got the gingerbread grotto ready in time.'

I pinch my eyelids with my fingertips, still leaning firmly against Patrick's chest. 'My head hurts.'

He rocks me a little from side to side. I let him. *This is easy*, I hear myself think.

'This is nice,' he says, and I know we're still as in tune as we were last night when we kissed for hours like teenagers, getting hotter and wilder until I guess we passed out, only meaning to rest for minutes. I remember thinking how I was going to follow him back to his place up School Lane and over the recreation ground. I remember thinking how nice it would be to take him to bed. And then, we were asleep.

'Oh God, imagine if the kids had caught us sleeping in Santa's grotto!' I say, hiding my face in his neck.

263

'I know.' His body rocks with a silent laugh. Nothing is loud or forced or exaggerated this morning. We're past all of the hard work of liking each other, and now we just get to do this. We get to be together, comfortable, quiet, relaxed.

Now it's my turn to say, 'This is nice.' And what I'm really thinking is, *This is how it's going to be from now on*, and I sigh into his shoulder, hold on to his waist and thank my lucky stars I wasn't too afraid to let Patrick in.

–

After the quickest cup of coffee, drank from one shared mug, he insists he's going to walk me home, which is totally unnecessary but extremely lovely, and it's not until we sneak through the side gate and onto the high street that I realise Wheaton is under some kind of invasion.

It's nine fifteen. The school-run traffic should have cleared by now but there are cars and vans on the double yellows all along the road and the traffic warden is on the march, writing tickets, knocking at drivers through their windows, saying, 'You can't park here.'

I can see Izz still in her long crossing coat holding her lollipop stick at the bottom of the village hall steps. She should be finished for the morning and getting the cafe open. What's she doing up at the hall? There are a few council vehicles along there with their orange flashy roof lights spinning, and there are people queueing all over the place.

A crowd with big cardboard boxes are waiting at the main school gates to be let in.

'Gingerbread builds?' Patrick says to me, still holding my hand as we call off our walk to my place and make our way along the street to investigate the hubbub.

I turn up my jacket collar, not that it'll do much good hiding my unbrushed hair and yesterday's face. I must look a fright. Patrick hasn't said a thing about it, but my eyes hurt from lack of sleep and my skin feels dry. I need a shower, a ten-hour nap and a whole bottle of moisturiser to set me right again.

'Excuse me,' Patrick says, getting the attention of one of the people in the school queue. 'I'm the school care-taker. Do you mind telling me what's in the box?'

'Oh,' says the young man, and the teenage girl he's with turns too. 'It's a gingerbread greenhouse and allotment.'

Of course it is.

'But why are you here?' I ask.

'We set off at four, from Carlisle. Wanted to make sure it arrived in time.'

'Right,' I say, astonished, and others in the crowd start sharing what's in their boxes. Some of these people, I recognise − they're locals, parents and grandparents of schoolkids. Others have come a long way to drop off their handiwork.

I spot Mrs Slaughter making her way from the school office across the schoolyard with the key to the gate to take delivery of their builds. I suppose there's plenty of room for them if we shove some of the others together a bit or add some extra tables. Think of the Pepperkakebyen, I tell myself, and all those gorgeous builds packed in side by side, a gingerbread city, not just a village. Ours will look the same. How wonderful!

'Let's go.' I pull Patrick away, not wanting the school secretary to see me and Patrick all unkempt and loitering about this early. She'd definitely put two and two together.

We make our way towards the village hall as car doors swing open across the pavement in front of us and, mostly, young people step out, telling drivers – their parents, I suspect – that they won't be long. Some are holding their phones up, already recording, narrating their arrival in Wheaton. There's a queue of them outside the village hall, presumably wanting to get a video 'for their socials', to quote Lucy.

I don't, however, notice the outside broadcast van parked right in front of the hall until we get closer.

'He's going to get a ticket,' says Patrick as we approach.

There's a camera operator and a presenter I recognise from the local news.

'First time *they've* ever set foot in Wheaton. I thought we were too local for the local news?' I say, but my wisecrack falls flat when I notice there's someone mic-ing up Izz as she stands on the steps of the hall. They're running a wire up inside her *Children Crossing* coat.

'Izz! You OK?' I shout over the heads of the people gathered there, snapping photos of her and of the council workers as they traipse in and out of the building. It sounds like some repairs are underway already, or is it the start of the demolition?

'They want me to do an interview,' Izz shouts back, her eyes wide.

Someone with headphones and a radio mic at their lips starts clearing the way through the spectators so the interviewer can ascend the steps to Izz.

'Is she all right?' Patrick asks me, looking concerned for our friend.

'She looks like a rabbit in the headlights. Should we intervene?'

'Sign here,' the headphone person's saying to Izz, showing her papers on a clipboard. 'And here.'

'Hey, what is that?' I shout out, but the crew take no notice of me.

'It's a waiver, I think?' Izz calls back over their heads.

'Standard permissions,' I hear Headphones telling her – a little tersely, to my mind.

Within seconds, someone's counting down, and there's a lull in the crowd's murmuring.

'Good morning, West Midlands,' the interviewer announces in a sprightly burst. 'I'm Annabella Gormley, and welcome to Wheaton Village Hall which was condemned last week by the local council who have plans to redevelop the site for luxury properties. I'm joined by…' – Annabella looks at the notes in her hand – 'Isobel Armstrong, local lollipop lady. Can you tell me what the hall means to you?'

Izz stares down at the microphone that the woman's thrust under her nose. The cameraman moves in closer.

'I, uh…' she begins tremulously, glancing over to me, helpless here in the crowd. 'I, uh… I danced here all through my teens. It was a big part of my life. Uh… we would watch movies projected onto the wall of the foyer.' She shakes her head, frustrated with herself, but the interviewer seems happy with that. She's already moved on to the next question.

Izz looks breathless. I manoeuvre myself so I can watch what's being broadcast in one of many little screens stationed around the cameraman. A red ticker tape of headline news runs along the bottom of the monitor while a *Cotswold's Focus Feature* logo rotates in the top corner. I throw Izz a thumbs up, though she doesn't see.

'Viewers might recognise you as the woman at the centre of a viral video in which you appeal against the hall's closure. Why do you think the hall should stay open for the community?'

Izz is shaking her head over the mic. She gulps, her eyes darting around across the crowd then back to the interviewer in a silent appeal for mercy. 'I... I...' she stammers. 'The hall is ours,' is all she manages, before the interviewer, sensing failure, turns away from Izz, leaving her unsure what to do in the back of shot.

'Also joining us this morning are Councillors Scavenger and Carruthers, the men behind the controversial planning process that could see this historic community asset gutted and turned into luxury dwellings. Good morning, gentlemen.'

'It's Scrimengor,' grumbles the old baker as soon as the camera finds him on the edge of the crowd.

'How do you feel about Ms Armstrong and her viral fundraiser bringing one hundred thousand pounds in donations from across the world in a matter of days?'

'Have they?' gulps Mr Scrimengor, looking a tiny bit impressed in spite of the shock.

'According to their fundraising totaliser this morning, they have,' Annabella tells him.

I recall Fern filming the exhibit late last night. She must have posted it already. Could that be the reason for this latest jump in donations?

Rodney Carruthers takes the mic from the interviewer like this is his TV show.

'That's not going to be enough to save the hall, sadly. It would require more than double that to carry out the repairs needed and get it up to a standard safe for community events. We're talking dangerous levels of corroded pipework, falling plaster, ancient electrics and now a perilously water-damaged floor. The place is a death-trap. What it needs is investment with a construction partner willing to plough in funds. We're working with the very best architects to see our planning application come to fruition and conserve this magnificent building for generations to come.'

'Yes, the shell, maybe.' Izz steps up, surprising me with her courage. 'You want to gut the place. It won't be a community space any longer. We want to be having clubs and sports and parties and dancing here for another seventy years.'

The small crowd cheers.

Annabella turns back to Izz with a gleam in her eye like this woman isn't quite the lost cause she thought she was. 'Ms Armstrong, there's been much speculation about the whereabouts of one village resident, Alexi Thorne. I'm hearing in my ear that the studio are running some of that viral footage of the pair of you now, so if any viewers have been sleeping under a rock and don't recognise you, they'll be able to see the video. You were romantically linked with Alexi Thorne? Are you hoping for a reunion now you've made Wheaton famous?'

'What?' Izz gasps, her hand at her chest, all her confidence bursting like a bubble.

'And what do you say to rumours that the claims made by some members of the public online, that Alexi has been located living in England, are merely the work of malicious trolls?'

'Trolls?' Izz repeats.

'Hoaxers? Liars?' Annabella presses.

'That's enough,' I shout, barging through the crowds and up the hall steps to rescue my friend.

Patrick, refusing to drop my hand, comes with me and we form a sort of human shield between Izz and the interviewer.

'And who are you?' the woman asks me.

It's at this moment I realise the camera is right in my face. Upon the monitor over the cameraman's shoulder, I see myself plastered with yesterday's mascara in Alice Cooper streaks down my face. My Avon extra-lasting lipstick in 'Devil Red' has, since I reapplied it at nine last night, made its way across my mouth in a wide smudge, and my hair is tufted up at the back where I slept on it. I'm trying to sort it out with a rake of my hands and a tissue scrubbed at my face but the damage is well and truly done and there's a mic in my hand somehow.

'Thanks for asking, um, Annabella. I'm Margi Frost.' I look at the crowd and not the camera. 'My mum set up the Wheaton gingerbread village display to fundraise for the community over sixty years ago.' I'm getting into my stride now. 'The grotto was staged here in Wheaton Village Hall until it was condemned by the council, and now me, Izz and Patrick here, we run the gingerbread village together. All of Wheaton got involved this year and we're set up at our temporary venue in the school gymnasium where friends of the Wheaton Village Hall are still queueing up to drop off their gingerbread bakes to add to our wonderful display.'

It's safe to say I'm enjoying myself now and I decide to plant my feet and make the very most of this free fundraising opportunity.

'The exhibit opens today at three thirty and runs every afternoon until Christmas Eve. There'll be mulled wine and gingerbread cookies on sale. Tickets are available on the door. Come down and help save Wheaton Village Hall and support a fantastic local community enterprise.'

There are whoops and cheers from the crowd and Patrick squeezes my hand. This is it, my moment of triumph. God, I hope Mum and Dad are watching, and Lucy too.

I'm not done yet. The crowd spurs me on. 'For once, we're getting the attention we deserve,' I yell, gripping on to the mic even though Annabella's trying to yank it from me. 'Save Wheaton Village Hall!' I cry, and the crowd echoes my words back at me just as the interviewer wrestles the mic away.

I'm too elated to care. I got my point across and we're live on the telly. The vloggers and TikTokers and Instagrammers are catching every word on their phones too so we'll be live across the country right now, no, live all over the world, wherever there's Wi-Fi.

'And you? Patrick, did you say?' Annabella is asking, turning her attention to my boyfriend. *Yes, I said boyfriend.*

She's being a bit smiley and forward with him, I notice. Far more smiley than she was with me or either of the old buffers on the council.

Patrick nods sharply, and looks from me to the camera lens, preparing for the question on Annabella's lips.

'So, Margi's your mum. What do you think of her fundraising? It's not every day a village's retired community steps up in protest at their local authority's decisions, is it? You must be a very proud son.'

'His *mum*?' I've shrieked it already so there's no stopping the giggles and shocked looks from the crowd.

'That's not my mother,' Patrick says, his cheeks reddening. 'She's my... uh, she's...'

I stare at him, unblinking, frozen in panic. What the hell's he going to say? She's my girlfriend? A friend? A colleague? *Say something, Patrick.* Is he going to lay claim, live on telly, to the mad woman who was just shouting nonsense into the mic? The woman with the sticky-up hair and yesterday's make-up smears? The woman who got all carried away, yet again, and convinced herself one thing was happening when in fact the reality was something completely different?

Patrick's opening and closing his mouth, hesitating, and looking to me like I might have the answer that's evading him. He doesn't have the words for what I am to him. And if he does, he's too ashamed to say them out loud.

'Oh God,' I say. 'Oh no.'

And that's when my feet tell me to get the hell away from all these cameras and the amazed, wide-eyed people dying from second-hand embarrassment.

'They're not *together*, are they?' I hear someone in the crowd, a young woman, saying. And I cover my ears, guessing what's coming next and not wanting to hear it. *Eww! Cringe!* Just like those girls said at my street collection.

I'm dragging Izz by the hand, darting through the onlookers. Behind us, Annabella signs off, 'Back to the studio,' and with our heads down, Izz and I disappear out of sight, round the back of the hall, and in through the back door. I'd only returned the key to the front door and now I'm glad of my stubbornness.

We only stop when we're panting against the cabinets in the hall's kitchen cubby. I'm already replaying what just happened, my brain picking over the memory, my mouth dropping expletives in a filthy string.

'Oh shit, oh shit, oh shit. He was horrified! He was embarrassed.' I look down at my body, seeing yesterday's grubby clothes, and I scrunch my nested hair in my hands with a groan. 'Of course he was.'

But Izz, in spite of her grip on my arm, isn't hearing me.

'Trolls?' she's saying. 'Hoaxers? So... Alexi's *not* going to be found? They're lying? The people on the internet?'

I snap out of the storm in my head to pull her close to me.

'I'm so sorry,' I tell her. 'What a mess I've made.'

And we hide out, wide-eyed in the unlit kitchen, trying to figure out what on earth we're supposed to do now.

–

'So? You're... hiding?'

Lucy is justifiably incredulous when she comes to our rescue bringing two bacon baps from Izz's – Fern is doing a good job of running the cafe in Izz's absence, it seems – and hot tea in takeaway cups.

'We're... regrouping,' I say, trying to sound dignified.

At least the council workers seem to have cleared out of the hall building, probably warned off by their bosses about the snooping people gathered outside. It makes me wonder if they have the authority even to be in here when the place is still at the start of the planning application and we still have our stake in saving it.

'Has everyone gone?' asks Izz, unwrapping her breakfast.

'The TV people have. There's still a bunch of gawpers out there, and a minibus of dudes in suits from Historic

England? They were keen to talk with Scrimengor and the other one.'

'Carruthers,' I say miserably. 'Good, let them all talk, as long as we're left alone. You didn't see it, did you?'

She knows exactly what I mean.

'I think everyone's seen it,' she says, nodding. I don't want to think about what she means by 'everyone'.

'Am I the village laughing stock again?'

'Don't be silly,' she says unconvincingly.

'Lucy?' says Izz. 'Can I borrow your phone?'

'Sure.'

'Make it go on the village hall video thing. The one where the person said they were Alexi's grandchild?'

'You sure?' Lucy asks, but Izz only gestures for her to hurry.

We draw up two chairs at the very edge of the hall next to the kitchen door and we look at the tarpaulin-covered hole in the ceiling and the spot where our gingerbread display was. Now, presumably, it's all in a council skip on its way to landfill.

Lucy plonks herself down beside me and we let Izz wander away to scroll through the comments. She leaves her food untouched.

'Want a bite, Luce?' I say, holding out my sandwich, but she declines, so I get to work on it hungrily. 'I haven't had anything since yesterday lunchtime.'

She only looks at me. 'I figured you were busy.'

'Don't give me that face,' I say, not wanting to laugh when it actually hurts so much. 'It's not even a thing now,' I tell her. 'Let's just forget the last few days with him, OK?'

Lucy takes this in, surveying my face. 'What do you want to do now? You can't hide in here. I mean, this place could literally fall down on top of you.'

'What do I want to do now?' I repeat.

It's now or never.

In fact, I can't think of a better time to tell her I'm decided. I'm going to cut and run. Do a Don.

'Lucy,' I say, wrapping up the roll and setting it aside. 'There's something I need to tell you.'

'OK, me too,' she says.

'Well, me first, because it's big, and I haven't said anything because I wasn't sure, but with everything that's been going on...'

Lucy's drawn her hands over her mouth and her eyes are big, round, worried circles. 'Are you sick?' she says, and her voice wobbles.

'No, God no.' I pull her hands down and hold them. 'I'm leaving Wheaton.'

The slightest shake of her head shows she's processing.

'I'm going to put Mum and Dad's cottage up for sale. It's mine now, they signed it over to me when they went to Spain, so it's not *terrible* to sell up, you know? And I'm going to move.'

'OK,' she says. 'Where?'

'Well, I've been to see a nice little place, actually. In Birmingham.'

She doesn't speak, so I press on.

'I wouldn't bother you all the time if that's what you're thinking. I'd just be nearby because, uh, you probably don't know this, but when your mum and dad left for New Zealand, Lydia, um, she asked me to take care of you.'

Lucy's looking down at her hands in mine. I think she's going to cry.

'And up until now, looking after you meant us being mates and hanging out together and you've not really needed looking after, as such.'

Lucy's lifting her gaze and shaking her head.

'But now you seem so sad and lost and… if I was in Birmingham we could look after each other, and maybe you'd be a bit happier with someone who's always… right there. Lucy? You're not glad?'

She's drawn her hands away from mine and onto her lap. 'Auntie Margi, I don't understand why you'd leave everything you love. You love Wheaton. You belong here.'

'No,' I say. 'I used to, but now I'm just the crazy old lady who foists gingerbreads on a community and keeps throwing herself headlong into ridiculous love affairs that end in disaster, and I feel like everything I touch goes bad. I mean, look at Izz,' I whisper, 'and the whole viral video thing. If I hadn't roped in Fern, and if I had *tried* to protect Izz's privacy a bit more, she wouldn't be over there crying into your phone.'

We glance over at Izz leaning against the mural, her eyes fixed on the phone, her thumbs scrolling, waiting for news that will never come because contrary to what everyone thinks, the internet isn't some cure-all oracle or a harbinger of justice. It is in fact a shitshow.

'And now, not only have I dragged Izz into this mess, I've done the same to Patrick, when for ages I've been trying to protect him from me and the way I spoil things. So, I'm selling up. I'm getting out, and I'll be able to live somewhere anonymous and quiet and grow my own potatoes in my own potagerie.'

Lucy sighs.

This isn't going how I wanted it. I thought she'd be a tiny bit pleased.

'I've spoiled us as well, haven't I?' I say, my lip wobbling. 'I've interfered and I've intruded, and, oh my God, I've been a clingy old lady. Of course you don't want your auntie as a neighbour!' Now I have my hands over my mouth in horror.

'No, no. It's not that at all. I'd have loved that a year or two ago.'

'What's changed, then?'

'I should have told you,' she says, dread sneaking into my heart. 'When Craig left, I gave my landlord notice, and I came here to clear my head a bit. You've been asking about my supply teaching and I didn't know what to say, but I just needed some headspace to sort it all out before I told anyone.'

'Told us what?'

'Mum and Dad have found me a flat near them in Auckland. I'm going to teach on supply there until I can get a permanent art teacher job.'

'In New Zealand?'

'Yeah. I still have to sort out my stuff and book flights, but...' She goes quiet.

I sit for a long time, unsure what to think or feel. *Abandoned* springs to mind, but that's not fair on Lucy. I hadn't mentioned my Birmingham escape plan so why should she have shared her big New Zealand getaway idea?

'Are you still selling up?' Lucy asks eventually, and all I can do is shake my head.

I have absolutely no idea what I'm doing. A veg bed and a compact end of terrace in the outskirts of Birmingham doesn't have quite the same appeal now I know it'll just be me rattling around in it. No Lucy, no Patrick, and God knows if Izz will forgive me once the dust has settled and we're all taking stock in January.

Staying here doesn't feel like an option either. Patrick told me not to blow this, and I blew it anyway. I'm in way over my head in all of this. What a bloody shambles.

We're interrupted in our misery by the shout of Mr Collins from the council, the surveyor. He's back in his hard hat with the torch on the front, and he's not happy.

'Izz Armstrong?' he's shouting.

'Yes, yes. We're leaving. We know,' I yell out.

I stand and make my way towards Izz.

'Take one last look,' I tell her sadly. 'They're going to take my key off me, for sure.'

Lucy's behind me too, her hand on my elbow, hovering.

'Let's go back to your place,' she says. 'I have to start packing – get back to Birmingham soon.'

'Are you Izz?' Mr Collins shouts again.

'I am,' she calls back. 'What wants to know?'

'Someone's here for you. It's more than my job's worth to go scrabbling around condemned buildings looking for old ladies,' he mutters, and he trudges off, grumbling.

'What's got into him?' says Lucy, but nobody answers because there are two strangers standing in the doorway of the foyer, one a young woman in a slanting hard hat that clearly doesn't fit, and she's holding the arm of a man – a man Izz's age or thereabouts – who is looking around at the room like he's stepped inside a haunted house.

'No,' Izz says in a sharp whisper. 'It can't be.' And I watch as my friend walks towards them at the foyer doors.

'What's happening?' I ask Lucy, but she's crying for some reason.

'Quick,' she says, dragging me in Izz's wake.

We keep our distance as Izz reaches them and the man breaks away from the young girl who is also, weirdly, crying, and it's only now I see it.

I see the years falling away. I see the village hall in bright light and full colour. I see coloured bunting strung along the walls and generations of the same families laughing together, tea poured from the big silver urn, and Izz, my dear friend, I see her walking tall and lithe, her head tipped a little to one side in that girlish way she's always had, and she's stepping bravely towards the man who had held her captivated so long ago, a man who's holding his arms open to her, his chest rising and falling heavily, but with a look on his face like he's greeting his closest loved one, like no time has passed at all, and they fall into each other's arms.

Chapter Nineteen

Shutting it all out

I haven't shown my face at the gingerbread grotto, but the word on our social media streams is that they're queued round the block to get in.

Leo Bold makes an excellent Father Christmas, by all reports, and I was sent a lovely picture of Sully laughing his head off sitting on his knee.

I can smell the mulled wine in the air even from my cottage door, so I'm guessing Lolla's husband is going great guns at his stall by the school gates. Lucy tells me they're charging three quid a cup, so that'll boost the coffers even more.

I've stayed away. Haven't been needed, really, not now the exhibit's set up and everyone's got their jobs to do. I'm surplus to requirements, as I should be.

Patrick will probably have gone to Dunham for his night shift last night as usual, and goodness knows where he is now.

I've taken a day off. The first of many.

Mum was the first person to phone and congratulate us on raising the hundred grand. Even though, as Mr Carruthers suggested, it still might not be enough to stop the planning application, it's still way beyond anything we'd ever dreamed of raising, and it could go some way to throwing a spanner in the works with the luxury redevelopment.

Mum was kind enough not to say anything about Patrick. She saw it all on the expat news channels, of course. So she gets it – why I'm hanging up my apron, surrendering the measuring bowl.

Her recipe is still at Sully's bakery, so he'll know what to do when it comes to it next year. I'll be blissfully unaware.

I'm done. Had it. Knackered. Retired.

'Tea?' Izz asks.

'No thanks,' I say, lifting myself from the sofa in the den where I've sat all day watching the fire and avoiding all the phone calls.

I made the mistake of picking up the first few times. One of the glossy magazines had somehow got my landline number, wanting to do a story on age-gap romance. I'd not meant to laugh so unkindly before I put the phone down on them. Probably should have tried to be more dignified, but hey, what's dignity anyway?

Then there was a tabloid after a quote for their feature on 'going viral for all the wrong reasons'. I let Lucy handle that one, and she had a few choice words for that journalist, none of which they could quote in a national newspaper.

After that, we turned off all our devices and unplugged the landline, and it's been nice and quiet, apart from Izz and Alexi talking late into the night at the kitchen table.

We'd sneaked them out the back of the hall and into Mr Collins's van – which was very sporting of him considering the trouble we've caused him recently. Izz's cottage is reportedly still besieged by the press, and it's all been a bit much, so she's staying here another night until it all calms down.

'They can't stay in town forever,' Izz said this morning after she and Alexi did a bewildered meet-and-greet down the high street, shaking hands and being hugged by folks their story has struck a chord with. 'They'll have to go home for Christmas eventually,' she said, grateful to have my cottage to retreat to where she could talk with Alexi in peace.

Alexi's granddaughter left this morning, needing to get back to work. I'd promised her we'd take good care of him. No sooner was she driving away than Alexi turned to us and said, 'Thank goodness for that. She's a wonderful girl, but she does hover so.'

We managed a decent bit of dinner last night, but I felt increasingly like a gooseberry in my own home, and surrendering the two bedrooms for their use, Lucy and I crashed in the den. My second night out of my bed, and doesn't my back know it! I've a knot in my spine that aches every time I move, much like the knot in my heart every time I think of Patrick lost for words when asked to confirm if I was or wasn't his dear old mum or in fact his new girlfriend. Lucy's told me a hundred times we don't look like there's an age difference; it was just my unfortunately migrating make-up, and when people under thirty see natural grey hair on a woman they make stupid assumptions. None of it helped, but it was nice that she tried.

Fern arrived a few moments ago, tiptoeing inside as usual.

'It's amazing to meet you,' she says to Alexi, and she jumps back a little when he reaches out a hand to shake.

'You're the one we owe our reunion to,' Alexi says.

'I think it would have happened anyway,' she says. 'You'd have got in touch somehow.'

'Not without a push,' Izz says. 'So, shall we get this over with, then?'

It doesn't take Fern long to set up the shot, her phone mounted on a tripod with a selfie ring which, it turns out, is just a circular light that makes everyone look ten times better-looking than they are. I must get myself one for FaceTiming with Mum and Dad, see if they notice.

'Do you know what it is that you want to say?' asks Fern, and they both say they do, they've worked it out between them. They're ready.

'OK,' she says. 'So you're live when I press this button. Just wait a few minutes for viewers to join.'

I come to stand behind Fern's phone so I'm not in shot, and Lucy comes to my side, putting an arm around me. She'll be leaving soon and I don't know how I'm supposed to go on breathing. How can I have lost her and Patrick in the space of a few hours? I hold in the sob that wants to burst out of my body, and pat Lucy's hand where it rests on my arm.

Fern's giving them the nod and we all wait in silence.

Izz looks at Alexi who I imagine must be a calm, dependable, solid sort of man in his normal life. Here, though, there's been a fair bit of damp eyes and whispered conversations I wasn't privy to, and I can see the toll it's taken on him too. He looks as tired and journeyed as Izz.

'Hello,' Alexi says and looks to Izz with a nod of encouragement.

They're holding hands just out of shot.

'Hello,' my friend repeats, looking into the tiny dot lens. 'I'm Izz Armstrong. And this is Alexi Thorne.'

He smiles into Izz's eyes, and I might be wrong but they seem to get lost in each other for a second, just beaming like best friends and a little bit abashed with one another.

'We, um, we were reunited because of you,' Alexi goes on, turning to the camera once more. 'You all tried to find me because of some images you saw of us from over fifty years ago.'

'Long time, fifty-eight years,' Izz says to Alexi.

'A lifetime.'

'I was surprised that anyone was interested in our story,' Izz says, again like she's addressing Alexi.

'The first I knew about it was my granddaughter showing me the film made by a very talented young woman called Fern Brash.'

We all look at our new young friend as she watches her subjects on the camera screen and blushes.

'She recognised something in us that a lot of you recognised too,' Izz tells the viewers.

At this, Izz and Alexi fall wordless, and I can tell Alexi is finding it hard to go on. Izz lifts his hand from where she'd held it out of shot and brings it up onto her lap, cradling it now in both hands, sending quiet encouragement to him.

Alexi clears his throat. 'You could all see how much we cared for each other.'

Izz nods gently and takes over. 'And you felt for us when you found out that we had to separate.'

Alexi speaks, his voice shaky. 'I thought if anything was going to clear my head of Isobel Armstrong, it was serving my country at an army posting miles away in Malta. I hoped the sun would bake her out of my brain.' He laughs a whispery laugh. 'But I thought of you every day of my life from that point on.'

Izz and Alexi let the next part go unspoken, but I can see they're leaving a silent space for it as they look into each other's faces. The years when Alexi met a local girl, a nurse, and they had a son and lived a settled life where he'd been the provider because that's what men were supposed to do and because part of him wanted to as well. He'd said all this last night over dinner. And he shared with us how he'd told his wife about Izz and she'd been clever enough to know Malta was a world away from the Cotswolds and was contented enough to be the second love of his life, and they'd rubbed along together until she passed away leaving him a widower who filled his retirement with grandkids and gardening and trying not to reminisce.

'I lived,' Izz says, 'always wondering where the other half of me was, thinking I'd never find out.'

Alexi sweeps a tear from his own face then one from Izz's and the pair sniff and smile, and they huff a soft laugh of astonishment that this is actually happening.

'There's a lot to be said for a quiet life,' Alexi adds, and Izz nods in agreement before speaking through a big rush of smiling tears.

'But I think there's a lot more to be said for a great big unapologetically happy life where you don't care if people disapprove of you.'

Alexi pulls Izz closer and they hug, but my friend breaks away to speak directly into the camera again like she can't contain her words a moment longer.

'I've spent five decades pretending, plastering on a smile and trying to be kind and gentle the way people forgot to be kind and gentle to me when I was young and in love with someone I shouldn't have been...'

This is broken by a lot of tears from Izz that sends my hand flying up to my mouth so I don't spoil their live stream for all these viewers, over eight thousand of them, according to the little counter on the top of Fern's screen.

Izz goes on, recovering herself. 'I'm not doing that any more. No more pretending half a life is enough for a person.'

Alexi's been nodding the whole way through this, and he's smiling when he speaks next. 'When love comes for you, you have to let it happen, all you people watching,' he tells the world beyond the camera, 'you have to *let love happen*, and hold on to it. In the end, love and the things that bring happiness are the only things that matter.'

'Auntie Margi,' Lucy whispers. 'Are you OK?'

I realise my face is streaming with tears. I feel like my heart wants to burst right out of me. The whole time they were speaking I felt their words like a boxing bout.

'Where are you going?' Lucy asks as I try to find a tissue and my boots, all without getting in the way of the camera, but knowing if I'm going to get across my kitchen and out that door, that's just not possible, not if I don't have a second to waste.

'We're inviting you all to help save the Wheaton Village Hall,' Izz is saying now.

'Where we fell in love on the dance floor,' adds Alexi, and my heart swells for these two, bearing their souls like this.

'The council have condemned it,' Izz tells the audience of unseen strangers.

I'm scrabbling for my coat in the boot room, causing an avalanche of cagoules and windcheaters, which, first thing in the new year, are all going to the charity shop.

'But it's part of Cotswold history,' I hear Alexi say.

'Of our history,' Fern shouts — yes, *shouts* — and everyone laughs in surprise.

I've got my bag. I fix my face in the kitchen mirror, but it doesn't matter really.

Izz is saying, 'And we need your help. Please.'

'Got to go, sorry,' I say, nipping behind them, knowing this will prompt a stream of comments asking if that was the panda-eyed lady who was on the news yesterday holding that younger guy's hand and making a complete fool of herself. And I don't even care.

Let them laugh if they must.

–

I'm running, actually running, right down the high street and past the queues of people waiting to get into the school, some of them with their heads bent, watching the live stream from my cottage on their phones.

There are banners tied between lamp posts and street signs. They read, *Save the village hall*. One in the shape of a big gingerbread man says, *Don't discriminate against gingers*. One has my face on it – how did they make that so quickly? – and it reads, *meme mom says he's not my son*. I don't really get it, and I don't care either. It doesn't matter whether they think I'm a funny person they admire or if they're simply making fun of me. All that matters is love and the things that make you happy, and right now, I need to do a whole lot of work to get those things back because I blew it.

Wheaton looks like something between a Christmassy protest and a festival, and it's actually starting to snow and there's some singing coming from the church and if this didn't feel so urgent I might stop and take it all in but I can't.

'Have you seen him?' I shriek at the people in the queue.

I don't recognise a single one of them, but a few recognise me, and someone shouts after me, 'I saw him at the gingerbread thing.'

It's hard to get through the revellers, especially without spilling their cups of hot chocolate and mulled wine. Everyone's smiling. There are a few pieces to camera still going on. I know some people are holding their phones up as I dash past, filming me. Again it doesn't matter.

Sully's at the school door and I reach for him.

'This way,' he says, pulling me inside, and he trails behind me as I jump the queue, following the scent of gingerbread.

'He's just taking over from Leo in the grotto,' says Sully.

I keep pressing on, past the dining hall and the PE cupboard and into the gymnasium, my eyes adjusting to the dark, my brain only just registering how delighted everyone looks, drifting around the candlelit tables, admiring the builds, fingers pointing at little details, kids sneaking sweets out of the dried icing and into their mouths, just how it should be.

An elf, one of the new volunteer mums, is about to stop me barging into the grotto, but she realises what's happening and stands aside to let me onto the little stage.

'Father Christmas is on his way,' she tells the waiting kids. 'He'll be a few minutes,' and there's a little cheer.

I draw back the red curtain and trip the last step into the darkness of the grotto because what does pride matter anyway when there's me and Patrick at stake?

And he's there.

In red velvet breeches and black boots, buttoning his red coat over a white T-shirt, just how he looked that night two years ago at The Salutation when I realised he was really kind of amazing but I was too distracted doing what I thought was expected of me, thinking Don was the only answer for me, not understanding at the time where the hell I was going wrong.

'Margi?'

He blinks at me, once, twice, and his mouth hangs open a little.

'I know we don't have long,' I tell him. 'There's a queue of kids out there desperate for some budget stationery and a bear. But I had to see you.'

'You didn't answer my calls,' he says, and I see what that's done to him. Hours of waiting are etched in his face.

'I was… hiding,' I say weakly. 'All this time I've felt like a laughing stock in the village, and now I really am a laughing stock. I'm a meme, apparently.'

'Oh, God.' Patrick drops his head. 'That's my fault. I just didn't know what you wanted me to say. I didn't know if you wanted me announcing live on the news that I was your lover, after you'd been so cautious, knowing you felt so embarrassed after Don. You'd made your feelings pretty clear about how you thought Wheaton saw you. And we hadn't spoken about what we were to each other after sleeping here and everything…'

'I know,' I blurt. 'You couldn't have known what I wanted you to say. You were put on the spot, and I realise you were thinking of me.'

Patrick goes on, words rushing out. 'It's been so hard, liking you, when you're so fixated on this age difference thing. I've never known how to play it when it has never once, not for a second, been a big deal for me.' There's a note of sternness in his voice. 'I don't understand when you became so worried about age.'

'I don't know,' I say. 'It just happens. I hit sixty, and *poof!* I suddenly turned invisible and irrelevant with no warning whatsoever, you know? Now nobody can see me, and if they do, they're seeing a doddering blur of elderly aura and nothing else.'

'Not true.'

He's finding all this exasperating, I can tell. But he asked the question, so I'll answer it truthfully.

'And then everything just got so bloody hard,' I go on. 'When I was left on the scrapheap by Don, and after I'd been planning on being fabulous all through my sixties before rocking my seventies and positively slaying my eighties. I had such big ideas about how I wouldn't let numbers define me and I'd work on being happy and confident, but then that just… disappeared, around about the time my husband ran out the door with the words "I do" still fresh on his lips.'

His eyes narrow like he's thinking, and after a moment, he snaps. 'Well, Don can't have you. I won't allow it. He swept in and took you? Fair enough, you wanted him.' He shrugs in acceptance. 'But I won't let him have you now he's buggered off. He can't have all the years of the rest of your life. *I* want them, actually. Sorry if it sounds unbelievable and stupid to you, but there you are.'

I peer at the crease between his brows and his jaw flexing away.

'Are you cross?'

'Little bit. Maybe.' I see him feeling ridiculous, then recovering himself. He surrenders with a smile. 'I can't help feeling this way. You're the one telling me I'm too young for you, but you're giving me no say in deciding for myself, and I'm sorry, but I already decided, actually, on the day I met you. I've tried to show you ever since, in my actions.'

I have to give him that. He really has. 'That's true,' I say. 'I haven't run short on logs for years. And you've baked all those gingerbreads with me.'

'I don't even like gingerbread,' he says.

'*No!*'

'It's true. I'm a Tunnock's Teacakes kind of man. Look, I'm standing here dressed as Santa, for God's sakes. I've been showing up for you for years.'

'I know, and I've kept you at arm's length. I'm sorry.'

'So...' he begins, and I wait, screaming inside: *Don't let him give up on me now. Let him still want me.* He swallows. 'So, what do you want to do?' he says.

'It's not up to me,' I say. 'I've pushed you away and told you over and over you deserve someone... fresher, someone who hasn't been around the block with two husbands. But I know now that none of that matters, and it took all this,' I gesture around me, 'a village of volunteers, a hundred thousand people on the internet, two entire years of being distracted... to figure out what matters is that you want me, and I want you.'

He runs a hand over his head but doesn't move.

'Do you?' he says. '*Do* you want me?'

I step closer to him. 'I want you out loud and in the open and with nothing hidden.'

That's all I have time to say before he closes the space between us in one stride and pulls me to him.

I lift myself to kiss him just as the elf, who I'm sure has been listening in, pulls open the curtain and the whole world sees us as our lips meet, and we're awash in whoops and cheers and whistles.

Patrick laughs, and I do too, because this is what matters, us setting out on our great big unapologetically happy life together, letting love happen.

Epilogue

Summer

Winter's legacy is still everywhere in Wheaton, if you look for it.

Even though every trace of Christmas has been packed away in storage for next time, even though all the curious grotto visitors and Izz-and-Alexi supporters have gone home, even though you wouldn't necessarily know just from looking at us that our tiny little Wheaton village caused an internet sensation, sparking apparently endless memes and one great flood of generosity – despite all this, there is still, out there, every day, between all of us Wheatonites, a new, special spark that connects us.

We won't forget in a hurry what it was like last December when we were all reminded of what really matters and we woke up as if from a long sleep under individual roofs, behind individual locked doors, and we joined together to do something good.

The snow lay for two whole weeks over Christmas, most obligingly, really setting off the grotto exhibit perfectly. The mulled wine ran dry, and Santa Claus ran right out of teddy bears and candy canes and had to send an elf to the cash and carry three times to keep up with the demand for presents.

The totaliser on Fern and Shell's website froze for a while and Patrick made a guess that the server had crashed due to volume of traffic, but when it came back online on Christmas Eve, we'd not known how to contain the explosion of joy inside ourselves at the sight of that number: 300,000 pounds and still climbing.

It was Izz and Alexi's broadcast that had done it.

There's merch now, would you believe? *Let Love Happen*, the T-shirts say, Alexi's words. Pink's the most popular colour, followed by forest green, Fern's suggestion. And we've got a logo too. Lucy designed it.

And yes, she *is* currently in New Zealand, but only on a holiday to see her mum and dad. She's felt the legacy of our Christmas shake-up too.

She'd been sketching scenes in the school gym of the kids looking at the gingerbreads, when the Wheaton art gallery owner just happened to be in. Peering over Lucy's shoulder, she asked, '*Local* artist, are you?' and Lucy's moment of hesitation in replying – wanting to say that yes, she was a local, actually – had told Lucy everything she needed to know about where she wanted to be.

She's got her first two paintings displayed in the gallery windows already, and if you need to ask the price, you already know you can't afford them. She's terribly exclusive now, you see, my Lucy.

It's not all artists' smocks and artsy Cotswolds glamour, however. Half the week she's engaged in a new community project behind the scaffolds at Wheaton Village Hall, working with the young people to paint a new mural to complement the original – a snapshot of life in the village now – and I've only heard the parents singing her praises about how she's encouraging a whole new generation of little artists.

Anyway, the grotto committee is still going strong, only I've handed the reins over to the new volunteers. There's so many of them, all guided by Fern, who, I have to say, has really come into her own now she's taken over at Bizzy Izz's. She hasn't changed a single thing about the chintzy retro cafe, other than making the place 'internet famous' with her socials and adding her own freshly baked bread to the menu – which she makes in rustic small batches every morning, the way Sully taught her.

Shell's often to be found in there, holding the phone and filming Fern's live cooking demos, when she's not up at Brambledown helping Tommy Brash and proving herself to be an excellent apprentice farmer, that is.

But listen to me, chatting on when there's an event to get to.

I've worked my hair up into a mass of silvery waves over my new undercut style, something I always wanted to try but talked myself out of so often, thinking everyone would think it was too young for me, until I asked myself was I really going to let that stop me? I only need to approve of myself these days.

I've made up my face following the girls' tips, and I'm zipping up my new floaty dress and making for the door, in my Docs, of course.

If I run, I'll make it.

Wheaton's never looked nicer. Not even in the snow.

It didn't take us long to string the rainbow bunting all down the high street, not when everyone pitched in to help, and I mean everyone, even old Mr Scrimengor and Rodney Carruthers, who accepted defeat, if not gracefully, but with all the fortitude of men utterly thwarted by the budgeting, which was all that mattered in the end.

We presented our costings and our balance to the nice people from Historic England who found themselves in agreement with us that a village hall must remain a village hall if there's public backing and a huge wodge of ready money. The scaffolding will be coming down in a few weeks now the roof's almost been restored, just as it was before.

'There you are!' Izz shouts from her cottage garden as I approach. 'You're late.'

Alexi emerges from a froth of roses and alstroemeria in the borders. He's transformed the flower beds since he started visiting and staying longer and longer each time, and now Izz has freshly cut flowers on the kitchen windowsill every day as they make the most of each second they've salvaged together.

Alexi drops the secateurs into a basket. 'Shall we?' he says, and we all join the wandering stream of locals making their way out into the sunshine and past the school where the Gingerbread Christmas WORLD exhibition (and grotto) will be held again this December – applications for display spots on the tables have already closed and we've been promised donated builds from all over the globe once again this year.

We pass the hall where work continues noisily inside on the heating system; all presided over, you'll be pleased to know, by the recovered painting of the goggle-eyed King George by an unknown artist of limited talent but great enthusiasm sometime in the 1950s. We're promised a grand reopening next autumn, if all goes well; a dance party for the whole village, and I know who'll be first to take to the floor.

'Oh, I see them,' says Izz, more sprightly than I have ever seen her, now she doesn't have to pretend. So much of her happiness nowadays comes from the well within her that replenishes itself with Alexi who, it turns out, is a pub quiz master and the Stubborn Greys have become the team to beat. You can try, but it won't happen.

We're just in time. Sully is waiting by the doors of his newly refurbished bakery, and there by his elbow is his grandfather, wearing something closer to a smile than anything I've ever witnessed on that man's face, and Leo Bold, the village's super head teacher – well, we think he's super: we didn't need a turnaround report from some inspector or an uptick in pointlessly stressful exam results for our little ones to tell us that. He's already planning his first nativity for the kids, to be held in his own school gymnasium, since we'll have the grotto back in the newly refurbished and properly heated village hall – which is booked out every December in perpetuity for the ginger-breads.

The rest of the year there'll be all manner of clubs and societies in there – including a watercolours class for grown-ups, a little side project of Lucy's, and Bobbie's boot camps, as well as all the old book clubs and baby groups, and there's rumours of a new local history society headed up by Tommy Brash who we see around the village more often these days, now he has a little help at the farm. I've heard Leo's being roped into that little venture too.

Not that he minds. Not that he minds anything at all. He was even bold enough to tell the board he was reverting Patrick's contract back to the full-time variety, so there's been no need for any more late-night shifts in Dunham Gravey or any other place that takes him away from me and our weekend dates all over the Cotswolds.

I don't think I've ever seen a man so transformed as Leo. He's even wearing a *Sully's Bakery* apron to match the new proprietor's who thought 'Scrimengor and Grandson's' didn't quite cut it any more, not now we've all been through our big transformation, and Wheaton village is thriving on community spirit and confectionery.

Patrick arrives by my side at the back of the crowd just as they cut the ribbon and the whole place erupts in a happy cheer. He's been walking Cinnamon, our rescue pup. She's a Spanish sort-of sausage dog, possibly with hints of beach-stray-beagle in her. Mum didn't know for sure. When she showed her to us over FaceTime in the spring, all matted and skinny, we knew she was ours and started the paperwork immediately.

It turns out we are excellent puppy parents, Patrick and I. He dotes on her almost as much as I do. I scratch at Cinnamon's smooth head and she immediately flops onto the pavement for a tummy tickle. Patrick crouches to oblige her.

'Silly pup,' I tell her as her tongue lolls out of her mouth and her tail whips in a frenzy of puppy joy.

'Free gingerbread men for everyone!' Sully cries, and the customers flood into the now baby-blue bakery with its new fixtures and fittings. And I see his grandfather shaking his hand warmly and attempting something like a grandfatherly embrace, even if it is a bit awkward because he's still getting used to showing his feelings, before trying the same thing with Leo who pulls him in close for a proper hug and makes the old man gasp in surprise.

'Are we hanging around for our free gingerbread man?' Patrick asks me, and we stop fussing Cinnamon and stand to watch the crush to get inside Wheaton's newest success story.

'Still not a fan of the gingerbread?' I ask him.

He scrunches his nose. 'I can take it or leave it.'

I laugh and let him lower a kiss to my lips.

'They look busy,' I say, glancing again at the hustle and bustle. Sully's popping corks and handing out Prosecco now.

'We could pop back later when it's quietened down?' he says, and I know exactly what he's thinking. He confirms it with another kiss, this one even softer than the last.

'Let's go,' I whisper, slipping my hand in his, and we sneak away, out along the road to the little cottage we share, once my mum and dad's and now ours, where we've had a proper clear-out and a bit of a paint, and there's an airy freshness through the whole place and a new sense of beginning.

We walk all the faster as the gate comes in sight, Cinnamon running her little legs off, and we laugh at how we still can't seem to stop doing this, not being able to keep our hands off each other, and we push through the gate, past the new sign that Patrick hung in the spring that reads *Gingerbread Cottage*, a new name for a new start, and we kiss our way up the path, thinking of our soft white bed below the oak beams.

Patrick makes sure to bolt the door behind us, and we escape into our own little world once more, where life is guaranteed to be as sweet as Christmas gingerbread and where no matter the time of year, we let love happen.

A letter from Kiley

The first thing you need to know about this book is: nobody dies. Unlike *A Christmas Carol* nobody is dead to begin with. Not one person catches so much as even a sniffle or takes a tumble (unless we're talking falling head over heels in love). Margi's lovely mum is there at the beginning of the book and accounted for at the very end. I promise this book is wall-to-wall unmitigated kindness and Christmas feels, very much in the vein of my first festive novel, *Christmas at Frozen Falls*, OK?

OK, good. Now that's out the way, here is my letter to you, Dear Reader.

When my (really pretty feisty) gran turned ninety, I remember her telling me she didn't feel ninety at all. She couldn't believe that number belonged to her and that there'd been some kind of mistake because she was just a girl really. She was chuckling and shaking her head in amazement as she told me. I'm not sure I totally understood what she meant at the time.

Now, however, the older I get, the younger I realise 'old people' are.

It was thinking about this that made me want to write a book about intergenerational friendships where I did justice to women characters in their sixties and seventies (which is SO young!), letting them be rounded humans before anything else.

Still, I did want to explore some of the knotty problems about society's expectations around how women are supposed to age (preferably quietly, without a fuss and remaining as pretty and palatable as possible while we do it), and I wanted to unpick the paradox of ageing women's invisibility even when they're the ones keeping society's wheels turning, doing so much and for so little recognition and for so bloody long!

So I wrote this book celebrating women and friendship and ageing noisily and without shame and loving ourselves first and foremost so we're all the better at giving and receiving love when it comes to those around us.

I hope you like Margi. She's been through the wringer a bit, but she's got some seriously kick-ass, rebel spirit, even if she's forgotten this when you first meet her.

As I wrote her, I was channelling the magnificent Dame Vivienne Westwood (whom the world lost in 2022, on my 44th birthday, as it happens), urging Margi to remember who she really is and encouraging her to defy society's expectations of what her life should look like. Margi and her pals are, to use Westwood's word, 'seditionaries' in their own wonderful ways.

You'll still find plenty romance and cosiness, and lots of community spirit and festive feels amidst all these women figuring out how exactly one acts their age when the ageing rule book has been torn up, doused in petrol and set alight.

I really hope you enjoy my Christmas offering and if you feel moved to share a review I'd be thrilled. Taking the time to write a review is the biggest thing you can do to support authors, and I really appreciate every minute of your time. Thank you!

Oh, and I'm on social media too, come and say hello @KileyDunbarAuthor on Instagram or at the Kiley Dunbar Author Facebook Page.

Finally, Happy Christmas! I hope it's a time of friendship, sweetness and success for you too!

Love from Margi and her gingerbread gang, and from Kiley, x